MARS [P9-DTA-205]

Bloodcurdling, bizarre, and banned . . . until now!

"Collectible gore."
—Newsweek

"Guaranteed to evoke a frisson of terror and guilty delight."
—Science Fiction Age

In 1962, at the height of the cold war, the Brooklyn-based Topps Chewing Gum Company released a set of trading cards that combined a classic H. G. Wells–style alien invasion with the graphic atrocities of war. The result was the legendary *Mars Attacks*® cards, and the reaction was immediate.

National uproar.

Deemed too gruesome for innocent young minds, the cards were quickly suppressed.

But even as they disappeared from the market, their cult status grew . . . and grew. Finally, in 1995, Topps rereleased the set, adding new—and equally gruesome—cards. The invasion began anew, leading to comic books and now, at last, novels.

Don't look now: The Martian wave is spreading across the land!

Mars Attacks®
Published by Ballantine Books:

MARTIAN DEATHTRAP
by Nathan Archer

MARS ATTACKS!®: THE ART OF THE MOVIE
by Karen R. Jones

WAR DOGS OF THE GOLDEN HORDE
by Ray W. Murill

MARS ATTACKS®

WAR DOGS OF THE GOLDEN HORDE

RAY W. MURILL

A Del Rey® Book
BALLANTINE BOOKS • NEW YORK

A Del Rey® Book
Published by Ballantine Books

http://www.randomhouse.com

Library of Congress Catalog Card Number: 96-96758

ISBN 0-345-40954-X

Manufactured in the United States of America

First Hardcover Edition: May 1996
First Mass Market Edition: March 1997

10 9 8 7 6 5 4 3 2 1

FOR JEANNE,
WHO COULDN'T WAIT
FOR THIS BOOK
TO BE FINISHED

PROLOGUE

In the aftermath of the Martian Occupation of Earth, the planet was divided between Martian Holdings and Free Earth by the World Wall—an immense fortification girdling the globe, jointly constructed by the cosignatories of the Earth-Mars Non-Aggression Pact.

Virtually all of Canada, Europe, and the old Soviet Empire fell within Martian influence, while in the Southern Hemisphere the lower halves of South America and Africa also suffered under an alien yoke. In the West, significant portions of the continental United States clung contentiously to freedom.

But in the Far East, virtually unnoticed by the forces fighting to resist further Martian encroachment, lay underdeveloped Mongolia—a barren steppelands boasting only one city of significance and populated by nomadic herdsmen whose culture had all but atrophied.

In the uneasy armistice between Terra and Mars, the free-riding, unambitious Mongols were dismissed as noncombatants.

Until a disgraced member of the Martian Ruling Council became curious about another, more ancient wall which divided Western Free Mongolia from the unoccupied provinces of northern China.

And a Khalkha Mongol named Dog rode up from the Black Gobi to seek a new life . . .

1

THE WORLD WALL, OCCUPIED CHINA

Former Martian Ruling Council member Telian Piar stood looking west, beyond the World Wall to the vast lands designated the Profane Side, when the office door signaled a visitor with a shrill *breep*.

"All honor, Telian Piar," a servile voice said. "Major Mu'd requests permission to deliver requested intelligence."

Telian Piar did not turn from the window.

"Enter. The door is unlocked."

The skull-faced Gnard Martian from Intel/Div entered. His two red eyes burned, but his tone was respectful.

"Elder, I have assurances you will find the intelligence to be complete in every wise," he snapped through his scissoring piranha teeth.

"The essence of it, if you please."

"Your will." The Gnard paused, then began reciting. "The wall in question is known to the Terrans as the Great Wall of China and was constructed approximately two thousand Terran planetary rotations ago for the sole purpose of protecting the vast empire called China from the depredations of marauding Mongol nomads."

"Nomads?"

"Primitive barbarians, armed with sharp blades and rude but lethal, portable catapult constructs designed to loose wooden missiles known as arrows. They made war from the backs of four-legged beasts called horses."

"I know what a horse is. Continue."

The Gnard's two hell-red eyes blinked once, carefully. "Under a leader by name Temujin and by title Genghis Khan, these Mongols were welded into an army whose discipline, ferocity, and raw appetite for conquest was unequaled in Terran history. Before their decline, the empire of this khan had spread westward to occupy an area of this hemisphere greater than that we presently control."

Telian Piar turned, his trailing lavender robes shifting softly. Unlike the swollen-brained Gnard Martian, Piar's Paeec head resembled a mottled pink puffball whose needle teeth champed behind trembling facial tentacles. Two blank eye spots dominated the lower face, while a single scarlet orb peered out from the horny spinal bumps of an ivory sagittal crest.

"Did you say *greater*?"

"They controlled all of China, of which only this crucial eastern portion lies behind our World Wall."

"Greater," Telian Piar repeated.

"Yes, Elder."

The Paeec's single red orb was reflective for a long moment, the black pupil expanding and contracting in thought.

Abruptly, he looked up. "This Great Wall. Did it hold?"

"No. It merely endures."

Piar nodded. "These . . ."

"Mongols."

"Thank you. These Mongols you describe sound more like you Gnards than Terrans."

"They completely lack our advanced technology, our brainpans, our—"

Piar raised a quelling hand. "Yet they once controlled a greater landmass of this planet than any other indigenous army before or since."

"They conquered and subjugated nation-states almost as primitive as they were," the Gnard said defensively.

"No, they subjugated nation-states greater than that which they could ever hope to aspire," Telian Piar said, his voice flavored with interest.

"That is another way of perceiving it."

"It is the correct way. Tell me, how do the Mongols of this era differ from their forebears?"

"They display no appetite for conquest, being content to live off their herds and follow the changing seasons on horseback. For shelter, they carry portable domed huts called *gers* by wagon, and appear content with their miserable lot."

"Is this another way of saying they live as they always have?" Piar asked.

"Yes."

"Suffering the same privations, enduring the same diet, wielding the same weapons?"

"The percussion firearm has largely replaced hand catapults called the bow and arrow among those dwelling closest to their pitiful cities."

"But otherwise, these are specimens of the type who followed this Genghis Khan?"

"They are."

"Leave the intelligence package. I will study it at length."

"Your will."

The door hissed shut and Telian Piar turned to gaze again beyond the World Wall which looked out over the wild mountains of Free China.

At a point where the rust-red concrete and steel bulwark of the World Wall jogged into mountainous terrain, it became an ancient crenellated rampart of paved stone and mortar that rose and fell with the undulating Chinese landscape. In its way, the Great Wall of China appeared more formidable and enduring than the New Wall that now divided a conquered planet.

"Yesss," he breathed.

2

THE WINDING ROAD, OUTER MONGOLIA

On the Day of the White Tiger, in the Month of the Horse, in the Blue Rat Year, Qasar the Mongol, destined to become Qasar Khan, rode up from Inner Mongolia, alone.

He stood in the stirrups of his orange-painted wooden saddle as his snow-white, stripe-legged stallion trotted across the vast steppelands of what the Chinese emperors had long ago dubbed Outer Mongolia. He rode Mongol fashion, backside out of the saddle, his legs stiff and supporting, the rest of his body swaying to the relentless hammering trot of his mount.

A traditional fur cap sat low over a broad face like a brass gong that had been beaten out of shape by many tiny hammers. The color of his coatlike *del* was a sun-faded green, enlivened by a tattered sky-blue sash. On the thumb of his right hand was attached a pad of cracked leather.

The sky above was an eye-dazzling blue. To the northwest beckoned the Hentiyn Mountains, low and brooding like fallen giants. Behind him lay the pastures of his clan. Behind him lay his life.

Ahead lay destiny. Whether good or bad, Qasar did not know, and cared even less. He had ridden four days with no remounts. And his stomach ached for mutton. He cared about mutton.

Knife-slit eyes searching the endless barrens before him, he sniffed the crisp spring air. It was neither hot nor cold. It was not good air, he thought. Good air had a clean taste and a sharp temperature. It burned the lungs with its withering cold or settled heavily in the heat of summer. This air tasted of death and fear. It was not Mongolian air. Therefore it had blown down from the distant north where the slavish Russians bent their backs to the soil to grub for their sustenance.

Right now the only sustenance that concerned Qasar the Mongol was his own. But if it meant his life, he would not dig in the hard earth for roots. That was for Russians—and hungry Mongol ponies.

So his crinkling eyes combed the landscape as his Mongol soul drank in the Eternal Blue Sky, which even an outcast such as he worshiped. And his stomach growled like a steppe wolf.

A black kite circled on a high thermal, and spying it, Qasar reined his horse to a stop and eyed it hungrily. A kite was no meal for a Russian, never mind a Mongol. But at least it was not a camel, or worse, horseflesh.

Taking up his long-range bow of sinew and ram's horn, Qasar patiently strung it as he watched the kite wheel and circle hungrily. The bow resembled a nearly closed circle, but when he finished stringing it, its limbs were bent back in the opposite direction like tense antlers.

Taking a red-fletched arrow from his boxy saddle sheath, Qasar nocked it and, using the leather thumb pad, drew the shaft back at an acute angle, simultaneously raising the bow to his thick shoulders.

Tracking the kite, his arms contorted against the opposing tension—dead gut and sinew against living sinew and muscle. He let fly.

It was an impossible distance. Qasar knew this. But

hunger and an indomitable spirit forced the attempt. His keen eyes watched the arrow whistle and arc, only to fall short of its mark. The kite, startled, screamed once and made for the west on furious wings. The arrow fell behind a low hill up ahead.

Methodically unstringing his bow, Qasar resumed his trek. His stomach growled anew. His heart beat like a drum. But he would persevere. He was a Mongol.

Night began falling like the dying of the world, and Qasar's stomach still complained. It was almost a song now, an accompaniment to the clattering hooves of his stripe-legged stallion. The way became littered with black Gobi gravel, and the horse, used to low steppelands and desert, grew nervous at the uncertain graveled terrain.

Qasar smelled the blood before he came upon the long-faced Mongol bent over a black-faced sheep with a familiar red-tufted arrow in its flank, on the other side of the low hill behind which his arrow had fallen. The sheep lay on one side, its ribs laboring like bellows, its wool absorbing and discoloring its very lifeblood.

At his approach, the Mongol took up an ancient carbine rifle and called out.

"*Sain baina*, Mongol."

"*Sain bino,*" Qasar retorted in a neutral voice. Reining his horse, he dismounted casually, hobbling his mount by tying a strip of rawhide around three of its legs.

Leaving his unstrung bow on the saddle, he approached. The skirts of his *del* made steady whisking sounds.

"Did you shoot this sheep?" the other Mongol asked warily.

"I never miss," Qasar retorted.

"I was stalking him," the other Mongol said, hefting his carbine. "In another heartbeat I would have felled him." He had a red but unweathered face. It was very long and drawn, but his eyes were wise as walnuts. He wore plain mohair pants and a sheepskin coat made by a machine. A city Mongol. Qasar had seen many in his time, but never one so red. His nose was a raw bulb.

"He is mine," Qasar grunted.

The other refused to back down. "I will share him."

"That is for me to say, not you."

"I saw the sheep first."

"And I shot first. For that is my arrow in him. His meat is mine."

"He is not yet dead. Therefore you do not have the right to the kill."

The city Mongol made as if to point the muzzle of his ancient rust-pitted carbine at the sheep's head, but Qasar, moving in, took the muzzle in one big paw and pushed it away. It discharged into the air, frightening only its owner.

Pulling a dagger from his sash, Qasar knelt, slitting the laboring sheep from groin to throat. Then, reaching into the warm red cavity, he found the still-beating heart.

"What is it you do, Mongol?" the city Mongol wondered.

"I am finishing this sheep's life, for its blood is going to waste."

The heart pulsed twice in Qasar's hand. He squeezed it three times. It became still. In a moment the sheep's legs ceased to kick, then began to stretch and relax in death.

Standing up, shaking red droplets from his right hand, Qasar eyed the city Mongol and said, "That is the proper way to kill a sheep."

"A bullet in the brain is quicker."

"The head would be ruined."

"We do not eat the head in Ulan Bator."

"I knew you for a city Mongol from the moment I laid eyes upon you," Qasar said without feeling.

Interest flickered in the long-faced Mongol's thin eyes. "What is your name, Mongol?"

"Qasar."

"That is a good name for a horse Mongol—Dog."

"I am a Khalkha Mongol. And your name?"

"Bayar."

Qasar threw back his head and laughed mightily. "The father who named you 'Happy' must have been drunk on *airag*. I have never seen so mournful a countenance—or one so red."

"When I was a boy, my name fit my face. Now that I am a man, it is different." And taking out a well-used handkerchief, the Mongol whose name meant Happy blew a mighty blast. He wiped it off on one sleeve before pocketing it.

"I suffer allergies," he explained. Then swiftly reclaimed the handkerchief and re-created the explosion.

"It is the bad air coming down from Russia. It would make even a Tibetan puke up his soft innards."

"It is the pollen," Bayar said. "I have been told this by the doctors in the city. Nothing can be done for it. When it is sneezing season, I sneeze as often as I breathe."

Qasar made a metallic face. "Pollen?"

"The magic dust that makes many flowers out of few."

"If you paid these city doctors to hear such lies, I hope they entertain you to the end of your days, because it is the bad Russian air that is tormenting you so," Qasar said.

Kneeling, Qasar began to skin the sheep. Bayar watched this with ill-disguised interest.

"I was willing to share," he reminded.

"Have you a pot?"

"Yes."

"I have none. Therefore, I am willing to let you boil my dinner in your pot."

"I am willing to do this."

"In return, I will let you enjoy the smell of my dinner," Qasar said.

"It is better than nothing," Bayar said, digging at his handkerchief. He was too slow this time and sneezed all over his sheepskin coat.

An hour later, with the great north star known to Genghis Khan as the Golden Nail burning overhead in an onyx sky, Qasar and Bayar were hunkered over a campfire fueled by yak chips, while a rude pot boiled. The dead sheep had been rendered down to raw bone and packets of meat, some few of which tumbled gray and foaming in the boiling pot.

The horses were hobbled nearby, heads down, pulling at the tough steppegrass.

"Where are you bound, Qasar?" Bayar asked as they watched the pot bubble in silence. A wind blew through the black sands, disturbing the bluish yak dung smoke.

Qasar's eyes stayed on the pot as he answered. "To the place where I was born."

"Where were you born?"

"The Mountain Where the Wolves Give Birth."

"You cannot go there anymore."

"I go where I wish."

"The Mountain Where the Wolves Give Birth, like the capital, lies behind the New Wall."

Qasar looked up from the pot. "Wall?"

"I have not seen this wall, but no one has breached it—or if they have, none returned alive to speak."

"The Russians have built a wall?"

Bayar shrugged, not taking his eyes off the mutton.

"There are too many wild tales to believe a certain one over another one. Some say the Russians, some say the Chinese. Others talk of stranger things. But all agree that the New Wall is beyond penetration."

"I am going to the place where I was born. No wall built of Russians or even Old Man God will deter me."

Bayar studied Qasar's brazen face in the firelight. "Why do you seek the place where you were born?"

Qasar resumed staring into the fire. His eyes slitted until the red reflections in them smoldered low. His voice became quiet. "So that I may be born again."

Bayar adjusted his sheepskin cap. "This is a peculiar notion."

"When a man dies yet walks the earth, he is caught between being something and nothing. I did not care to walk the earth as nothing. So I will midwife myself into flesh once more."

"You are a ghost?"

"I am a masterless Mongol. It is almost the same thing."

"No clan?"

"I ride alone."

"Where did you come from, then?"

"Up from Dead Mongol Pass."

"That is not a place Mongols come from, but where they die. Especially in the winter."

"It was in Dead Mongol Pass that I died."

"Since the building of the New Wall, I doubt nothing my ears hear or my eyes see," Bayar muttered, his gaze going hungrily to the boiling mutton.

Qasar speared a particularly choice gobbet, brought it to his teeth and took a mouthful. With the edge of his blade he sliced off the portion before his teeth. The blade scraped his incisors and scaled the tip of his nose. He chewed vigorously, swallowed, and repeated the operation.

"There is enough mutton to share," Bayar suggested.

Qasar finished the last of his morsel and speared a

second. He said nothing as he chewed and sliced his way through that.

"I was willing to share with you," Bayar said hesitantly.

Qasar grunted. "You should have shot sooner."

"I thought there was time. I wished a clean kill."

"A rifle is no weapon for a horse Mongol."

"I was born in Ulan Bator."

"Even a city Mongol should hunt with a bow before he resorts to the rifle."

"A rifle shoots farther than a bow."

"That may be so," Qasar admitted through a mouthful of gray stringy mutton. "But of what value is a rifle once the bullets run out?"

"A smart Mongol never runs out of bullets."

"A smarter Mongol makes his own arrows. Bullets have to be bartered or bought." Qasar gestured to the barren surroundings. "If you are beset by foes out here and the bullets run dry, where do you obtain a fresh supply?"

"Off the dead."

"And if the foe is hurling arrows?"

Bayar thought a minute, seemed about to speak but launched into a sneezing fit instead. He blew snot into the boiling pot. Qasar noticed this but seemed unconcerned.

When Bayar had finished wiping his raw nose, he said, "If the foe is hurling arrows against my bullets, I may die, but not before I turn many of my foes into moaning ghosts like you."

Qasar laughed aloud. "That is a good answer. Especially for a city Mongol. There is a tiny collop of mutton you blew snot on. You may have that—but no more."

"Thank you," Bayar said, reaching in with his dirty fingers to claim the gray morsel. He blew on his fingers while passing the mutton between them until it was cool enough to consume.

At length Qasar said, "You may have the head."

"We do not eat the head."

"The head is good. Try the brains. And there is meat on the cheeks and jaw if you scrape deep enough."

"It is better than nothing."

"Mutton is better than any other meat," Qasar said amiably.

"I prefer the tail."

"The tail is mine. I will save it for a happy occasion. You may have the head."

A few minutes later the head was tumbling in the pot, the open eyes of the sheep clouding over like those of an old man going blind.

"Where are you bound?" Qasar asked Bayar.

"Away."

"Away? No Mongol goes away. He is always going to."

"I am going away from the night skies that are busy with falling stars that do not fall."

"All falling stars fall to earth."

"There are new jade ones in the sky that do not," Bayar said.

"Interesting. I do not believe you, but it is interesting that you think this."

"Some say that ghosts ride these falling stars and it is they who have built the New Wall."

"How could those ghosts build walls if the stars they ride do not fall to earth?" Qasar wondered.

Bayar shrugged. "I am only relating a rumor. But some say these jade stars are really *fei chi*."

"I do not know Chinese, except for curses."

"*Fei chi* means airplane. It is the same as our *namdu*."

Qasar nodded in understanding. "I saw a skyboat once. It flew very high or was very small. I could not tell. It seemed impossible that there were men inside it, but it made a great long roar as it passed through the Everlasting Blue Sky."

"These jade skyboats are silent, like ghosts. It is said the ghosts who ride them have dead faces like skulls with eyes."

"A skull cannot possess eyes, only empty holes. I do not believe this tale."

"Believe it or do not believe," Bayar said slowly. "That does not make it any less true."

Qasar was silent. Bayar speared the sheep's head from the pot with his own dull knife.

"Behind me," Bayar said as he scraped meat into his mouth, "many Mongols follow. They are refugees from the sky troubled by the jade stars that do not fall."

"I am not afraid to ride into troubled skies," Qasar scoffed.

"Then you are ill-named, for even a lowly dog has more sense than to ride into unknown dangers."

"I seek the cave of my birth. If I die on the way or after, it cannot be said of me that Qasar the Mongol did not struggle to redeem himself in new flesh."

"Why are you in need of redemption?" Bayar asked with sudden interest.

Qasar narrowed his dark eyes and studiously began to whet the edge of his dagger against the sole of one felt boot. The sound was a whispering, but in the vast emptiness seemed louder than the sighing night wind.

When enough time had passed, Bayar understood he was to be favored with no answer. He had eaten all the flesh he could and was digging into the puddinglike brains with his fingers. The last of them slobbering down his throat and chin, he looked at the remains and asked, "Do horse Mongols eat the eyes as well?"

"Only if their bellies demand it."

Bayar looked at the milky globes for a long moment, making a long face. "I will leave the eyes and instead travel with you."

"I am going the opposite way. And into dangers."

"True. But you travel with five days' supply of mutton, and I have only two blind eyes which will not sustain me one day, even if I can bring my mouth to capture them for my stomach."

"They will go to waste," Qasar said.

Bayar shrugged. "Take them if you wish."

Qasar grunted a laugh as he sliced the sheep's eye muscles and prodded them into his waiting palm.

"You must swear fealty to me," he said, pocketing the eyes.

"Why?"

"Because otherwise you will only travel four days' march and go your own way once we have sucked the last sweet sheep marrow from the last discarded thigh bone."

Bayar swallowed. "You expect much for your mutton."

Spanking dust off his *del*, Qasar the Mongol stood up and sheathed his resharpened dagger.

"Next time, you will not hesitate to shoot first," he said, grunting with amiable humor.

3

KOLYMA TOWER, FORMER SIBERIA

The Killerghost shuttle *Red Sands* skimmed over the rugged Kolyma Mountain Range, riding a navigation beacon to the imposing rust-colored tower that housed the Martian Ruling Council, as well as functioning as the Martian High Command's Earth headquarters.

At its approach, a ponderous bay door set high in the massive tower began lifting to receive it. Without any hint of deceleration, the iridescent green saucer slid into the gaping bay, froze, lowered its landing gear, then touched down gently. A hatch irised open, dropping a smooth tonguelike ramp that settled with a click.

His hands tucked into the sleeves of his lavender robes, Telian Piar glided down the ramp, where a Gnard honor guard from Sec/Div awaited him.

"All honor," they said in greeting.

"Escort me to Komo Dath's office," Piar instructed.

"Your will," the guard intoned. Turning smartly, they trooped down gleaming corridors charged with the thin components of the Martian atmosphere, Telian Piar floating after them like a stately religious figure. His gait was serene, but his mind was ablaze with possibilities.

For two years now a difficult truce had existed between the Terrans and the Martians. But a more difficult one strained the Paeec-Gnard alliance. Both of Mars, each faction was distrustful of the other.

Telian Piar was paramount among equals of the intellectual Paeec: First Council member, signatory of the Terran Truce, and, in times past, the chief liaison between the Council and the Gnard who functioned as Martian Military Commander, Komo Dath.

Now, for the duration of the present crisis, Dath had been given absolute authority over military operations, while the Council adopted an advisory oversight position. Telian Piar had retired from any active role in the Council, and was suffering under a relaxed form of house arrest.

Reaching a smooth portal adorned with the symbols of Komo Dath's high rank, the Gnard honor guard stopped, breaking formation. Two of them spun on their heels to take up positions on either side of the door. Their eyes fell upon Telian Piar, who glided to a stop a careful distance behind the third Gnard, who addressed the door with his spine rigidly at attention.

The silent Paeec ignored the smoldering gazes of the sentry Gnards. They were ostensibly subject to the Council, but their deepest loyalty cleaved to the Gnard waiting behind the door.

"Who is it?" the raspy voice of Komo Dath demanded through the door comm link.

"All honor. Telian Piar is here."

"Have him enter."

"Your will."

The third Gnard stepped off to one side with a grim precision. His radiant eyes followed like tracking lenses on a swiveling sensor sphere as Telian Piar glided forward. The door surrendered to his approach and he passed into the headquarters of Komo Dath.

Dath stood in an attitude of animal menace, hands clasped behind his back. He was pacing. Komo Dath was forever pacing, Telian Piar thought. On his shoulders fell the on-the-ground responsibility for the conquest and subjugation of Earth. Every Martian death incurred—whether because of inefficiency or lack of political will—burned into his warrior's soul.

A warrior himself, Dath fully understood that soldiers were capital, designed to be expended—and he expended them so lavishly that he threatened the force-level integrity of the Martian Military Command.

Head hung low, Dath whirled to face Telian Piar.

"To what do I owe the 'honor'?" he rasped.

"I have a solution to the impasse that exists between the Council and yourself."

"I will hear it," Dath said in a tone that suggested doubt, if not naked skepticism.

"The Council does not know of this."

Dath's red eyes sharpened. "Going behind the backs of the Council?"

"Exploring alternative paths on the march to victory. Is that not how you would phrase it?"

Dath continued his manic pacing, his posture that of a caged beast. Had he had his way, Terran resistance would have been crushed long before. But there had been mistakes. Both Martian factions had committed mistakes. Thus the current state of affairs.

"I am listening," Dath said.

"The Terran Truce protects us from openly acquiring more territory."

"Bah. The nuclear submarines that lurk beneath their great blue seas, prepared to annihilate us all, prevent us from grinding the so-called truce under our boots."

"Two perceptions. One reality," Telian Piar assented. "Our other attempts to circumvent this impasse have caused no seeds to grow."

"You are referring to the insect bombs."

"Yes. A good plan. Turn Earth's arthropoda into

gigantic marauding engines of destruction. But they proved uncontrollable and had to be exterminated by our own forces."

"At great cost," Dath spat.

"Done is done. I have a new engine of destruction for your consideration."

Interest flickered in Komo Dath's eyes. His teeth froze in mid-gnash, widened, then slowly closed as if over stunned prey. "What engine?"

"One as numerous as the ants, and as terrible in their own way. But infinitely more controllable. Much more controllable."

"You interest me . . ."

"What do you know of the lands south of here?"

"Barren. Almost empty of Terrans."

"Yet the World Wall stops short of these under-populated areas."

"It was necessary only to absorb the capital cities of the two south-lying nations, to neutralize significant insurgencies."

"Yes. Beijing, China. And Ulan Bator, Mongolia. What do you know of Mongolia, Dath?"

"Only that all this territory will be ours one day."

"But you know the land is harsh and thirsty, and there are red deserts as well as black deserts."

"Yes. I know these things. Get to the point, Paeec."

"The point is these dry lands to the south not yet under our domination are very much like the sands of our home planet, sands that gave rise to you Gnards."

"This is true. They will need little eco-reconfiguring when the time comes—Mother Mars grant it come very soon."

"In these harsh lands," Telian Piar continued, "a species of Terran more fearsome and more formidable than any seen on Earth before or since came into being."

"Terrans are Terrans," Dath spat.

"Not these Mongols. They are to Terrans what Gnards are to Paeecs."

"You insult me and every Gnard who died in the execution of his duty," Dath blazed.

"No dishonor intended."

"Dishonor accepted," Dath retorted, resuming his pacing.

"Attend my words," Telian Piar said, his voice shedding its scholarly lilts for the deeper tones of authority.

Dath ceased his relentless pacing. He stopped, squared his shoulders and looked full into Telian Piar's single red orb as if to outstare him through sheer will and force of personality.

Telian Piar returned the gaze unmoved. He continued in a firm voice.

"As I have said, they are called Mongols. Long ago, they dwelt in dome tents they carried on the backs of beasts of burden. They ate poorly, suffered from wind and rain and cold. They were indomitable. They killed with a savage blood lust you yourself would admire. And in Terran eras past, armed with the crudest of weapons but the mightiest of cunning, they united in a confederation that swept over a greater landmass than we now hold in this Terran hemisphere, accomplishing this with a highly mobile strike force of only 150,000 cavalry."

"What of it?" Dath growled.

"They are capable of doing this again. Properly guided."

"What are you saying, Telian Piar?"

"They breathe the heavy metallic air of Terra, which has been poisoned to our race by nuclear contamination. They are mobile. Even to this day their very name evokes fear and dread. And they dwell south of here, as had their city-conquering ancestors, in need only of a strong leader to bring them together once more."

"Me?"

Telian Piar nodded once. "In secret, yes."

"You speak rubbish."

"Are you aware of the old wall that winds around the southernmost section of our World Wall in this hemisphere?"

"Yes, I have seen it. It is the only Terran-built artifact that can be scanned from beyond this marshy world's orbit. A section was cannibalized and incorporated into the World Wall."

"It was built to keep out the Mongols of long ago, so terrible were they. A mighty civilization—by Terran standards—constructed it because, despite the wealth and vast armies of the land called China, an army of rootless cavalry, capable of riding for days, hardly stopping to rest, carrying its homes on its backs and driven by deep yearnings for blood and battle and the envious comforts of civilization, cannot be beaten back. They own no homes to return to. They possess no creature comforts to lure them back. They can only advance or die. There is no retreat."

"You almost speak of the Gnard when you say these things," Dath said slowly.

Piar bobbed his oversized head. "I told you there were similarities."

"I cannot believe that any Terran can equal a Gnard."

"There is a test I have in mind."

"Yes?"

"Let us test one of these Mongols. Let us see if the burning flame of their forebears still smolders in their unsatisfied hearts."

"And if it does?" Komo Dath asked.

"If it does," Telian Piar said, "perhaps we can fan this rude flame into an army that will conquer and consume all of the vast fertile lands below Mongolia."

4

THE WINDING ROAD, OUTER MONGOLIA

At the hour of the Black Dragon, Qasar the Mongol lay awake under a moon that seemed like a bowl of shaven ice. He had no felt tent to protect him from the elements, only a flap of felt to cut the wind and stop any rain that might fall. But no rain fell.

Stars fell. Qasar watched them as, off a ways, Bayar's adenoidal snoring came steadily.

Qasar watched for jade-green shooting stars. He saw none. The falling stars he did spy were blue-white and thin. Every one fell.

After an hour of this, he rolled over, heavy of lid, and slipped off into a troubled sleep.

The jade shooting star crossed the diamond web of the Seven Giants star constellation, veered west and circled to alight behind low sand hills and twisted pink-blooming tamarisks.

Some twenty minutes passed. A gritty stirring of sand touched Qasar's sharp ears, and without a grunt of surprise or other betraying sound, he rolled out from his makeshift bed and took up his bow, already strung.

Crouched in his thin undergarments, he fitted an arrow to the string and held the bow so that its angular limbs were parallel with the ground.

His slit eyes hunted. Bayar's snoring masked the sounds of the night, but in the pauses he heard the monotonous crunch-crunch-crunch of booted feet on loose black Gobi gravel.

Brigands, Qasar thought. Well, they would walk the sand no more after this night.

Something topped a rise and Qasar pivoted in his crouch, releasing the nocked arrow almost at the same instant he saw the head lifting into view.

The shaft whistled for two long breaths, and there came an unexpected sound, like glass breaking. An unearthly scream pierced the night and the gritty thud of a falling body mixed with breaking glass sounds.

Chof!

Something threw a flash of green. Making emerald shadows, it sped toward him. Qasar rolled as Bayar jumped out of his sleep.

"What! What!" he said, looking every way at once.

Qasar let fly with another arrow. A blind shot. The shaft flew, skimming the top of a dune with a hissing sound.

There appeared another head topping a rise. From the west this time. "Three brigands!" Qasar shouted. "Yours to the south!"

Bayar lunged for his carbine, got it in the crook of his arm, and, dropping into a crouch, began shooting indiscriminately.

Chof! Chof!

Bayar saw the flashes of fire and rolled clear. They skimmed the ground like fleet green marmosets and struck the rended sheep. It blazed up and began burning merrily, releasing the fragrance of its meat into the night air.

The carbine barked twice, kicking up sand and dirt.

Chof!

"Aim for the flash!" Qasar called, loosing another arrow as the upper edge of a globe peered over the hill.

The arrow creased the top of the bulb without breaking it. The globe withdrew, and Qasar let the sound of the shifting of enemy feet tell him where it was going.

At his back the carbine split the night once, cleanly. Another unearthly scream was followed by the sound of a body spilling face forward.

Qasar heard all this. His eyes were on the low rise. Arrowhead tracking his unseen quarry, he was as focused as a hunting falcon, waiting for that first perfect moment to strike.

A metallic hand slipped over the rise and a bulky silver device angled around blindly. From a hole at the front, racing rags of emerald fire spurted.

Chof! Chof! Chof!

Qasar held his low stance. The screaming emerald flashes zimmed by to startle the horses but do no harm.

The weapon angled again and emitted a single flash this time.

Chof!

Untouched, Qasar let out a howl of agony.

The foe jumped up like a jackrabbit, and before he could turn his weapon in a focused direction, Qasar's arrow broke his breastplate.

His scream was tiny and indistinct within the globe that encased his head. He fell backward, feet sticking up from the rise. Slowly, they slid backward to retreat from sight.

Nocking a fresh arrow, Qasar rotated his head, seeking sounds of menace. Hearing none, he motioned for Bayar to rise.

"Did you see their faces?" Bayar hissed.

Qasar shook his head. "Only eyes. Red eyes."

"They were ghosts," Bayar whispered.

Qasar grunted. "We will see."

Settling the horses with hard spanks to their rumps, they inspected the nearest body.

He lay sprawled face downward. His body wore a smooth white armor that shone like metal but was not a metal Qasar recognized.

Where the head should have been was a broken dome of transparent material out of which spilled exposed brains in a puddinglike flow.

"Look! I shot his brains out!" Bayar said excitedly.

Qasar shook his head grimly. "There is too much brain."

"That is because I am a wonderful shot."

Digging a blunt toe under the carcass, Qasar gave the body a flip. It rolled over easily, being lighter than a Mongol, exposing a shattered death's-head face and closed eyes.

Bayar jumped back. "Sorcery!" he rasped. "Look how it has already decayed."

Qasar knelt. His eyes were stern. "The face is like a skull," he muttered.

"Yes, just as you would expect of a ghost."

"But there are eyes. And warm brains."

"Yes," Bayar agreed.

Using the tip of his dagger, Qasar angled into the shattered globe and pried open one pinkish eyelid. The exposed orb was as red as blood and malevolent as death.

"That is no human eye," Qasar said.

"It is an eye. And that is a shooting star ghost such as I have heard other Mongols tell."

"Why does it encase its head in glass?" Qasar asked.

Bayar pondered this conundrum a moment and said what seemed logical to him. "Allergies."

Qasar scowled doubtfully. "Do ghosts breathe?"

"You are a ghost. Do you not breathe?"

Qasar stood up. "I am a different manner of ghost."

"And that is an even more different manner of ghost. One with very terrible allergies."

"I say it is a Russian demon."

"The Russians do not have demons. But the Chinese have many kinds of demon."

"If such beings as this built the New Wall, it is a Russian demon," Qasar insisted.

"It does not look Russian."

"Nor does it wear a Chinese face."

"In truth it wears no face at all," Bayar admitted. His eyes fell on one of the manlike thing's hands, and the gleaming weapon clutched by smooth metallic fingers.

Scooping this up from the dead hand, he curled his grubby fingers around its butt. "Look, Qasar. I have never seen one of these before."

"Leave it."

"It may be valuable."

"No one will want the property of an accursed demon."

"It looks like a ghost."

"All the better to leave it."

Bayar tested the heft of the weapon in his hand, his finger seeking the trigger. He realized he found it only after it erupted in his hand.

Chof!

A spurt of greenish flame raced by Qasar's shoulder and he whirled, knocking the weapon from Bayar's unprepared hand with a cry of *"Ai-Yah!"*

Bayar stared at the fallen weapon as if at a viper that had unexpectedly struck.

"Next time watch where you point that thing," Qasar warned.

"It is a gun," Bayar said, reclaiming it.

"It fires no bullets."

"It is a sneeze gun. You saw that it sneezed flame."

Qasar shook his head. "No, it spoke its name. It is a Chof."

"I have never before heard of a Chof."

"I am naming it a Chof, therefore it will be called a Chof."

"I prefer sneeze gun."

"It is a Chof. This is obvious," Qasar said, reaching the second body.

This one, too, lay with a shattered dome over its skull. They regarded it stonily under the effulgent moonlight. Both eyes were open. They gleamed like flat dead rubies.

Qasar claimed its weapon. He lifted it and tracked it with a practiced eye. Sighting a lonely scrub tamarisk, he pulled the thick trigger.

The weapon went *chof* and expelled a brilliant rag of iridescent emerald flame which raced away from them. The tamarisk burst into flames, and almost instantly fell to powder.

"See?" Qasar said. "A Chof."

"It is possible you are correct," Bayar allowed.

They moved on to the third body, the one that had slipped behind a dune.

It lay in shadow, the eyes half open, pupils thin slits of smoldering scarlet. Qasar's arrow stuck up from a cracked crater in its chest. It had fallen with one hand behind its back. There was no sign of its weapon.

"What manner of arrowhead penetrates metal?" Bayar asked.

"Iron."

"Iron does not pierce other metal."

"Therefore, this demonic armor is not made of metal but some other substance," Qasar pointed out.

"Demon's metal, perhaps," Bayar suggested.

A low hiss was escaping the chest crater, and Bayar saw that the jagged teeth were scissoring slightly.

"It still breathes," Bayar noted.

"I will fix that," Qasar said, stepping forward to stomp on the glass bulb encasing its hideous death's head.

The eye slits thinned, then quirked wide.

Out from behind the creature's back a hand jerked out the hidden weapon, snapped in line with Qasar's unprotected chest.

Chof!

The creature recoiled in flame and Qasar threw himself back, all but stumbling into Bayar. Bayar sidestepped and Qasar fell backward onto the seat of his *del*.

He stood there blinking as the creature blazed up in greenish fire and began curling its limbs inward like a scorched insect.

The ugly burnt-flesh stink forced Bayar back, holding his handkerchief over his gagging mouth. He looked to Qasar, grinned broadly and, waving his Chof gun, said, "I did not hesitate to shoot this time."

"It is good not to hesitate."

"It is very good not to hesitate," Bayar agreed.

"And for that you will eat roast mutton to your heart's delight." Qasar grinned, knuckling himself to a standing position.

Bayar grinned from ear to ear.

"But you still owe me your fealty," Qasar added, reaching into the pocket of his *del* for a sheep's eye, which he gulped down without chewing.

"You must be very hungry," Bayar commented.

"The eye of the sheep is a delicacy," Qasar said casually.

"I did not know this."

"Which is why I did not volunteer the information," Qasar replied, his face without emotion.

5

KILLERGHOST
<u>RED SANDS</u>

In the control room of the resting MAFB-2 Killerghost saucer *Red Sands*, Gnard Captain Lhyso watched the tactical replay of the defeat of the three-man Death Squad, his eyes livid.

"These Mongols are good, they are very good."

"They appear lucky," a sergeant said. His hands clenched and unclenched spastically.

Lhyso swiveled in his command chair.

"You would enjoy a crack at these barbarians, would you?"

"Honor me to lead a Death Squad."

"No. An Air Death Squad. Let us see how their luck holds now that you have studied their response patterns."

"Your will."

The sergeant stalked off, his fists like mallets of fused bone. His rage would guide him to utter victory, Lhyso knew.

Angrily, he reached for the yellow comm button on his command chair. Kolyma Tower must be informed. The mission was escalating already . . .

6

THE WINDING ROAD, OUTER MONGOLIA

Qasar the Mongol and Bayar stood around in the eerie shadow-streaked moonlight where the Winding Road wended up from Black Gobi to steppelands. They were eyeing all the six directions of space warily. The dead lay asprawl at their feet, their brains putrefying.

"It is a ghost. It wears a skull face," Bayar was saying.

"It wears armor. Therefore it is a demon," Qasar again countered.

"But not a Russian demon."

"If from the north, a Russian demon. Without question."

"The Russians do not have demons," Bayar insisted. "They are godless. No gods. No devils. It is simple logic."

Silence overtook the argument.

"These are the ones who built the New Wall," Bayar said with a touch of awe.

"Ghosts do not build things," Qasar countered. "They roam the caravan trails, unburied and unhappy."

"Ghosts do not have brains on their crowns. Or carry sneeze guns."

"Chofs," Qasar corrected.

Bayar scrunched up his mournful face. "Who decreed you khan?"

Qasar ignored the comment. He nudged the spindly

body with one booted toe. "It can be killed, therefore it cannot be a ghost, though it wears a ghost's dead flesh-stripped countenance."

"Perhaps it is a demon."

"There is one way to find out," Qasar said, dropping to one knee.

"What is that?"

"We will skin it."

"What will that prove?"

"Ghosts do not have bones. Demons have bones. If it possesses bones, it is a demon and there will be no further argument."

"That is a good theory."

"Which I will now prove." Suiting action to promise, the big Mongol began attacking the whitish carapace armor that sheathed the dead thing that was not human, whatever else it might be.

The armor refused to surrender. Qasar could not remove the gauntlets or the gleaming boots. They might all have been a single piece.

But there remained the cratered hole where the arrow struck. Qasar took the shaft and extracted it with a sharp tug. The arrowhead came out trailing goo that was not blood or recognizable viscera.

Eyeing this, Bayar said, "No blood is green."

"It is not blood," Qasar grunted.

"If not blood, then what?"

Qasar made a thoughtful face. Bayar sneezed without warning, blowing semiliquid matter in all directions.

"Hah! It is snot!" Qasar exploded, driving the arrowhead into the soft sandy soil for later retrieval.

Kneeling over the kill, he attacked the creature with his blade, and the fractured pieces began surrendering. It was hard, strenuous work. But Qasar went at it with a will.

Bayar turned away, saying, "I will claim my mutton now."

"First the oath," Qasar reminded.

"What oath?"

"I will say it for you, and you will repeat it."

"For roast mutton, I will speak any words," Bayar said fiercely.

Qasar nodded.

"Repeat my words: 'I swear eternal fealty and loyalty to you.' "

" 'I swear fealty and loyalty to you.' "

"Eternal. You must speak the word 'eternal.' "

Bayar swallowed. " 'I swear eternal fealty and loyalty to you.' "

"I will go as vanguard against the multitude of your enemies. All the beautiful girls and married women that I capture and all the fine horses, I will give to you."

" 'I will go as vanguard against the multitude of your enemies,' " Bayar echoed. " 'All the beautiful girls and married women that I capture and all the fine horses, I will give to you.' "

"When hunting is afoot," Qasar continued, "I will be the first to go to the battle and will give you the wild beasts that we surround and catch. If in time of battle I disobey your orders or in time of peace I act contrary to your interests, part me from my wives and possessions and cast me out into the wilderness.' "

Bayar swallowed hard. " 'When hunting is afoot,' " he recited, " 'I will be the first to go to the battle and will give you the wild beasts that we surround and catch. If in time of battle I disobey your orders or in time of peace I act contrary to your interests, part me from my wives and possessions and cast me out into the wilderness.' "

Qasar nodded with deep satisfaction. He never looked up from his bloody toil.

"What oath is that?" Bayar wondered.

"Have you had no schooling? Genghis's loyal cavalry swore such an oath to him."

"I have not read much of Genghis Khan," Bayar admitted.

Qasar looked up sharply. "What kind of Mongol are you not to know the life of Genghis by heart?"

"One educated under the old Soviet system," Bayar said promptly.

Qasar grunted. He had created a hole now larger than his fist. Lathelike ribwork lay exposed, sheathed by a sick pinkish flesh more like toadstool meat than human flesh. The seeping blood was redder than human blood.

With his knife, Qasar scored the breastbone lengthwise until the skin parted as if stretched to the breaking point over a framework of wooden sticks.

When attacked, the ribs broke easily, liked dried sticks. The sound was grisly in the night.

By now Bayar had reached the sheep carcass and was hunkering down to pick at it with his dirty fingers. He was silhouetted against the low terrain. He picked here and there, but when his fingers came away, they clutched hard pieces of black matter that broke with brittle snaps identical to those Qasar was obtaining from the exposed breast of the dead carcass.

With a howl, Bayar jumped to his feet and stormed over, his mohair-sheathed legs churning.

"I withdraw my oath," he spat.

"An oath cannot be withdrawn," Qasar grunted.

Bayar stumbled to a stop. "Nevertheless, I withdraw it."

"You cannot do that. An oath is sacred."

"I swore an oath in return for my share of roast mutton. No meat is left on the sheep's black bones. All is charred. You know this."

"I knew nothing. I merely extracted the promise at the appropriate time."

Bayar crossed his arms defiantly. "No mutton, no fealty."

"You have given your fealty. Mutton you will do without, just as I."

Bayar was looking into the open chest cavity. It was raw and thick with unfamiliar organs. "I spy bones."

"Bones, yes," Qasar said.

"Bones mean a demon, not a ghost."

"Bones mean a foe who is mortal."

"Of course he is mortal. We killed three."

"I killed two. You only killed but one."

"I killed the one who would have slain you, Qasar."

Qasar grunted. "For which you may eat all the mutton you can pick off the carcass."

Bayar seemed at the point of saying something pungent when he exploded into a sneeze, which he barely gathered into his handkerchief before it sprayed the dead thing.

As he wiped his raw nose, Bayar watched with a fascinated horror as Qasar plunged a big hand into the chest cavity and felt around among the viscera and the slime.

"What are you doing, Qasar?"

"Seeking the heart."

"Demons do not have hearts."

"I have heard this as well."

"So why are you seeking what is not even there?"

"Because I believe in what I find or not find with my own hands, not what I see imperfectly or is carried to my ears by the rumor-haunted Gobi winds."

At length Qasar paused. His cabled wrists contorted and he pulled out a great glob of red organ meat.

"What is that?" Bayar asked.

Qasar turned it over in his hands. "The demon's heart."

"Therefore it is not a demon."

"It is not a demon. Not even a Russian one."

"So what is it?"

"A man," Qasar said, tossing the heavy heart into the dirt and regaining his feet.

"No man wears a skull where he should have features. Nor brains where thick black hair should grow."

"Then it is not a man, but only resembles one."

"If it is not a man, what is it?"

Qasar looked thoughtful into the north distance. "It is a *Yasu-Tologoi*."

"A Bone Head! What is a Bone Head?"

"That dead thing."

"I have never heard of Bone Heads. Are they a Kazakh tribe?"

"If so," Qasar said, "they will rue the day they erected their accursed wall around the mountain where I was born and expect to be reborn."

Bayar looked to the set profile of Qasar the Mongol, then down at the dead Bone Head, and thought that he would not want to be a Bone Head in the coming days.

7

KILLERGHOST
RED SANDS

Gnard Captain Lhyso reported back to Kolyma Tower from his hidden Killerghost saucer.

"Death Squad Six is down."

On the comm screen, Komo Dath's reddening face loomed closer.

"Impossible," he rasped.

"The Terran barbarians overwhelmed them in less than ten Terran subunits. Houdi D'ud is being dismembered at this moment, possibly for food."

Komo Dath hissed through his wicked needle teeth. "Only because their orders were to probe and test Mongol response under fire."

"They were not frightened by our KA-77 fire."

"They are too stupid, too primitive to know fear."

"Instructions?" Lhyso asked.

"Double the size of the next Death Squad."

"Mission parameters?"

"Exterminate. They must pay for those Gnard deaths, and there are other Mongols to haul before that cursed Paeec, Telian Piar."

"Your will."

8

THE WINDING ROAD, OUTER MONGOLIA

Qasar was saddling his white charger whose black leg bands silently proclaimed its direct descent from the wild horses of Mongolia.

"We cannot sleep here," he was saying.

Bayar looked unhappier than usual. "Where will we sleep?"

"We cannot sleep at all. Other Bone Heads may lurk on the steppes. We will be safer on horseback and on the move."

"Since I have sworn a solemn oath to obey your every command, I must do as you say."

Qasar finished cinching his saddle. "Good."

"But that does not mean I have to like it," Bayar added.

"I do not care that you like it, only that you obey," Qasar returned.

Lifting his saddle onto his skittish gelding, Bayar noticed that the other horse was uncastrated. "You ride a stallion?"

Qasar nodded. "This is a good horse."

"How do you control him when he is around mares?"

"I control him with my voice and my will, for he, too, has sworn fealty to me."

"No horse can give an oath."

"This horse has," Qasar said, mounting his stallion. "He is the greatest horse I have ever known."

"I trust my gelding. I trust only geldings."

"A gelding is incomplete. A stallion has spirit. I will not ride a spiritless horse any more than I would take a spiritless woman."

Appraising the horse, Bayar commented, "That is a sand-bred horse, I see."

"I broke him on the steppes. He almost broke me."

"We are riding into mountains. You should have a mountain horse."

"I have Chino. He is equal to mountains or steppes and any land in between."

Incredulity lifted Bayar's eyebrows. "You have named your horse?"

"Yes," Qasar said, turning his mount. They started along the Winding Road.

Forking his gelding, Bayar followed him closely.

"You are a man named Dog and you ride a horse named Wolf?" he asked.

Qasar said nothing. The horses were ambling. Bayar's ear flaps slapped his ears, making a sound like the exhausted beating of bird wings.

"If you were not mad, it would be the other way than the way it is. You should be called Wolf."

"I have never met a man called Wolf," Qasar said.

"Nor have I. Although some talk of a wild Khalkha Mongol named Wolf who is infamous from the Red Gobi to the Hunger Steppes."

"I believe what I touch, not what I hear from rumor-mongering tongues."

"This Wolf is a killer."

"All wolves kill. It is their nature."

"A good point," Bayar said. "But this Wolf slew a fellow Mongol, which is a very bad thing. A Russian or a

Chinese is acceptable, but what manner of Mongol slays another?"

"Genghis slew his own brother," Qasar pointed out.

"That was Genghis. It is different now."

"Only the times are different, not the Mongols who exist in this time," Qasar replied.

They rode in silence as their horses picked up speed, Qasar standing in his wooden stirrups, while Bayar sat on his saddle and bounced with every hoofbeat, his head bobbling like that of a broken-necked corpse on a bouncing wagon. These were the only ways to ride a Mongolian horse—absolute control or abject surrender.

"That oath I swore," Bayar said at one point. "It spoke of enemies."

"It did."

"You possess many enemies?"

"Not as many as I intend to," Qasar said.

"I do not like the sound of your words."

"They are true words, like them or do not like them."

"I have no wives or possessions for you to deprive me of should I fail you in war or peace," Bayar remarked.

"Then I will deprive you of your worthless life if you fail me," Qasar returned without menace.

Bayar scrunched up an unhappy eye. "That was not in the oath."

"It was in my oath that I swore to myself," Qasar said.

"Have you wives and possessions?"

"No."

"Not one wife?"

"No."

"No one would have you?"

"I loved a woman once wrongly, or loved the wrong woman rightly. I do not know. So I have no wife. Only a stallion."

"A wife is good to have on a cold night, but a horse

makes a Mongol a Mongol. I would rather have a horse than a wife, all in all."

"After I am reborn, you will have both."

Interest touched Bayar's long face. "She must be fat. The wife, not the horse. I will not stand for a scrawny wife."

"I would not burden you with a scrawny wife, good for nothing except scolding."

"Her cheeks must be plump and her lips like sheep fat. And when I place her on my sleeping *kang* for the first time, she will not fight, except perhaps a little."

"That is between your fat wife and you."

"Of course."

The combined clicking and scuffing of hooves filled the silence that followed, until Bayar ventured a fresh thought.

"It is good that you found me, for I have always desired a wife. I was betrothed to the daughter of my cousin, but she died before her twelfth birthday. To find a wife without the help of one's clan is a very difficult thing. So I am glad that our paths have crossed."

"It is fate," Qasar said.

"It was a sheep," Bayar said.

"Fate sent the sheep."

"Fate is not always kind to Mongols," Bayar pointed out.

"That is why it is called fate."

"Those are true words."

"Those are very true words," Qasar said, his knife-slit eyes alert to every shadow on the road ahead.

He did not see the six figures rise up from behind a hill they had put behind them, to levitate into the air in a loose swarm, and then with a soundlessness that promised death float after them like trailing grasshoppers.

9

THE BLACK GOBI, OUTER MONGOLIA

Air Death Team leader Kuda B'ux took point, moving through the thin Gobi air in a vertical position, his legs dangling high off the ground, his gleaming KA-77 clutched in both gloved hands. He chanted into his helmet mike.

"Air Death Strike Three. This is Strike Point. Approaching designated targets."

"Proceed, Three," came the reply.

Kuda B'ux surged forward. The honor of the first blood would be his. If he moved quickly enough, he would scorch both Terrans and avenge Death Squad 6 before his trailing team members could trigger their weapons.

His bulky moon shadow raced along the parched ground ahead of him, the lunar disk at his back. Like rubies seen dimly at night, his hot red eyes were almost black in the darkness . . .

10

THE WINDING ROAD, OUTER MONGOLIA

The vast stretch of stars known as the Silvery River poured down white light that rivaled that of the moon as Qasar and Bayar rode along the shadow-haunted ribbon of the Winding Road. The Black Gobi was behind them now. They were into pastureland where hills lifted and the pocked marks of camel caravans showed plainly.

"How many marches to the next well?" Qasar was saying.

"One. Have you no *airag*?"

"I do not drink fermented mare's milk."

Bayar looked disappointed. "What Mongol does not drink *airag*?"

"One to whom *airag* is like a rage that carries him into trouble."

"I had hoped you carried *airag*, for I have none. Only a brick of tea."

"We will drink fresh water one march from now, if there are no *gers* or cattle stations along the way."

"The next *ger* village lies two marches."

"Then no *airag* for at least two marches."

"I would settle for mutton."

Chof!

At the sudden sound, Qasar flung his stallion around, crying, *"Ai-Yah!"*

The spurt of emerald flame melted into the ground at

the spot where he had been a moment before. It sizzled, turning the yellow sand to smoking amber glass.

Dropping into the saddle, Qasar muscled his horse around by the strength of his legs and he flung his hands up, a Chof gun clenched in each fist. His eyes locked on the floating figures. His mouth dropped open in momentary shock, then he was triggering both weapons.

Chof! Chof! Chof!

Whirling in his saddle, Bayar spied the flock of red-eyed Bone Heads and lifted his captured weapon.

Chof! Chof!

Return bursts were brief. The floating ghosts were consumed in midair, to plummet like brained birds. They dropped in ones and twos to earth, landing with sounds like dull unmusical gongs.

"You did not hesitate to shoot," Bayar said with admiration.

"To hesitate is to die. Tonight, we are not the ones to die."

"That is tonight. Tomorrow night may be different."

"This, too, is fate," Qasar said, urging his stallion back along the Winding Road to the place where the flying Bone Heads had crashed to earth.

There, he collected their weapons as best as he could. Some were shattered and unworkable.

"These are Chof rifles," Qasar said, hefting one of the surprisingly light devices in both hands.

"If you say they are Chof rifles, than that is what they are," Bayar said agreeably.

"You are a smart Mongol."

"I am a living Mongol. That is what counts on this strange night."

Remounting, Qasar cradled one of the big bulky rifles across the pommel of his traditional saddle.

"We are rich," Bayar cried. "These Chofs will fetch

many horses in barter. Then we shall be rich in horses, which are the greatest riches to own."

Qasar shook his head. "They are not for barter."

"Then what good are they?"

"They are for dealing death."

"And preserving our skins, do not forget."

"In dealing death, they preserve our skins," Qasar remarked. "For the Bone Heads wish to drop our charred bones into the Gobi."

"Are these Bone Heads among your multitudes of enemies?"

Qasar nodded grimly, his voice equally grim. "They are now."

"Riding with you is very interesting. But my stomach still growls for mutton."

"At least it growls."

"There is that, yes."

"You will watch the south and the east. I will warden the north and the west."

"You expect more Bone Heads?" Bayar prompted.

"First they sent three. Then six. Next they will send twelve," Qasar said.

"How do you know this?"

"This is how the Bone Heads think."

Bayar made a puzzled face. "I thought you never encountered a Bone Head before."

"I have not. But I know how a man thinks, and how animals think. And I have seen how a Bone Head thinks. Mark my words, next there will be twelve."

"Walking or flying?"

Qasar was silent a moment.

"Both. Six walking and six more flying."

"Are you certain?"

"I could be wrong."

"Then you are not certain?"

"Uncertainty is uncertainty. Look to the earth and the skies both. Watch to see the sheen of moonlight on their head bulbs or the fierce glowing of their wicked red eyes."

"I would be happy to see no more Bone Heads ever," Bayar said glumly.

"If they see you first, it will be too late for you."

And hearing the sudden thick tightness of Qasar's words, Bayar stole a furtive glance at the big Mongol.

Qasar held his reins in his teeth, a Chof gun in each fist.

Bayar decided this was a good idea, except that he had but one Chof gun. He slipped it into his *del* and, taking his reins between his teeth, brought his Chof rifle to bear. His eyes became busy scouring the impenetrable night shadows.

They were riding at a steady un-Mongol pace now. Speed would not be of use to them. Not with a foe who might steal upon them from any of the six directions of space to deal fiery green death.

11

THE WINDING ROAD, OUTER MONGOLIA

The combined Death Squad and Air Death Team emerged from the Killerghost *Red Sands* like gleaming locusts made of quicksilver and mercury.

The red-and-silver Death Team trudged toward the Winding Road through the harsh Mongolian terrain, atmosphere suits awash with moonlight, their night-vision helmets activated. They walked through the rich air they could not breathe with the gingerliness of persons in an unfamiliar environment.

The Air Death Team hung back on the ground, waiting for the go order. It came after the Death Squad trooped down a declivity of rock and sand to vanish from sight.

"Death Squad leader to Air Death unit."

"Copy, Death Squad leader."

"In ambush position."

"Acknowledged. Moving into retreat interdiction position."

Lifting one hand, Air Death Team leader Nrvus Tiq signaled his team of five KA-77-armed Gnards to lift off. Their backpack thrusters began hissing, sending the sand toiling up in faint clouds that the moonlight caught and silvered.

Like metallic spirits rising from high-tech graves, they shot into the air, achieved the predetermined covert altitude and advanced, their upper bodies straining forward with an intent eagerness, their spindly legs trailing.

They swept around in a wide arc, using the low hills to shield them from the Winding Road.

"Check point blue reached," Tiq reported.

In his helmet receiver the brittle voice of his counterpart, Death Squad leader Sitar Dux came bitingly.

"No sign of targets from ambush point."

"Acknowledged."

Beneath his dangling feet Tiq noticed the Gobi sands were stirring and lifting.

"Increase speed two percent," he said.

Behind him his Air Death Team accelerated in a disciplined group. Tiq's military heart swelled. This was what being a Gnard was all about. Discipline. Battlecraft. Certainty of victory.

In their turbulent wake, sand dust rose shimmering.

Qasar shifted the reins in his mouth, tasting the sweaty rawhide on his tongue. It was good to taste. His strong teeth clamped it into a fresh position nonetheless.

The Gobi was quiet. No sounds other than the steady clopping of unshod hooves reached his ears. But under that sound, Qasar knew that danger could crawl, and death slither unheard.

"I have a question," Bayar hissed.

"Ask."

"You who do not trust rifles now wield two Chof guns. Why?"

"A Chof gun is better than a European bullet rifle."

"Why better?"

"It spits fire, not bullets."

"What happens when the Chof guns run out of fire?"

"We throw them away and pick up the Chof guns that have yet to run out of fire."

"What happens then when our last Chof gun burns no more?"

"I still have my bow and you your European rifle."

"And if they are not enough?" Bayar wondered as he scanned the star-dappled skies on his side of the Winding Road.

"By then we are either victorious or dead," Qasar said simply.

"I would pray for another ending."

"There is no other ending," Qasar muttered, "for we are being hunted by Bone Heads, who live to kill Mongols."

"Did I mention that there are those who say the beings who built the New Wall came down from *Ulan Nud*?"

Qasar's gaze flicked to a burning red point in the night sky. "Red Eye?"

"Yes. The Red Eye star, which is supposed by those who study the stars to be a world like ours."

Qasar made no comment through his clamped reins.

"What do you think of that story, Qasar?"

"It is a story. Why waste thought pondering something one cannot ever hope to know?"

"You are a practical Mongol."

"I am a Khalkha Mongol. When the great khans laid waste to all the world, my tribe was the only tribe that refused to kneel before them."

"In other words, you are stubborn even in the face of a tiger?"

"Tigers know to run from the sweat-smell of a Khalkha Mongol," Qasar said.

"You are also full of your own spirit."

Qasar grunted. "Whose spirit would I be full of if not my own?"

* * *

The clopping of beasts of burden came through the acoustical receptors of the Death Team leader's atmosphere helmet.

"Quarry coming into audio range," Sitar Dux warned.

On either side of the Winding Road, hunkered-down Death Squad troopers unlatched the safeties on their KA-77s.

In his earpiece, the voice of Flying Death Squad leader Tiq hummed.

"Setting up retreat blockade."

"Acknowledged."

Addressing his men, Dux said, "You know the drill. Wait until they come into cross-fire position. On my signal rise and open up."

The dead air hissed.

"And stay strictly within your preassigned firing corridors. A wild shot could take out a teammate. I want zero casualties. Understood?"

No one answered. No one had to.

Qasar saw the faint moonlight and starshine shimmer that floated over a western hill. His dark eyes narrowed in his brazen face.

"What lies behind those hills, Bayar?" he muttered.

Bayar shrugged. "More hills. It is the Gobi."

"No trail?"

"I know of no trail beyond those hills."

"Then why does the sand dust rise as if camels and horses have passed?"

Bayar looked to the west.

"We would hear camel bells or yak grunting if a caravan or herd were passing," he muttered.

"But not flying Bone Heads."

His eyes tracking the path of the shimmer, Qasar saw

that it was greater and higher up ahead of them. Less high behind them and to the west.

"The Bone Heads are circling around behind us," he warned, his voice a dog's growl.

"How many?"

"That is not the question. The question is, what lies before us?"

Bayar peered down the Winding Road. It wound to the north behind a hill, like a dark ribbon washed here and there by moonlight filled in by granite shadows.

"I see nothing," he said.

"That does not mean nothing is there."

"More Bone Heads?"

Qasar's knife-slit eyes tightened. "Walking ones, if I know my Bone Heads."

Bayar sipped a quick breath. "They intend ambush?"

Qasar nodded.

"But command me, and I will ride where you say," Bayar said fervently.

"That is very brave of you, city Mongol."

"I speak not from bravery, but because my heart tells me that where you ride, danger may swirl but will not touch me."

"I do not know this to be true."

"I see in your eyes and hear in your voice the determination to seek the place where you were born. You will reach there. If I follow you, so will I."

"If it is your destiny to die by the side of the Winding Road, nothing a Khalkha Mongol can do will alter your fate."

"That is why it is called fate. But I will take my chances with you."

"Then listen to my instructions before the Bone Heads fall upon us with their Chof guns . . ."

* * *

Air Death Team leader Tiq stood in the center of the Winding Road. He could see only so far, even with his night-vision dome activated. Arrayed on either side of him stood his team, their KA-77s at the ready. They stood like statues, burnished by the alien moon whose light was too harsh, too metallic for their comfort. The Martian moons gave a softer, more stealthy light.

Time passed.

"Air Death Team Three to Death Squad leader. Mission status check requested."

"Stand by."

"Standing by," Tiq said, thinking the trap was about to be sprung.

The next transmission made him clutch his weapon more tightly.

"Here they come . . ."

After that, all transmissions were chaos.

Chof! Chof! Chof!

The sounds came out of his earpiece, but the greenish flashes of close-quarter combat were visible just over the next hill.

"Looks like we may not be needed, men," he remarked.

Chof! Chof! Chof! Chof!

The firing went on, growing in intensity.

In his earpiece Tiq heard a conglomeration of sounds—hissing, sizzling, spitting crackles. A Gnard death-scream. Definitely a Gnard death-scream.

"I'm hit! I'm hit!"

Then came the terrible hissing of an atmosphere suit disintegrating under Terran atmospheric pressure.

"They're taking casualties!" Tiq raged.

Muttering curses came from his poised team. They ached to take to the air. But their discipline was too strong. Even with their fellows dying useless deaths on this alien planet, they stood resolute.

Payback would be theirs if any unfriendlies survived the Death Team attack. And if not, there were other Mongol Terrans on which to take out their justifiable rage and frustration.

A long silence followed the last burst of electric green and the final sporadic choffing of KA-77 fire.

Tiq called into his helmet mike. "Air Death Team Three to Death Squad. Engagement check."

In response, the slow hiss of an atmosphere suit came steadily. It was a creepy sound. In his mind's eye Tiq could see the skull of a Gnard decompose on contact with the hellish Terran oxygen-nitrogen mixture.

"Tiq to Dux. What's happening up there?"

The hissing could be any Gnard's, but in the protracted silence, the knowledge that it was Dux's filled Nrvus Tiq with a cold grimness.

"Attention Air Death unit," he said with a tight clarity of enunciation. "Forward march. Let's close this gap."

Assuming walking fire formation, they started forward, KA-77s trained on the road ahead.

The thunder of alien hooves filtered into their helmets before the twin beasts came charging around the bend in the road and into view.

"Kneel and shoot!" Tiq howled.

They dropped into kneeling fire positions, fingers touching triggers.

"Hold your fire!" he said suddenly.

There was no disobedience. Not a shot was triggered.

"No riders!" a Gnard called out.

The horses bore down on them, eyes wild, their manes flying, decorated saddles empty.

Moving fast, Tiq called out orders.

"Make way! Let them pass. Two of you, Kwsp and Kaw'ke. Take to the skies. Locate those Gnard-killers!"

The Air Death Team rushed to clear the road while the Gnards on each tip of the skirmish line rose to the nearly silent hissing of their propulsion units. Reaching surveillance altitude, they broke apart, executing a circular sweep pattern designed to scan the largest area in the least time.

As Tiq watched, Kwsp suddenly convulsed, his arms separating briefly. They clapped together over his chest, his KA-77 falling to earth. A moment later Kwsp joined it.

Then the horses blew past. They let them go. Horses were not threats. And they had to be alert to ambushes.

Nrvus Tiq learned his mistake as he watched Kaw'ke zigzag in the air as if dodging enemy fire. But there was no fire, no sharp crack of the primitive Terran metal bullets that could shatter the polymer atmosphere suits.

"Kaw'ke. Report!" he called out.

"I am taking fire."

"What kind of fire?"

"Missile."

"Can you spot the enemy?"

"Negative. There is no muzzle flash. Instructions?"

"Random pattern of return fire. Your own flashes may pick him out."

"Acknowledged."

Kaw'ke's KA-77 began choffing wildly. The man was in a panic. It was unbelievable. A Gnard panicking because he faced wooden missiles he could not track from an enemy he could not spot.

Then one caught him in the face plate and Kaw'ke's helmet exploded outward in all directions.

Tiq was watching him fall to the ground, helpless, when the full significance of his tactical blunder came to him in the form of exploding helmets on either side of his command position.

The sharp percussive crack of rifle fire came from behind. It was impossible. But Air Death Team members were falling to the road, their brains flying like so much discarded bio matter.

Tiq whirled clumsily—and saw one Terran firing carefully, expertly making each shot count from the saddle of one of the horses whose saddles had been empty a moment before!

Tiq was blown backward, and the awful hissing of his life-giving air supply reached his stunned brain through his auris. Leveling his KA-77, he acquired the target. He was a heartbeat too late. The target had already acquired him.

The bullet struck his KA-77, and it exploded in his hand, sending screaming metal shrapnel into his chest and faceplate and giving Nrvus Tiq his first terrible taste of pure Terran air.

It made the lungs scream in agony, and Tiq was screaming in sympathy with their anguish as he pitched forward.

He was spared the sight of his surviving men wilting before a cross fire of bullets and arrows, and never understood how the Terran sharpshooter had gotten behind him . . .

Bayar stood up after the last Bone Head had fallen with one of Qasar's red-tufted shafts shivering in his air-supply backpack.

"We are victorious!" he cried.

"Are you certain?" Qasar called from his shadow-haunted shelter of the hills.

"None are standing."

"I see no Bone Heads in the skies."

"Therefore we are victorious."

Qasar came down off a rock outcropping, seemingly materializing like a man of stone shaking off an ancient hibernation to walk the earth once more. They met at the point where the flying Bone Head had died without taking to the air.

"You were correct, Qasar. Six walking and six flying."

Qasar surveyed the Winding Road. "Now twelve lying dead."

"They failed to see me clinging to the side of my horse as I rode past them."

"Chino also shielded you from their eyes."

"It is an old trick. I am surprised it worked on Bone Heads."

"That is why they are called Bone Heads."

"Now that we have conquered twenty-one Bone Heads without dying in the bargain, what will they do next?"

"Not even the Bone Heads know the answer to that question, so how can we Mongols?"

Bayar frowned in the moon-touched Gobi blackness. "That is a good answer."

"It is a very good answer."

"Much better than 'I do not know,'" Bayar added, grinning more widely.

Then they walked back down the Winding Road to collect their laboring steeds.

12

KILLERGHOST
RED SANDS

Killerghost Captain Lhyso reached for the yellow comm
button on his command chair and pressed it without
looking. His thin ruby eyes were fixed on the tactical
screen before him.

"Report."

"I have a tactical feed for you, Commander Dath."

"The operation was successful?"

"The tactical feed will answer that question better than
I," Lhyso said dully.

"Transmit."

"Transmitting."

Lhyso pressed the tactical feed button that squirted the
recorded chaos of the obliteration of the combined Death
Squad and Air Death Team units by a pair of primitive
Terrans.

Arms clutching the command chair armrests, Lhyso
waited, his thin eyes still fixed on the now-black tactical
screen. He breathed with the labored regulation of a man
at the end of everything—pride, commission, life itself.

The rasping voice of Komo Dath came not long after.
"Lhyso."

"I am prepared to relinquish command of this ship,"
Lhyso said hollowly.

"And I am prepared to accept it in return for your
abysmal failure. But I offer you a final chance."

Lhyso sat up, the fire returning to his eyes. "Listening."

"Take those two Terrans. Alive."

"Alive?"

"If even one dies, it will be your commission, perhaps your life."

"Alive? But they are Gnard-killers."

"And when I am done with them they will be Terran-killers."

"Your will," Captain Lhyso said, vaulting from his chair. He called over to a factotum.

"Pull a KA-77 from inventory for my use. White Card load." Then, hitting the intership comm button, he barked, "Next Death Squad on the roster, assemble for mission briefing. Now!"

13

THE WINDING ROAD, OUTER MONGOLIA

Qasar eyed the eastern horizon. It was tinged with a gray haze that chased the diamond-hard brightness of the low-hanging stars.

"It will be dawn soon," he said.

"I will welcome the dawn," Bayar said, his voice hollow.

"Bone Heads fear the dawn."

"They will not come by daylight?"

"I did not say this," Qasar amended.

"The Bone Heads walk by day as well as night?"

"I have never seen one walk by daylight."

"You have never seen one walk by day *or* night before this strange night."

"This is true," Qasar admitted.

They rode along in silence for several *li*. The spidery tamarisk trees were shedding their shadow-clotted night webs to reveal pinkening blossoms.

"How are your allergies?" Qasar asked at one point.

"Do you hear me sneezing?" Bayar retorted, his voice buoyant, if still hollow.

Qasar looked back. Bayar was riding up in his saddle in the fashion of a true Mongol. It was the only way he could keep the Bone Head helmet perched on his shoulders. Even so, he held it in place with one hand while the other clutched the reins of his gelding.

Qasar smiled. "Perhaps you were right about these allergies," he allowed.

"We are men to be feared now. We are fierce killers of Bone Heads."

Qasar shook his head. "We will be hunted men when the clan of the Bone Heads begins to miss their warriors."

"After tonight I fear no Bone Heads or any other foe," Bayar said loudly.

"Then you are a fool."

"You know fear?"

Qasar nodded. "I acknowledge it in my heart."

"That is honest."

Qasar made a closing fist. "Then I crush it without mercy."

"I would rather not feel fear in the first place."

"Fear feeds a Mongol's courage. Without it he is but a woman."

"I have known courageous women."

"I, too," Qasar muttered, eyes slitting. "Too well . . ." he muttered under his breath.

"Of course," Bayar added, "it goes without saying that none of them have known me . . ."

"This will change."

Bayar perked up. "I look forward to this with great anticipation."

They rode along in silence. Little by little Bayar's stiff legs began to weaken, then buckle. When the seat of his trousers came into contact with his saddle, he began to bounce wildly in time to the rollicking gait of his horse.

Try as he might, Bayar could not hold the great helmet over his head. He kept hitting the inside with his bobbling skull.

Eventually he flung it off. It banged along the side of

the road, then came to rest against the collapsed skeleton of a caravan camel.

"A Mongol must be made of iron," Qasar remarked thinly.

"My legs only have so much iron in their marrow," Bayar lamented.

"The iron in your legs is midwifed by the steel in your brain."

"My brain is made of brain."

"Then you are no Mongol, but a mongrel," Qasar said flatly.

After a while the dust of the road tickled Bayar's exposed nostrils and he began sneezing severely.

Qasar laughed. "Which is preferable—sneezing or standing tall on your mount?"

"I am a creature of habit," Bayar lamented. "I cannot change, and was a fool for thinking that I could."

At that, Qasar threw back his black-haired head and laughed so hard his stallion seemed to shake in riotous sympathy.

They neither sensed nor heard the ghostly thing slip up behind them, skimming along the Winding Road as if somehow connected to it. It veered around a great purple-gray massif and lined up on them, closing the distance at many times the top speed of a horse.

Its growing shadow foretold its coming. At the first cool dark touch, the horses sensed danger.

"Ai-Yah!" Qasar yelled. It was the signal to break off. But it was too late. The shadow was over them, and the horses became uncontrollable.

"Aiieeee!" Bayar cried, looking up. A glowing green shape hovered overhead. It was greater than anything he had ever seen. It resembled a great pavilion of jade and emerald, chased with golden lights and turned upside down, more opulent than the pavilions of the old khans.

Where the roof wheel should have been, a portal opened and down filtered a swarm of flying Bone Heads, their red eyes avid and intent.

"Dismount!" Qasar cried, jumping off his stallion. He spanked it away and it ran for its life, eyes screaming.

Bayar rolled under his own mount, still clutching the reins. The gelding bucked and reared but held its ground as Bayar fumbled to get his Chof gun into position.

Chof! Chof! Chof! Chof!

The sounds came in a cannonading wave, but instead of green fire, the skies were filling with a spreading murkiness.

Something black and busy enveloped the head of Bayar's horse and wrapped around it. He looked up. It resembled a spreading black net with balls swinging from different knots in its weave. Upon landing, the balls began beating at the horse's head, bouncing off with mad ferocity.

Another net landed nearby, like a spiderweb filled with armless black spiders that bounced in futile anger.

The reins came out of Bayar's hand, forcing him to roll aside ahead of the snapping hooves in danger of beating down upon his head. Coming to his feet, he fired into the air wildly.

A black net landed hissing and burning very close to his position. Bayar chanced running a few paces east, then south, then west to confuse the swarming Bone Heads. "Qasar! Where are you!" he cried.

No answer came. Frantically, Bayar peered around. He saw the white stallion charging off, its topknot whipping back and forth like a flail, as if flagellating itself for cowardice in the face of danger.

Another round of the black nets fell and one caught Bayar's left boot, throwing him to the ground.

Squirming on his back, he strained to get the boot

extricated. Seeing it could not be easily done, he fought to remove the obstructing boot when a thousand slick ropes gathered him up, and he felt the incessant battering of the bouncing balls against his ribs, back, and helpless skull.

They knocked the senses from his mind. But not before he looked over and saw Qasar, lying on his back, enmeshed in a similar snare, trying to rise as a hot-eyed Bone Head dropped from the sky and pressed the blunt muzzle of his Chof gun to the Khalkha Mongol's helpless forehead.

Through the nets, Qasar's brazen profile burned fiercely like hot metal under stress, his unflinching eyes glowering up at his assassin.

If I am to die here, at least my last sight of life is one of courage, Bayar thought as all sight slipped away.

The last thing he heard was the rude *chof* of the weapon pressed to Qasar's brow, and when the big Mongol's face turned, his eyes were staring wide and there was a white brand on his brow—like a death's-head scar.

14

THE WORLD WALL, OCCUPIED MONGOLIA

On the endless steppes of his unconscious imagination, Qasar the Mongol, born on the ninth hour of the ninth day of the ninth month of the Year of the Serpent, rode for his life.

The sky was the impossible hue that all Mongols worship as Menke Koko Tengri, the Everlasting Blue Sky. It stretched forever, so vivid it made a man drunk to ride under it, so jeweled it seemed to press down upon the steppes like the pulsing womb of eternity.

Qasar rode, because that was the way of the Mongol. It had been the way of the Mongol since before the era of Genghis. Even after the fall of the last khanate, the Mongol man continued to ride from the day he was weaned from his mother's breast to the very hour—if he was a fortunate Mongol—he laid his bones amid the manure-rich soil of his ancestors.

He rode for his life, but could not remember why. Qasar only knew that his life was forfeit if he did not ride hard and far, and so he spurred his stallion along under the everlasting sky that seemed to call to him with the sounds of the Mongol *hoomi* long songs—songs so wondrous and beautiful they were not of this Earth, but belonged to some heavenly realm.

Among the Hentiyn Mountains lay safety, Qasar knew. He rode for those mighty massifs. There, on the peak called Burkhan Khaldan, it was said, Genghis had found refuge during his troubled youth. There, too, at the end of his days, he had been interred in secret. No Mongol knew exactly where. It was a holy place. Qasar understood that if he could reach that mountain, the spirit of Lord Genghis, the Heaven-sent, Overlord on Earth, would protect him from the evil that followed him unseen.

As he rode the great blueness of heaven began to change. It darkened to cobalt, shadowed to indigo, and ultimately turned a jet-black with a thousand constellations, of which none were recognizable to man or Mongol.

The stars in the great black slate of heaven were also a terrible color. Jade. All were jade. There were no ruby, topaz, or golden stars. And certainly none the true star color of diamonds. Their unremitting greenness seemed like the eyes of a thousand malevolent jade-eyed idols hovering over Mother Mongolia.

Bathed in their unholy radiance, Qasar spurred his muscular white stallion Chino to greater speed. As great as was his heart, however, Chino was capable only of running as fast as the fleetest horse.

Then the jade-green stars began to fall and trouble the unfamiliar night sky. They were hunting him, Qasar knew. He understood it instinctively. He understood it perfectly, not with his senses, but with his Mongol soul.

He did not know why the shooting stars were seeking him. He could never fathom why. But he alone, of all men on earth, was the prize they sought.

Crisscrossing the skies madly, they at first seemed blind. Then one froze, reversed its track and arrowed after him.

As if the word had gotten out that there rides Qasar the Mongol, others fell in along its path, following in a sinuous jade necklace.

They swelled in the sky. And more quickly than it takes to draw four breaths, the air over Qasar's head was ringed with great glowing shapes like sky pavilions of smoldering jade and gold.

Together, they began descending, as if linked by unseen ropes.

Qasar reined in his horse. The stallion reared up, its tossing head silhouetted against the jade falling stars that were no more stars than Qasar the Mongol was Kublai the Great Khan.

In these sky pavilions there were windows, and within, burning red eyes shifted in the shadows and watched him. Turning his frightened horse, Qasar saw red eyes all around him, peering stonily and shifting in the shadows.

What was strangest of all, Qasar saw before an unknown darkness overtook his mind, was that some of these eyes moved, not in pairs, but singly. This was impossible. Eyes came in pairs. When one moved, so did its mate. It was unnatural to see flaming red eyes shift and blink, independent of others.

Qasar awoke as if a thunderclap had rattled through his mind.

His eyes snapped open, focused instantly, and before the pupils had finished dilating, he strained to move.

He could not move. His arms were somehow fettered, and his ankles chafed under a resistless thrall. Even his heaving chest labored stiffly. He could hear the crackle of the rib cartilage as his lungs fought to draw in oxygen.

His brow burned as if touched by a hot coal. A memory arose in Qasar's mind. He remembered falling under weighted nets, remembered, too, a fierce-faced Bone Head placing a Chof gun to his brow and pulling the trigger.

But that was all Qasar remembered. He sucked in a

deep breath. *I am not dead,* he thought. *I should be a pile of cooked meat and bones, but I am not. This is a good thing.*

His eyes began wandering.

Above, there was light. It was not good light, possessing neither the color of sunlight nor moonlight, nor even the sick yellow guttering of yak-butter candlelight.

The light shook and beat down, as if to dry the uprising of sweat from Qasar's pores.

Into the light moved a black shape. A man. No, not a man. The head was too big to belong to a natural man.

As his eyes grew accustomed to the backlighting, Qasar saw form and details resolve, and in his deepest soul place he felt a cold clutch and a growing fear.

It was not a Bone Head. It was different. The color was the same, but the sharp-toothed mouth was smaller and ringed with worms that writhed and twitched intermittently.

Where the eyes should have been were two flat blank ovals, greater by far than any eyes should be. And above them a single red orb burned red and hot and intolerable, remindful of the Red Eye planet in a midnight sky.

The orb stared with endless detached curiosity. Qasar tried to look away, but the eye held him.

"Begone, demon," he muttered through his discomfit.

The orb continued staring.

"Back to hell with you. I want none of you, Red Eye."

The head shifted slightly, the single eye moving around Qasar's face, then down to his naked chest, as cool and unhuman hands reached down to touch the iron hardness of his muscles.

I am to be eaten, he thought.

Unexpectedly, the hand withdrew and the head retreated. The ungodly light returned in full force, leaving Qasar to stare up at it, and to listen to the drumbeat of his racing heart in his chest, which threatened to push up from his ribs out of sheer fear.

Closing his eyes, Qasar concentrated on isolating that fear. Soon he would crush it to powder and blow it away with a single casual breath.

But after that, he did not know what his fate would be . . .

"The consistency of its muscles is five times more fibrous than that of other Terrans we have examined," the Tech/Div analyst was saying.

"The Mongols of past eras lived in their saddles. This is such a Mongol," Telian Piar said sibilantly.

"He is very strong," Komo Dath admitted. "And cunning."

"A killer," Piar agreed.

"A killer we can bend to our will with the proper . . . augmentation."

"No. This is as much a wild animal as a thinking being. It lives by instinct as much as by sinew and brain. He can no more be controlled by neural implants than can the giant arthropoda created by Tech/Div. We will discover another way."

"I would like to test its raw animal strength."

Glancing at the control board, the medical analyst noted, "Its constant straining against the inertia field has produced a surprising three percent power decrease."

Telian Piar and Komo Dath exchanged crimson glances.

"Arrange what you wish . . ." Piar said. "I do not fear for this Mongol's safety."

"Your will," Komo Dath hissed.

Qasar grunted as he attempted to lift his upper body without success. He could not see his bonds. He felt no chill of metal or abrasion of rawhide or hemp. He was unable to move—it was as if the sweat of his back had adhered him to the place on which he lay.

Abruptly, the table tipped forward and he was in a standing position, but still unable to stand. His feet did not touch the floor.

Before him stood a smooth steely wall, polished to mirror finish. He saw himself. He was nude. But his nudeness was not what startled him.

In the center of his forehead was a mark.

To Qasar, to whom beholding his face reflected in a mirror was a rare event, it was a soul-freezing sight.

Squint as he might, he could not resolve the shape or meaning of the mark. It had the look of a Chinese pictograph, but Qasar could read only the old Uiguhr script and some Russian Cyrillic, not Chinese signs.

A moment later the humming in the room stopped and his feet smacked the cold floor. He caught his balance and started toward his reflection, his eyes on the unfamiliar mark on his forehead.

Abruptly, he froze. For he saw that it was an angular white skull, outlined in red, partially eclipsing an ivory moon. The skull resembled a Bone Head skull, but with hollows instead of eyes.

Then two doors opened on either side of the room.

And four living Bone Heads stepped out.

They wore no bulbs of glass over their heads and carried no weapons that Qasar could see. They approached with flat-footed, wide-armed stances impossible not to recognize as threatening.

They had spindly arms that suggested the gnarled branches of the Phoenix tree—and suggested, too, a method of rendering them helpless.

Standing his ground, Qasar let them come. He set his

feet wide apart, lifting his arms, and made his big weathered hands into hooks.

"Do you know Mongol wrestling, Bone Heads?" Qasar challenged. "I have snapped many a neck in my day."

His foes made mallets with their hands. Their living eyes in their dead faces burned with a raw hatred that Qasar returned with a hooded glower of his own.

Quickly, the big Mongol found himself encircled by venomous red eyes.

Taking a backward step, he encouraged the two Bone Heads to advance confidently. At the moment when their feet were half off the polished floor, Qasar exploded in a paroxysm of violence.

His feet came off the floor, kicking backward. They encountered stiff resistance, and a Bone Head went squealing in a flurry of limbs. Qasar bounced forward, his big hands going for the wattled throats of two of his advancing enemies.

Feeling the hardness of their necks in his horny hands, Qasar brought them together. Two heads struck like Chinese spring melons. They came apart like melons, too, sharp-toothed mouths emitting high-pitched death-screams as their brains turned to jelly.

Feet hitting the floor, Qasar turned in time to see one Bone Head stumbling backward under the lash of his kicking foot.

The fourth shifted away and circled, his eyes turning raw in his bloated skull face at the sight of his two fellows laying pulped of head on the floor.

Qasar taunted him with a crooking finger. "Come, Bone Head. Come and fight like a Mongol."

The Bone Head continued to shift until the stumbling one finally landed on his back, and bounced up again.

Warily, they began circling him. Qasar moved with

them, maneuvering to keep both in sight at the same time. They understood his strategy and moved to defeat it, one stopping while the other continued feinting.

Tiring of the sport, Qasar suddenly lunged, caught a Bone Head wrist. His foe's snapping teeth sought his throat. Suddenly and inexorably Qasar broke the forearm like a rotten branch.

Backpedaling with the clutching hand and dripping wrist segment still grasped in his own fist, Qasar laughed. "You are not as dangerous as you look, Bone Head. Not without your weapons. A Mongol does not need weapons to be dangerous."

And Qasar flung the arm back into the face of its owner.

Dry fists began beating at his back. They felt hard, but the strength behind them was the strength of wood. Not metal. Not rock. And certainly not iron Mongol thews.

Reaching around blindly, Qasar struck a glancing blow that set the Bone Head stumbling. Pivoting on one bare foot, he kicked out, knocking the other foot out from under his opponent.

It was a simple matter to reach down, gather up the off-balance creature, and break its spine over his knee.

Snap.

The body slid off the Mongol's knee like so much uneaten mutton.

Standing up, Qasar surveyed the room. The maimed Bone Head was beating at a closed portal, whining ugly sounds, seeking escape.

Padding up to him, Qasar gave him his escape. He took hold of his neck in both hands and snapped it with an audible crack.

"Bone Heads have no iron in their bones," he shouted. "Send me more Bone Heads. I will break them all until there are no more. Then I will ride on to the place of my birth."

A low humming—different from before—had filled the room. It now stopped, and a sibilant voice, an unhuman voice, began speaking to him in an imperfect version of his own tongue.

"Why do you seek the place of your birth, Mongol?"

"To be reborn."

"I do not understand the concept."

"That is because you are a godless creature."

There was a brief silence.

"If you could have all your desires fulfilled, what would they be?" the sibilant voice asked.

Qasar thought about that for a long moment. "I would desire above all my horse."

"And?"

"I would desire also to ride my horse to the place of my birth."

"What would you do there?"

"I will know that when I reach the Mountain Where the Wolves Give Birth."

"If these things are made possible for you, Mongol, would you do as we instruct?"

"Why should I bend to your will when I am capable of seeking my destiny without your help?"

"Because you are a prisoner."

Throwing back his head, Qasar the Mongol laughed out loud.

"Why do you laugh?" the sibilant voice wondered.

"If I am a prisoner, why do your minions lie shattered and dead at my naked feet?"

"We have more soldiers."

"I will break their wooden bones, too," Qasar boasted.

"Some have weapons. You have none."

"Then I am a dead man and will not reach the place

where I was born. Therefore, I will never do your bidding."

"There are ways to change your mind."

"I will refuse all food. I will not taste water. I will disdain the very air needed to sustain my life."

"We can force you to accept these things."

"Then you are a fool, thinking a spiritless Mongol is good for anything useful."

The humming resumed.

"It is very smart for a Mongol," Komo Dath was saying.

Telian Piar lifted his gaze from the monitor screen. "Do not underestimate its intelligence. One just like it subjugated most of this hemisphere in a single lifetime."

"If it cannot be forced into the role of uniter, there must be something it wants above all other things."

"I will ask," Telian Piar said.

When the humming died again, the sibilant voice returned, asking, "Mongol, what is your name?"

"Qasar."

"Qasar, my race has conquered most of your world."

"You have not conquered Mongolia, therefore it does not matter what else you have dominion over."

"We have conquered your capital, Ulan Bator."

"Hah. Only citified Mongols live there."

"We have the power to conquer Mongolia."

"You cannot conquer me. How can you conquer all others like me?"

A different voice cut in, harsh and biting, the raspy accents strange. "Mongol, ours is a warrior race. What we do not want, others may take for themselves."

Qasar frowned darkly. "I hear your words."

"How would you like to be king of the Mongols?"

"You cannot make me khan. Only other Mongols can do this."

"You have not answered my question."

"I love Genghis, who razed the proud cities of the world that he might unite it. Genghis was a great civilizer. It was only through the weakness of those who followed that his empire does not endure to this day."

"Your people need a new Genghis."

Qasar's eyes slitted and burned with a smoldering pride. "Yes. I have often thought this."

"You could be that leader, Mongol."

"That is between me and other Mongols. Not Bone Heads like you," Qasar flung back.

The raspy voice crackled. "I am a Gnard. I am of a warrior race. I am like you."

Qasar swept the room with his hand. "If you are like these, I will break your spine, too!"

"Abysmal fool!" Komo Dath hissed. "You wear the White Card tattoo I ordered burned into your forehead. You belong to us!"

"Defile your mother, Gnard!" Qasar spat back. "You who dare compare yourself to a Mongol."

The humming resumed.

"It insulted me!" Dath hissed, his face all but pressed into Telian Piar's impassive, unwinking visage.

"You were getting to it. You have its interest."

"It is too—too—"

"Strong-willed?"

"Yes."

"I would think you would admire that in another warrior."

"I need to control it."

"Sometimes pointing a wild creature in the direction

of its natural prey is all that is required to achieve an objective."

"Spare me your intellectual prattle," Dath spat, waving the Paeec away.

"You have touched the Mongol's pride, let me goad it in a fruitful direction," Piar returned.

The humming stopped and the first voice sounded softly.

"Name your every desire and we will consider granting them all."

"Why would you do that?" Qasar asked, his rough voice flavored with skepticism.

"Because we have the power to do this, Qasar."

"That is not an answer."

"It is the best answer you will receive."

Qasar paced the floor, thinking, his head low, his eyes smoldering like black opals lying on a heated grate. His black hair fell over his eyes, obscuring the mark on his brow. He let it hang.

At length he pivoted to face the source of the voice. "First, I wish to visit the place where I was born. Second, I wish my good horse, Chino, to be returned to me. Third, I wish for mutton."

"Mutton?"

"I am hungry."

"You will receive mutton."

"And tea. I must have strong hot tea."

"You shall have tea."

"Then I wish faithful Bayar to be at my side."

"He is not strong like you."

"I wish for Bayar because the next khan must have followers, and he is the only one foolish enough to swear fealty to a masterless Mongol like myself."

"This is acceptable."

"Finally, I desire that three special desires be granted."

"State these desires."

"I do not know what they are."

"I cannot promise to fulfill three wishes without knowing what they are."

"Then I will sit here, not eating, not drinking, and not breathing until I am dead and useless to you," Qasar the Mongol said.

There was a silence, then the humming resumed. The humming lasted less than twenty heartbeats.

"These three desires will be granted if it is possible to grant them," the sibilant voice said evenly.

"Then swear all this by any Bone Head oath you have," Qasar said, grinning with triumph. For he now knew for a certainty that Bone Heads were not supernatural but natural. For only fools granted a Mongol three desires without knowing their nature.

15

NEAR THE MOUNTAIN WHERE THE WOLVES GIVE BIRTH

"Are we to be eaten?" Bayar asked nervously.

Qasar shook his black-maned head. "No. We are to be freed."

"Why would the Bone Heads free us after going to such lengths to capture us in the first place?" Bayar whispered.

"Because they are Bone Heads."

"Of course. This is self-evident."

They were walking under guard through a maze of rust-red metal tunnels that had the look of being made by machines. Qasar was once again attired in his emerald *del*, his silver dagger attached to his sky-blue silk sash. His boots made soft padding sounds in rhythm with the whisking of his legs against the *del*'s long skirts.

"Why is your hair hanging over your forehead?" Bayar asked suddenly.

"Because it is."

"You do nothing without reason," Bayar remarked.

"I did not say I had no reason."

Bayar nodded, saying, "The last sane memory I have is of a Chof gun pressed to your naked forehead."

"I remember this, too," Qasar said, his bronzed face inscrutable.

"I remember also the sound of its choffing."

Qasar strode on, his skirts noisy.

Finally, they came to a great portal with what appeared to be Chinese ideographs burned into the surface. The Bone Head guard took up positions on either side of the door.

"Can you read Chinese?" Qasar undertoned.

"Some."

"What do those characters say?"

Bayar squinted. "Those are not Chinese characters."

"You are certain?"

"Absolutely."

The door hummed open and they were motioned in.

"They are not looking at us in friendship," Bayar said as hot Bone Head red eyes tracked them stepping into the room.

"How else can they look at us? Their faces are dead, but their eyes are filled with blood and malevolence."

"This is true."

The room was spare and gleaming, filled with unfamiliar electronic devices and objects. One end was dominated by a long window looking out over a vast mountainous area.

Waiting expectantly were two Bone Heads, one in a silver and green military-style uniform, the other possessing a single red eye, and dressed like a Buddhist monk.

"Why does that one possess but one eye?" Bayar hissed.

"Because," Qasar said.

"In other words, you do not know."

"Nor do I care. If it matters to you, ask him, not me."

"I will accept him for what he is—whatever he is," Bayar said nervously.

The Red Eye spoke, and his sibilant tones were instantly familiar. "I am called Telian Piar, and this is Komo Dath, whose rank is Military Commander," he intoned.

Qasar eyed both beings without interest or fear.

Komo Dath walked around him, his burning eyes appraising and resentful. No word passed between the two. Then, with a curt nod, Dath signaled the other to speak.

"Show us the place where you were born," the Red Eye named Telian Piar said, indicating the long window.

Ignoring Dath, Qasar stepped up to the window. He scanned the horizon, taking in the unfamiliar terrain at a glance. Great domes of clear glass stretched as far as the eye could see. Under them reared up towers and minarets and other unfamiliar structures.

Drawing close, Bayar muttered, "They build their cities under *gers* of glass."

"I do not know this place," Qasar growled.

The Red Eye spoke. "This zone lies east of the ruins of Ulan Bator. You are looking at the mountain range you seek. Do you see the Mountain Where the Wolves Give Birth?"

"I only know it is east of the capital."

Bayar spoke up. "I know the mountain."

"Show us," the Red Eye said.

Bayar pointed, his dirty finger trembling. "That is the mountain. That low angry one."

"If Bayar says that is the mountain, then it is the mountain," Qasar told the Red Eye. "I do not recognize it, for I was born very young."

"And now you will be reborn," Bayar said, breaking into a nervous grin.

* * *

They were taken to a chamber where one of the sky pavilions sat quiescent, certain lights about its oblate form winking expectantly.

"This vehicle will convey you to the place where you were born," the Red Eye announced.

Qasar nodded.

They stepped aboard, the Red Eye leading, and were shown seats set in a corner of the busy interior. Bayar promptly settled into what appeared to be the most comfortable one.

Qasar frowned down at him. "Mongols do not sit in chairs."

"Khalkha Mongols do not sit in chairs," Bayar returned. "I prefer chairs."

"You may do as you wish," Qasar muttered, taking a seat on the cold metallic floor.

They watched armored Bone Heads busy themselves at many blinking machines. The ramp retracted and the sky pavilion sealed itself like a magical wound healing up.

The air became charged with a low electricity that made the hairs at the back of Qasar's thick neck lift eerily. Then they had the sensation of movement.

Through screens they saw the progress of the sky pavilion as it passed over the many glass domes where towns were built.

"Why do you build your settlements under bells of glass?" Qasar asked.

"So that we can breathe the air of our homeworld," the Red Eye explained.

"What is wrong with Mongol air?"

"Too rich and poisonous."

"But you are breathing Mongol air now."

"No. You are breathing air scrubbed and formulated to sustain both of our species."

"A species is a kind of clan," Bayar whispered in Qasar's ear.

"These Bone Heads are not even human," Qasar shot back.

"That is their problem, not ours," Bayar suggested.

The flight was short and the rugged peak of the Mountain Where the Wolves Give Birth filled all of the screens at once, so Qasar knew they had reached their destination.

"It is time," the Red Eye said.

Qasar nodded. "I seek a certain cave."

"There are several caves."

"This one faces south."

The Bone Head Military Commander spoke to another Bone Head, who sat in a central chair directing still other Bone Heads.

The ship began to circle the mountain until it faced the peak's southern exposure. The portal opened and the ramp slipped out like a protruding tongue of silver.

"Here."

Qasar stood up. Bayar started to follow, but Qasar's arresting hand stopped him.

"Stay. This is my karma I must face."

"You will come back?"

Eyeing the passive Red Eye, Qasar growled, "I have additional desires to collect."

And with that, Qasar the Mongol stepped out of the floating skyboat and padded down the ramp to slip into the dark shadowy maw of the south-facing cave.

His silent bulk was soon lost to sight.

The air was cool and bitter as Qasar padded into the cave, where the light was dim for the first twenty paces, then became dark, and finally impenetrable.

Gritty detritus crushed under his felt boots. His hands

swept out to touch the cool rock sides, which felt very dry. He had expected them to be wet. The place where he was born, his father had said, had been very wet. Now it was dry.

The darkness reverberated before his wide-open eyes. Here, in caves and ledges all over this peak, the wild wolves came up from the steppes to bear their cubs and suckle them. It was wolf season, and it was likely there would be a she-wolf with cubs at the farthest extension of the cave.

Presently, Qasar heard a low growl.

"Ho, mothers of cubs," he said softly. "I am not here to harm you or your whelps."

The growl intensified.

"I come only to smell the old air of the place where I came into this world, for I no longer belong to the world of my clan."

The growling stopped.

Qasar resumed speaking, his own voice a soothing growl.

"My father told me I was born clutching a clot of black blood. My uncle told me this also. My mother was silent on this subject, neither telling me that it was true nor denying it. I never understood her silence until I began hearing tales of Temuchin, Lord Genghis, who was also born clutching an identical clot of black blood."

The wolf growl came again, low, not threatening, almost like a feral song.

Qasar addressed the impenetrable blackness. "Am I the next khan, O Cave Where I Was Born?"

The cave gave back only silence. Even the she-wolf respected the void of sound.

Qasar grunted. "I will interpret your silence as assent."

The growl again.

"And your growl, bitch, as sign that I am in danger."

A stirring came at the farthest end of the cave. There was another way out, Qasar had been told. Perhaps another wolf was stealing in. Perhaps the mate of the bitch was returning to visit his cubs.

The scratchy *pad pad pad* of an approaching low presence brought Qasar's alert senses around to a focus point. The distinct scent of a steppe wolf reached out.

"I was born the proud son of the Khalkha clan, but now I am only a masterless Mongol named Dog. If you think that you stalk a mere dog, come forward. But beware, lest you challenge a wolf far greater than the bravest wolf you can be."

The padding hastened, picked up speed. Somehow in the impenetrable blackness, tiny sparks of feral green eyes glinted as a shadow hurtled at him. Feet planted far apart, Qasar stood his ground to meet it.

Snapping jaws sought his face. But the big Mongol's hands grasped the rough scratching fur, clamping down on the pulsing throat. Pivoting, he spun. The wolf in his hands became horizontal with the force of his spin. Twice he spun. Three times as the snapping fangs sought soft throat tissue and jugular.

At the apex of the third spin, Qasar released the spasming wolf and he went flying, a snapping, barking bundle of ferocity stumbling back down to the cave mouth.

Quickly padding after it, Qasar fell upon his foe while it was still spinning along the rocky floor. It was struggling to regain its spindly legs when the big Mongol reared up and brought down a crashing fist.

Its skull broke under the first blow, then shattered with the second. The wolf's legs collapsed and it lay down to die.

Using nothing more than his bare hands and his silver

dagger, Qasar sliced open the belly and peeled the gray-black pelt off the still-living body until he had a short blanket of wolf fur that was still sticky and pink on the inner side.

Bayar sat quietly in the chair as the Bone Head leader and the Red Eye moved busily about the sky pavilion. Their eyes, when they fell upon him, were demonic. But after a while it was possible to become used to their merciless gaze.

From the cave came the furious snapping and snarling of a wolf falling upon its prey, and the Bone Heads were visibly startled. Unintelligible orders were rasped, and three Bone Head soldiers surged down the ramp, clutching Chof guns.

Bayar jumped to his feet. "Qasar! Qasar!" he called. "Do not die again!"

The Bone Heads rushed into the cave. They were hardly out of sight before they were backing out again, not turning, but stepping warily backward. When the heels of their boots reached the bottom of the ramp, they turned and scrambled up.

A tall muscular form stepped into the light.

He stopped on the ledge before the cave maw. He wore the hammered face of Qasar the Mongol, and the emerald *del*, too. He stood with his head held high, a fiery light in his eyes. His hair was swept back, and there was a mark on his forehead.

Bayar saw this clearly. It was a white death's-head outlined in red, over an ivory moon.

Raising his voice, Qasar called out in a thunderous voice, "Hear me, O Eternal Blue Sky, for I am reborn! I am no longer Dog, but Qasar-Bagatur—Qasar the Strong —destined to be the next khan!"

Hearing these words, a shiver of destiny rippled

through Bayar's body and from one eye came a bitter tear of Mongolian pride.

He abased himself before the horse Mongol to whom he had sworn eternal fealty.

16

MOUNT
BURKHAN KHALDAN

"I demand my first desire be fulfilled," Qasar said after the ramp had been retracted and the sky pavilion was resealed and in the lapis lazuli skies once more.

"What is this desire of yours?" Komo Dath rasped, fists tightening.

"First I must have my horse."

"He has been found."

"Bring him aboard."

"He is in a secure place."

"He is only secure when he is with me."

"Very well," Telian Piar said, nodding in compliance.

The sky pavilion shifted course and was soon on the ground in a place made of strangely colored steels and irons—or so it seemed to Qasar's untutored eyes.

In a pen composed of shimmering light beams, Chino reared and snorted as Bone Heads milled around in concern, their frightening eyes looking themselves frightened. One clutched a hoof-shattered forearm.

Qasar started forward. "I will settle him."

The horse quieted down. Qasar took him by the reins and walked him back to the waiting vehicle.

"You cannot bring that animal here," Komo Dath hissed.

"Where he goes, I go."

And so saying, Qasar led Chino up the ramp and

hitched him in the largest open space therein. The white stallion immediately began dropping dung.

"He is a good horse," Bayar said, patting Chino's withers.

"He is the horse of the next khan," Qasar growled.

"Now what is your first desire?" Telian Piar asked as the ship lifted off again.

Qasar faced the Red Eye, towering over him.

"I seek the burial place of Genghis Khan, which according to legend lies on or near Mount Burkhan Khaldan."

"Guide us to this mountain, then," Telian Piar said.

The trip was of short duration, and although he had never before seen the Mountain Where the Wolves Give Birth, Qasar knew full well the stark shape of the summit of Burkhan Khaldan, nestled among the Hentiyn range, its mighty shadow falling over the winding Onon River.

"That is it," he said.

"Yes. That is it," Bayar confirmed.

"Where is the burial tomb of this Genghis Khan?" Piar asked.

Qasar shrugged. "No man knows."

"This is true," Bayar echoed. "Genghis was buried in secret."

Qasar looked to Bayar with interest. "I thought you did not know about Genghis."

Bayar shrugged. "I know that much."

Qasar nodded. Addressing Piar and Komo Dath, he said, "It is known that Genghis is buried somewhere here. Muster all your soldiers and give them picks and shovels. If we refuse to give up, we will discover the tomb in time."

Komo Dath emitted a rattling sound, one Qasar

understood to be laughter only after it had trailed off like a ratcheting machine losing power.

"There are more efficient ways," Telian Piar murmured.

The ship stationed itself over the mountain, and Bone Heads busied themselves with their labors as, in the corner, Chino made more manure. The Bone Heads avoided this whenever they could, but one unfortunate had to reach around the horse to adjust a control and slipped on a grassy lump of offal.

"What is that mark upon your forehead?" Bayar hissed at one point.

"It is the Mark of the Next Khan."

"You did not have it when you entered the cave."

"Be sure to tell this to every Mongol you meet, so that all Mongols know that Qasar the Khalkha Mongol walked into the cave where he was born and emerged as Qasar the Strong, the Next Khan."

"What burned that mark upon you within the cave?"

"That I will never reveal," Qasar said, face inscrutable.

"Some things it is better not to know," Bayar agreed.

Then, satisfied on that point, they watched the Bone Heads go about their cryptic and doubtful work. All around the sky pavilion's interior they worked at screens. These screens displayed the mountain and the surrounding land, seen from various angles. As they plied their controls, the mountain seemed to melt and show its interior.

Bones of men and animals appeared through the peeling layers, as did discarded tools and weapons and other things, some made by Mongols and some not.

This toil went on for the eighth part of a day and seemed to bear no fruit.

At last a Bone Head spoke up in the gibbering tongue

that the Bone Heads spoke. Telian Piar motioned to Qasar. "Come here, Mongol."

On the screen, Qasar saw a shadow-clotted void, and nodded. "That is it. The tomb of Genghis. This is a great day, that it was found."

"A very great day," Bayar agreed. In a hoarse voice he asked, "What is the point of this?"

"You will see."

They opened the earth in a fashion that smacked of sorcery. The spot was selected and the earth touched by rays of blue-white light. The light caused the soil to froth and turn to gas. Layer upon layer of soil was skimmed in this fashion as Qasar and Bayar watched in silent anticipation, their chests rising and falling in controlled excitement.

"I have never seen such sorcery," Bayar hissed.

"It will be nothing to the wonder of standing within the tomb of Lord Genghis, breathing the very air that contains his spirit."

"I tremble at the thought."

"All mankind will tremble before I am done with my life. And Bone Heads, too," he added in a low whisper.

Bayar nodded. He continued watching.

Soon, the last layer of earth was sublimed and a dark cavity lay exposed. There was no more soil, no more rock. Only a great square hole that held an impossible blackness within it.

Qasar started toward the door confidently. "I must be the first to enter."

"I will be the second," Bayar said.

Telian Piar stepped before them, his single scarlet orb curious the way a fish's eye is curious. Remotely so.

"What do you seek there?"

"The symbol of my coming power," Qasar returned.

"The instruments with which I will prosecute my will over all who live under the Eternal Blue Sky." His eyes smoldered.

Piar nodded. "Go, then."

Stepping to the edge, Qasar peered down. The sun was beating into the hole, yet he could see little but shadows and a floor of trampled earth. Kneeling, he took hold of the edge of the hole and levered his legs over until they dangled. With his iron forearms he lowered himself farther still, until he hung in space. Then he let go.

It was a shorter drop than expected, but long enough to bend both legs' muscles double.

Rising, he drew in a deep breath. The air smelled of must, and earth, and death, and other dank things. He looked around.

All was darkness except for a patch of ground the slanting sun rays touched. The skeleton of a horse lay there, its collapsed cobwebbed bones partially covered by leather armor that showed blue and gold through a coating of ancient, undisturbed dust.

Calling up, Qasar said, "I need light."

"Is that one of your desires?" Komo Dath asked.

"Never mind," said Qasar, who was no fool.

"I am coming next," Bayar said after a little while.

He dropped down like a bundle of unhappy bones, rolling clumsily.

"I brought a light," he said, coming to his feet.

Qasar grunted. "What did the Bone Heads extract for it?"

"A promise that I would clean up after your stallion."

Qasar laughed. "You made a good bargain. Give me the light."

"It is my light."

"And I am your khan."

"You are not yet khan."

"Hand me the light or when I am in truth khan I will punish you severely for not handing me the light."

"You speak like a khan, therefore I will do your bidding. Not that I like it."

"It matters only that you obey your khan," Qasar growled.

The light blazed, and every object and shadow in the tomb of Genghis Khan sprang into sharp relief.

There were bones. Human and horse bones. They lay half sunken in the earthen floor, and Qasar nodded in silent satisfaction.

"It was said that his favorite slaves and horses were buried with Lord Genghis, as well as the most beautiful daughters of his favorite princes."

Bayar looked amazed. "No coffins?"

Qasar grunted. "What do slaves or horses need of coffins?"

Here and there stood pikes, swords, and other implements of war. Great hardwood chests, locked with massive chains, stood about.

Qasar rushed to the weapons, knelt, and his eyes blazed wide.

"These are the very war tools Lord Genghis himself held."

"They are very beautiful," Bayar agreed, accepting the light back.

"They are filled with power," Qasar said as he reverently took up a short curved sword. The tang of the sword was bent.

"It has been damaged," Bayar pointed out. "Too bad."

"Fool. Do you know nothing of Mongol customs? The bent tang signifies this fine weapon has been ceremonially buried. Truly, it is no less than Genghis's personal sword."

Standing, Qasar cut the air with it. The fine blade

fluttered and swished with each slicing pass, as a good sword should.

"Yes, this is a blade of true steel," Qasar boasted. "And now it is mine."

Bayar was sweeping the tomb with his light and it fell upon something long and gleaming through a coating of earth dust.

"I spy silver," he breathed.

Qasar whirled. His breath came in a low, urgent rush. "I congratulate you, for you have discovered the silver coffin of Lord Genghis."

They padded toward it, Qasar taking the lead.

Coming to the long box of hammered silver and fantastic design, Qasar stood in reverent silence, then knelt. "O Lord Genghis, truly did you speak when you said, 'After us the people of our race will wear garments of gold, eat sweet greasy food, ride decorated horses, hold the loveliest of women, and will forget the things they owe us.' "

Qasar took a deep hot breath and his voice shook.

"All that you built is dust. All the blood you shed was in vain. Your sons and daughters own no land, occupy no cities, and have suffered under the successive yokes. And though they have not lost their Mongol spirit, neither have they taken up the challenge of your life. They are Mongols in name and by blood, but they scorn bloodshed and disdain battle. Because they have not kept up the ways of the Golden Horde, they suffered under the yoke of men who are not even men but wear the faces of death and see with the eyes of demons."

A silence came.

"But if it is true that I was born with a clot of black blood in my right hand, then I take this as a sign that the old ways are not dead, only slumbering. If it is my destiny to do so, I will awaken those old ways and gather all good horse Mongols together and sweep forth to reclaim our lands, and then all other lands that suit me. If this meets with your favor, Temuchin, give a sign to Qasar the Strong."

The fantastically filigreed coffin lay agleam. Bayar looked at it intently, his flashlight trembling in his hand.

"He does not speak to you," he breathed.

"He cannot speak, for he is long dead."

"Then what sign can a dead man give to the living?"

"That is up to the dead man."

Bayar switched the flashlight around. The beam picked out metallic glimmerings. "There is gold and silver here, I see."

"Gold is heavy and silver too light. We are Mongols. We need only ourselves, food, women, worthy enemies to slay, and cities to pillage."

"If I have a fat wife and good horse and sufficient mutton and *airag* for us both, I need not pillage," Bayar said.

"You are a Mongol. You will pillage."

"I am not a pillager."

"I will teach you. When I am done, your blood will yearn for pillage."

"If it is your wish that I pillage, then I will pillage. Do not expect that I will like it."

"I do not expect you to like it, only to do it."

Bayar nodded. "That is settled, then."

"I am still waiting for my sign," Qasar said. He began pacing around the silent silver coffin whose designs were rich and cryptic.

"Will you open it?" Bayar asked.

"I am wondering that myself."

"It is not good to disturb the dead."

"Unless one wishes to speak with the one who is dead."

"It is still not a wise thing to do. There may be poison barbs or traps to foil the unwary despoiler of graves."

"I intend no despoiling. I seek a sign."

Dropping to one knee, Qasar laid a heavy hand upon the dirt-filmed surface, feeling it with a quiet reverence belied by his thick scarred fingers.

"Here lie the bones of the greatest Mongol who ever rode a horse," he said.

"Timur was a good khan."

"Pagh! Timur was lame. And a Mohammedan."

"He conquered."

"All khans conquer. Timur founded no empire. That was Genghis. Genghis blazed the glory trail. Timur only followed the path already beaten. Genghis was the greatest of Mongols."

"The fame of Kublai still resonates even to the west."

"Kublai allowed it all to turn to ashes. After Kublai there were no more great khans. Genghis was the khakhan—the Khan of Khans. Genghis! Genghis!" Qasar said, slamming his fist on the silver coffin with each invocation of the revered name.

All at once there came a whispery shifting sound at Qasar's back. The Mongol leaped aside—just inches ahead of a descending object which threw the dust of the centuries billowing ahead of it.

It struck the silver coffin like a mallet pounding a gong.

The coffin spanked up dust; the heavy thing rolled aside and hit the earthen floor, where it rolled heavily and briefly.

"What was that?" Bayar asked, his flash sweeping.

"I do not know."

"A snare, perhaps."

"I do not know, but if it was a snare, it failed to snare Qasar the Strong."

Carefully, Qasar approached the beaten silver coffin of Genghis Khan. The heavy object had fallen on the far side. Snatching the flash from Bayar's unresisting fingers, he used it liberally.

It fell upon a long pole of hard wood, very stout, which was driven through a great round mass like the roof wheel of a *ger*, but was very thick and had no spokes. Nine white yak tails were affixed to its rim. The entire thing was topped by a three-pronged trident of hammered brass and silver.

Qasar gasped. "It is the sign," he muttered.

"A club of wood almost brains you and that you take for a sign from heaven?" Bayar muttered.

"It is not a club, nor a death trap. But the standard of Genghis Khan, and is imbued with his spirit."

Bayar drew close; the light was fixed upon the thing lying in the settling dust. "That?"

"Yes. Carried by a Mongol, it was lifted over the field of battle as the proud symbol of the Mongol nation."

"I see no gold or gems encrusting it."

Qasar shook his head violently. "It is not a toy for a palace, but a striker of terror on the field of war. Wherever the khan rode in the thick of battle, this followed him so that all knew where their khan fought and that he lived."

Kneeling, Qasar laid hands upon it. They strained.

"It is heavy?" Bayar asked.

"It is very heavy."

"Then how could one Mongol carry it on horseback?"

"A city Mongol could not lift it, but a Khalkha Mongol can."

"It does not look to me that even a Khalkha Mongol owns such strength."

Qasar grunted. The standard shivered, shedding earth

dust. He strained. The cords of his neck burst out and his features turned red.

Slowly, he unbent his knees and the standard came off the ground. With one hand he levered the heavy wheel aloft until the nine yak tails hung straight down. Reaching his full height, Qasar stepped forward and back as the standard attempted to pull itself down. He compressed his lips before tight-set teeth.

Bayar goggled at the display of raw strength. It looked as if the heavy thing would come crashing back to earth, but Qasar, his corded neck and arms straining, refused to allow this.

Finally, his entire body streaking sweat over earth dust, Qasar blew out a satisfied breath. His next words were tight.

"Now I know my destiny. I am the next khan. I possess the strength to hold aloft the standard of the Golden Horde, and once other Mongols see this, they will rally about me."

"And if they do not?"

Qasar grunted a hard laugh. "Then I will brain them with this mighty club and take off their useless heads with Genghis's own sword."

And Qasar's rollicking laughter lifted higher and higher, like that of a man drunk on the intoxication of his own spirit.

17

MOUNT
BURKHAN KHALDAN

When Qasar climbed out of the tomb of Genghis Khan, he was wearing elaborate leather and steel armor of blue and gold.

Bayar, too, was dressed more lavishly than before. But his sheepskin *dacha*, looted from the tomb, fitted him imperfectly. He carried in his outstretched arms weapons that had been interred with the first great khan of the Mongols. He all but groaned under the burden, but his long face beamed with ill-concealed pride.

Telian Piar and Komo Dath met them on the ground. They wore the armor of standing locusts, glass bulbs over their heads.

"What are those?" Piar asked, single eye flicking here and there to the sword and other ornate weapons.

"The weapons with which I will begin my conquest," Qasar growled.

Komo Dath met his burning gaze with a fierce glare.

"And that?" he rasped, indicating the heavy standard of Genghis Khan.

"The standard by which I will rally all Mongols around me."

"A flag?"

"No. Any man may raise a flag, just as any other may

tear it down again. Only a Mongol may carry this into battle."

"You cannot fight wielding such a clumsy device," Dath spat.

"And I will not. It is the duty of the standard-bearer to carry the standard into battle. I must find such a Mongol before I launch my first campaign."

Telian Piar drew closer, sole eye fixed. "Then you are ready to proceed?"

"After your Bone Head lackeys have removed the other war trophies from the tomb," Qasar added.

Komo Dath stiffened.

"Have this done at once. See to it the silver coffin is undisturbed." And with that, Qasar marched past the two Martians and returned to the ship, Bayar in tow, his eyes looking neither right nor left.

Red eyes following him, Komo Dath trembled like an angry leaf. "Who does he think he is to speak to me that way?"

"The lord of all Mongols, greatest warriors of Terra," Telian Piar murmured.

"We have made him what he is!" Dath hissed.

"No," Piar returned. "We have pointed a mighty missile in its true and inevitable direction. It will be all we can do to keep it on course—our course."

Dath eyed Piar hotly. Piar's odd single eye met the gaze with only a slow blinking.

"You seem to understand this Mongol's psychology exceedingly well," Dath rasped.

"Why not? It is identical to yours."

And as Telian Piar floated up the ramp of the waiting Killerghost saucer, Komo Dath made tight angry fists with his hands, and his breath made the interior of his helmet's faceplate moist and cloudy.

In the end, he rasped out orders that sent Gnard soldiers dropping into the tomb to loot it of further artifacts.

"Mind that nothing of worth is damaged!" he called down.

18

THE WINDING ROAD, OUTER MONGOLIA

Ariunbold the herdsman was tending his sheep when he heard the clatter of hoofbeats coming down the Winding Road. He looked up, expecting to see a dust-smeared, grimy-faced traveler, but instead saw a vision that made his pulse quicken and his straggle-bearded jaw drop.

Two men were riding, one astride a white charger, the other on a gray gelding. They wore not wind-weathered *dels* or felt buskins, but the hardened leather lamellar armor of a Mongol who had ridden out of time, medieval peaked iron helmets on their heads.

Stunned by the sight, Ariunbold at first thought he was witnessing passing ghosts. Not dead unburied ghosts but the imperishable spirits of the days of the great khans who were too hot-blooded and virile to die complete deaths.

Leaving his flock, Ariunbold walked to the side of the trail to witness this spectacle more closely.

"Who rides this road?" he asked.

The lead horseman turned his big head around to eye Ariunbold with steely interest. On his brow was a strange device—a white skull, outlined in red, over a full moon.

"Do you not recognize me?" he said, his voice a struck gong.

"I have never before seen you," Ariunbold replied. "Should I know you, traveler?"

"I am called Qasar the Strong."

"If your name is truly Dog, you are plainly a dog with an exceedingly fine coat."

A grunt that passed for a laugh came from the horseman named Dog. "You possess wit, herdsman."

"I am called Ariunbold."

"True Steel. That is a worthy name."

"My father gave it to me before he died."

"Then you have inherited riches."

Ariunbold nodded. These were good words.

"My companion and myself seek rest," the armored horseman said.

"My *ger* lies yonder," Ariunbold said, pointing to the dome of white felt where two shaggy brown yaks grunted contentedly. His eyes fell upon the tall standard that Qasar held at his side, its base resting on a pendant saddle stirrup of iron.

"I have heard that Genghis Khan spread terror and Mongol civilization equally beneath a nine-yak-tail standard such as this."

"You have heard truly."

"And that is the standard of Genghis himself," the second rider offered. He sat swathed in a sheepskin *dacha* of exceeding fineness.

"Who are you?" Ariunbold demanded of the long-faced Mongol.

"Bayar."

"A good name, if ill-fitting—as are your garments."

Bayar nodded in acknowledgment. "Thank you."

"Why do you think that standard is the true one?" Ariunbold asked Qasar the Strong.

"Because I myself extracted it from the tomb of Lord Genghis," Qasar said.

"If you speak truth, I must kneel before you."

"If you insist upon kneeling, do it quickly, for I must

ask you to take the standard from my hand so that I may dismount."

"I would kiss your boot for that privilege."

"I offer it freely and without price."

Carefully, Ariunbold took the staff in both hands as Qasar lifted it from its saddle holster.

"You have it?" Qasar asked.

"Yes."

And Qasar let go.

The staff wobbled in Ariunbold's hands. He stepped back, then forward and to one side, the yak tails shivering and shifting as if riding on camelback or the rolling deck of a ship.

Soon he held it steady.

"You are strong," Qasar said, dismounting.

Ariunbold looked up at the blowing yak tails. "I was a blacksmith once."

Qasar nodded, leading his horse along.

"You are very strong," Bayar said conversationally. "The last three herdsmen could not hold it vertical, never mind carry it for several paces, as you do."

"I could carry this standard forever. It fills my heart with such pride that my spirit strains to burst the bonds of my ribs."

"Would you carry it into battle?" Qasar asked in an even tone.

"If there were any battles for a Mongol of today, yes."

"What if I promise you battles beyond count?"

"Why should I battle? I have a *ger*, three horses, a herd, and a loyal wife."

"Have you riches?"

"My good name is my wealth, as you yourself have said."

"I mean gold, jewels, trappings."

"I need none of these things so long as I clutch my present possessions."

"Have you a fine house?"

"I have a *ger*."

"Have you courage?"

Ariunbold made his mouth grim. "I have courage."

"You have some courage. A herdsman's honest courage. I could teach you true courage."

"I am a man with a courageous heart, for am I not a Mongol?"

"I have never met a Mongol with a heart filled with milk, it is true. But I seek a Mongol who will carry that standard into battle knowing that by doing so he will light the hearts of Mongols everywhere."

"It lights my heart," Ariunbold said.

"I intend to unify the Mongols."

"For what? We live where we live."

"The capital, Ulan Bator, lies in ruins."

"I have never been there, though I have heard talk. All in ruins. The fine statues of Genghis shattered. The men slaughtered, the women enslaved, the children put to the sword, or bent to worse fates."

"I do not know these unfortunate Mongols. They are not of my clan."

The trio came to the *ger*, whose smoke hole was pouring out fragrant sheep dung smoke. The scent of tea came with it. It was a combination that made a Mongol feel warm in the deepest cold.

Pushing aside the felt tent flap, Ariunbold entered, as the horses were tethered. He had to stoop to carry in the standard, and at once his wife began to scold him.

"Take that out of here!" she snapped, her long braided pigtail swinging like a whip as she turned, her cheeks red as apples.

"It is the standard of Genghis Khan. I cannot dishonor it by leaving it outside where rain might touch it."

"I want it out of my *ger*."

Bayar poked his head in and smiled. "You have a plump wife."

"Thank you," Ariunbold said shortly.

"But her mouth harbors a sharp tongue."

"And your head wears a long face," the wife spat.

"I am called Happy."

"You are called wrongly, Long Face."

At that point Qasar entered. When he unbent himself upon stepping through the wood door frame, he dominated the interior of the tent.

"Who is that one?" the wife said, gasping out the words.

"Qasar," Qasar said.

"You resemble a wolf more than you do a dog," the wife of Ariunbold commented, her eyes akindle with interest.

"You are very perceptive. I am a dog of war and I stand for no female tongues troubling my conversation."

The wife turned aside quickly. "I will make tea."

"See that you make it hot," Qasar growled.

Ariunbold's wife got busy at the fire.

"You have a way with women," Ariunbold said approvingly.

"Not all women," Qasar growled as they took seats on the rug-strewn floor. The standard was set in a place of honor, leaning against a tall chest.

At length, tea salted and creamed with yak butter was poured steaming into fine china bowls and they drank it up greedily.

"You are constructed like me," Qasar said after a long period in which no one spoke.

Ariunbold accepted this comparison. "Yes."

"My clothes could fit your frame."

"They could."

"I have extra clothes."

"It is good to have extra clothes," Ariunbold allowed.

"My extra clothes were taken from the tomb of Ssutu-Bogdo, the Heaven-sent."

Ariunbold looked up from his tea, his eyes growing sharp. "What are you saying?"

"I need both hands free to conduct my wars. I need a strong horse Mongol to carry the standard of Lord Genghis. Such a man deserves to wear the clothes that once belonged to Temuchin."

"This is an intriguing thought."

In the corner the wife hissed long and low.

"Silence, woman!"

They drank more tea as Ariunbold's wife swept the floor with furious diligence.

"You bear intriguing notions into my *ger*," Ariunbold allowed. "But I have a wife."

"No children?" Qasar asked.

Ariunbold cast his eyes downward. "I am not so blessed."

"Thus, your burdens are relatively light."

"No man with a wife can be called free of life's burdens."

The wife swept dirt at Ariunbold's feet, and he remonstrated her with a sudden kick of a felt buskin. She returned to her sweeping.

"Can she ride?" Qasar asked.

"Of course. She is a Mongol wife."

"Can she fight?"

"She has fought with me, but I always win."

"Once I have united the Mongols, it is my intention to sweep south and harry the soft cities of China."

"Why?"

"Because they are there. Also, because they made serfs of the people of lower Mongolia, just as the Russian oppressors did of higher Mongolia."

Ariunbold spat in contempt. "The godless Russians are nothing now."

"And the soulless Chinese dwell in rich cities cut off from their former capital."

"I have heard of the New Wall. It is said demons built it as punishment for ancient Chinese wrongs."

Qasar's voice sank to a muttered growl. "Not demons. Something else."

"Bone Heads," Bayar said.

"Bone Heads? Are not all men and Mongols bone-headed?" Ariunbold asked, rapping on his skull with one callused knuckle.

"Their faces are masks of death, their crowns naked brain, yet they possess living eyes and speak good Mongol," Qasar explained.

Ariunbold started. "They speak Mongol?"

"Not perfectly, but it is understandable."

"You intrigue me, but I have no use for Chinese cities. I am a free-riding Mongol. With a wife."

"A barren wife," Qasar said.

This time, the busy wife kicked dirt toward Qasar.

"Your wife is very spirited," Qasar commented.

"You may cuff her if you wish. Just do not cause injury. She may yet bear me a son."

The wife spat and hissed like a cornered cat.

"I will refrain from striking her if she will refrain from her spite," Qasar said.

The wife subsided, turning sullen as a pot at low boil.

"In the Chinese cities there are Chinese women," Qasar said quietly.

"I have heard this."

"Chinese women with fertile wombs."

"What would I want with a son who is half Chinese?"

"Half a son is better than an empty *ger* when your hair is snow and your belly empty."

"This is something I have contemplated of late."

"You could still keep your present wife. Genghis had many wives and concubines."

"If I have a son by a Chinese wench, it could be raised by my good Mongol wife."

"If you are a sacker of Chinese cities, other Mongol women will seek out your seed to fill their empty wombs. You will soon become rich in sons."

"There is that," Ariunbold said thoughtfully.

"I myself prefer to have one wife. A fat one," Bayar remarked.

"Fat wives are good to have on a bitter night," Ariunbold agreed.

"But a horse is a true ally in life."

Ariunbold asked, "How will you raise an army, Qasar?"

"I will simply ride south through every town and cattle station, and the growing army will cling to my train like iron fillings trailing after a powerful magnet."

"It will not be that easy."

"So far I have two," Qasar said pointedly.

"I have not yet given you my decision."

"I see it in your eyes. You do not have to give it."

"But I will." Ariunbold met Qasar's stern gaze with a frank admiration. "My horses are yours."

"Good. I will need extra horses. For a horseless Mongol will more readily follow my train."

"You will ride south with the dawn?"

"No. I will ride after I have filled my belly."

"I would prefer a last night with my good wife, whom I will sorely miss."

"To what purpose? Even if her womb favors you this

night, it will be nine months before you know whether you have a son or daughter. By that time, you will be awash in willing wombs or moldering in your young grave."

Ariunbold shivered.

Qasar raised an eyebrow. "I thought you possessed courage."

"I do. I shiver with the thrill that no Mongol has known since the days of the last khan, Timur the Lame."

"Mongolia sleeps. But we shall awaken it."

"Make him swear fealty," Bayar hissed.

"I trust this man, my strong right arm, Ariunbold. Fealty can wait until after supper."

"If he is your good right arm, what am I?"

"A city Mongol who will follow me blindly," Qasar said, finishing the last of his tea and slamming down the bowl as a signal to the hovering wife.

In tense silence she poured fresh hot tea, but her dark eyes blazed.

"She has spirit," Qasar commented to Ariunbold.

"Spirit, yes, but no fire."

"Perhaps the long months alone will cause it to flare up."

Ariunbold nodded. "It will be good to ride to new lands."

"It will be better to conquer them, for did not Lord Genghis say this: 'The greatest joy a man can know is to conquer his enemies and drive them before him. To ride their horses and take away their possessions. To see the faces of those who were dear to them bedewed with tears, and to clasp their wives and daughters in his arms.' "

All agreed that Lord Genghis Khan spoke truly when he spoke those words so long ago.

*   *   *

They set out within the hour, their bellies full and the wife of Ariunbold the herdsman running and spitting after them.

"I dislike leaving my wife," Ariunbold said, kicking at her clutching hands.

"She will love you all the more passionately upon your return," Qasar said as the wife stumbled to the road and rent her hair, screaming imprecations.

"I have never heard her curse so foully. She thought highly of my poor dead mother and now listen. She is calling down curses upon her sleeping soul."

"At least you left her the *ger* and a mare to ride and milk. I would not leave a barren woman a brick of old tea."

Ariunbold gazed up at the nine yak tails shaking with each step of his horse. His other horses followed, as did two sheep.

"I feel transformed whenever I look at what I hold aloft."

"It is not you who will be transformed," Qasar said, peering down the Winding Road. "For we are a horde now."

Bayar blinked. "Three? A horde?"

"A small horde."

"A very small horde."

"But a good one," Ariunbold said, giving his standard a hitch and a shift to balance it better.

"And soon it will string out in a line as far as the eye can see," Qasar Khan vowed.

And neither man doubted his word or his resolve.

19

THE WINDING ROAD, OUTER MONGOLIA

At an *ail*, the New Golden Horde, though only three strong, tripled its force.

The clopping of their hooves was the first portent. Then over the dunes came the nine yak tails of which every Mongol had heard, but none had ever in reality seen.

When Qasar Khan topped the rise, splendid in his blue and gold lamellar armor, his steed similarly caparisoned, the young men and boys came out of the village *gers* and began shouting. Others fell in behind, pacing the three horsemen and their heavy-laden packhorses.

"Who are you, Skull-brow?" someone cried.

"He is Qasar Khan," Bayar called back.

"A Dog khan?"

"He wears the armor of Lord Genghis and rides south to harry the Chinese," Ariunbold added.

"This is a good thing," a laughing boy shouted.

"Yes, the Chinese are sorely in need of harrying," a one-eyed man added.

"Up from Dead Mongol Pass, he came!" Bayar shouted. "He went into the cave where he was born and emerged from it carrying the pelt of a wild wolf and wearing the death's-head mark you see upon his brow. No one knows what placed it there as a sign for all to see. It matters only that it is there."

Qasar's wind- and sunburned features remained inscrutable.

"Who will ride with us?" Ariunbold thundered.

"I am riding with you now," the young man proclaimed.

"Then fall into line!"

Entering the *ail* at a brisk bouncing trot, Qasar Khan lifted his voice for the first time.

"I will trade a fine horse for the loyalty of the bravest Mongol who is not married," he cried.

A herdsman stepped forward, clutching an old rust-pitted Enfield rifle. He spoke up. "I am the bravest man in this place, but I am married."

Qasar eyed him appraisingly. "Will you abandon your wife?"

"She is with child."

"Stay with her, then." Lifting his voice anew, Qasar bellowed, "I offer a horse for the next bravest Mongol who is not married."

A ruddy-cheeked Mongol stepped forth. "I am Ochinbal. I have no horse since last winter's smothering snows."

"Will you devote your life to conquest, in return for your pick of horses?"

"Without a horse, I have no life."

"Well-spoken. Select your mount."

The Mongol trotted alongside the straggling mounts, himself straining to keep up. "How can I pick the best when you will not stop?" Ochinbal said in exasperation.

"If I offer you a free horse, it is up to you to pick the best. If you cannot, I will leave this privilege to the third most brave Mongol, for the most brave will not come with me."

Ochinbal slapped the closest horse without further delay. "This one, then."

"Fetch your saddle and follow us," Qasar said, signaling Bayar to release the reins of the selected gelding.

Once the men of the *ail* saw one of their own throw his high wooden saddle onto the gift horse, others caught the fever.

Mothers wept. Wives screamed out in frustrated rage. Children danced and sang or fell down to cry, depending upon their disposition.

But the men—even those left behind—wore broad smiles and wept true tears, the true tears Mongols had not wept since the last khanate fell.

When they rode out of sight of the *ail* less than twenty minutes later, they were trailing a long dragon of dust and horse droppings and were more than a dozen strong.

"Now we are a horde," Ariunbold boasted.

"A modest horde," Bayar remarked.

"But one already to be feared," Qasar growled.

At every cattle station and village of *gers*, they acquired more men. Some were bought with fine weapons, others with fragments of Genghis Khan's wardrobe. Only the young and the strong were accepted, for the ride would be long and hard and no stragglers could be countenanced.

Along the road, Qasar Khan made his first field promotion. "Ariunbold, you are hereby promoted to the rank of *arban*."

"That is a good rank to have. What does it mean?"

"You are a captain of ten."

Ariunbold raised an eyebrow. "That is almost half the entire horde."

"Now."

"Who will captain the rest?"

"You will. For I cannot count higher than ten."

"But what will you captain, Qasar Khan?"

"I will captain you."

"This is a good system," Bayar said, venting a rare smile. "Who will I captain?"

"You will captain yourself."

"At what rank?"

"I have not yet decided this."

Bayar's face settled back into its glum lines. He sneezed once. He had not been sneezing as much. The farther south they rode, the less he sneezed. Qasar Khan took pains to remind him of this.

"It was the bad Russian air, after all."

"I think the strange Bone Head air was good for my sinuses."

"I do not know this word, sinuses."

"It is another name for the inside of the nose."

"The inside of the nose is called the inside of the nose. Why does it need another name?"

"I do not know. But I do not care as long as I sneeze less, for the sleeves of the garments of Lord Genghis that I wear are too fine to use to wipe my nose."

"Genghis will strike you dead in battle for wiping your nose on his sleeve," Qasar grumbled.

"That is what I just said. I will not do this."

"See that you do not. If you die in battle, it will reflect badly upon my generalship and my honor."

"Never fear. I am planning on dying in the plump arms of my wife to be. Possibly many times," he added, grinning.

They rode into the night. The stars came out. And in the brilliantly black heavens above, the occasional shooting star fell like a trailing yellow-green spark.

"The Bone Heads are about their cryptic business," Qasar muttered, gazing skyward.

"They are watching us," Bayar said.

"Let them watch. They should have slain us when they

had the chance. For at this rate, we will outnumber them within a week."

"Perhaps."

"A month, then."

"We do not know the true numbers of the Bone Heads," Bayar pointed out.

"I myself slew four with only my naked hands. Therefore, one Mongol is equal to four Bone Heads."

"But you are khan," Bayar pointed out.

"This was before I was khan."

"This is so," Bayar agreed.

"It is not numbers that will defeat the Bone Heads. It is our courage and our weapons."

"But we have no Chof guns. The Bone Heads took them away."

Qasar's face darkened in thought. "We have acquired Chof guns in the past. We can acquire more."

Bayar looked back. Many of the Mongols rode with Kalashnikov rifles at the ready, butt stocks resting on their iron thighs, muzzles pointing heavenward. Some wore clinking ropes of bullets across their chests.

"We are rich in rifles and bullets, but poor in bows and arrows," Bayar said thoughtfully.

"I hereby appoint you maker of bows and arrows," Qasar Khan said.

"I do not possess this skill."

"I will teach it to you."

"Is it not better that you make these things?"

"The khan has more important things to do, but if you prefer to retain your rank of Lowly City Mongol, I will arrange for another to do this important thing."

Bayar flinched. "What will be my new rank?"

"Arrow smith."

"That is a rank?"

"In my Golden Horde, it is a very important rank,

which includes an extra portion of mutton every third day."

"Am I not already entitled to a portion of your mutton in return for my fealty?"

Qasar Khan was silent for part of a *li*.

"It is possible that you may come to be called Arrow Prince, if you perform your duties well," he said quietly.

"I accept," Bayar said, long face brightening. "I think I am going to enjoy belonging to this horde, since I understand I am destined to be Jebei Noron Bayar."

"That is very good, because at present there is no other horde."

And down the straggling line of Mongols genial laughter broke out. The laughter grew infectious and, as if unleashing their spirits, they picked up speed and were soon riding tall in the saddle—all except Bayar, who bounced and bobbled as was his way.

Above their heads jade-green traceries came and went.

20

KOLYMA TOWER, FORMER SIBERIA

"They are forty strong," Telian Piar said.

Commander Komo Dath received this news with interest. "That insolent Mongol is a born leader. But they are not yet an army and have much ground to cover on horseback."

"They ride without relenting, gathering additional horsemen at each habitation, and practicing cavalry maneuvers along the road."

"They train as they ride?"

"I have been watching them. They are like a swarm of Terran soldier ants, growing by the hour."

"I must see this for myself," Komo Dath said, sweeping past the passive Paeec.

Telian Piar's soft admonition trailed him like a smoky promise. "Watch, and learn fear . . ."

21

MOBALIG,
OUTER MONGOLIA

The Golden Horde of Qasar Khan was over two thousand strong by the time it wound through Dead Mongol Pass six days later.

"This is a bad place," Bayar muttered, looking around.

"I know," Qasar grunted. "I died here."

Jet-black walls reared up on either side, decorated by lichens of burnt orange and gold. The slice of sky directly overhead was an eye-stinging blue.

Bayar shivered and looked to Ariunbold, whose hand was like a graven bronze claw on the shaft of the nine-yak-tail standard. Six days of this had given him a grip that could crush a man's finger bones to gravel. It was suspected by all that he had possessed such raw strength before, and the standard had merely increased the speed with which he could grind living bones to dead bone chips.

They brandished Kalashnikovs, muskets and revolvers, hardwood bows, and a sprinkling of ancestral swords. Some *ails* were found empty when they arrived. In other places, men, women, and children lined up to see them pass in glory. At almost every place, they collected new recruits.

The Golden Horde was now divided between *arbans* and *jaguns*—captains of ten and one hundred, all subservient to their khan.

"Soon, we will be invincible," Bayar said proudly.

Qasar Khan shook his head slowly. "We do not need to be invincible. For we are already indomitable."

"I will feel better when we are invincible."

"No Mongol is invincible, only the horde itself."

"I do not fear death."

"You ride through Dead Mongol Pass and you say this?"

Bayar shook his sheepskin shoulders. "I swore an oath. I go where it takes me."

Qasar nodded. "You sound less and less like a city Mongol with each *li*."

"I feel like less and less a city Mongol with each *li*," Bayar said proudly, riding up on his stirrups—only to drop back to his typical bobbling posture after his legs gave out.

As they wound their way between the high crags which in the dead of winter were impassable to man and beast alike, Qasar Khan grew more silent than usual. He had dropped to a canter, and the other horses, as if attuned to the lead stallion, quickly fell into step.

"You are silent," Bayar remarked.

"I am usually silent."

"You are more silent than usual."

"This is an unusual moment."

"How so?"

"I am a dead man riding back from the dead to the seat of my clan."

"I scent trouble."

"You have sneezed your nose to an exceedingly fine sharpness."

"An elderly camel could smell this danger through his nose bag. It hangs in the air like a stench."

"Here we will fight our first battle or increase our power."

"I would not wish to wager on either result," Bayar said quietly.

They rode farther, coming to a high crest. Down in the valley stood a cluster of white *gers*, looking like a field of assorted pale mushrooms, smoke holes pouring out the pungent fragrance of sheep dung.

"They possess many horses," Ariunbold said.

"All ours," Qasar said.

"And *gers* and wagons."

"Ours as well."

"And women in plenty."

Qasar Khan looked over his shoulder. "Bayar, you may select your wife from this stock."

"And if I find none?"

"Take one that will have you, for after this our lives are forfeit."

"Are our lives not forfeit in this valley?" Bayar asked.

"No. I know this enemy."

"How can your own clan be your enemy?" Ariunbold demanded.

"When they have cast me out like a cur," Qasar Khan muttered.

Drawing to a stop, he looked right, then left. Ariunbold led a company of men on a westerly arc; Ochinbal took his troop to the east.

They rode single file, briskly, but not so rapidly as to stir alarm. The two claws of the pincer were clearly going to meet at a point exactly opposite the mounted figure of Qasar Khan, on the other side of the valley. But by the time this became apparent, it was too late for the herdsmen who were milling about the *gers* to react.

A few, already mounted, seeing the imminence of their predicament, spurred their geldings toward the hole at the far side of the valley. They reacted too late. The circle closed like a vise of horseflesh and they drew back, their courage cowed.

By now every *ger* had emptied. Faces looked north. They looked west, south, and east. All knew their position. None suspected their fate. This was written on every face, young and old, tender and wind-weathered.

"What do we do?" Bayar asked.

"We wait," Qasar Khan grunted.

"For what?"

"For their fears to take root and sap them of all will to resist."

"This may be a long wait. They are Mongols."

"But they face the New Golden Horde."

An hour later the shadows were long and streaky, and a clot of Mongols, one very old and two young, approached on horseback. They carried their rifles across the pommels of their saddles, but fear—not fight—lay deep in their narrow eyes.

"You have come far enough!" Qasar Khan thundered.

Abruptly, they drew to a halt, horses rearing.

"Who are you, apparition?" the old man called out.

"I am called Qasar Khan."

"I have never heard of you."

"But I have heard of you, Dampildorj."

"How do you know my name?"

"It was your voice that spoke my death warrant."

"I? I know no man named Dog."

Qasar made his voice low and full of portents. "I have not always been known as Qasar."

The old man peered long at Qasar Khan's beaten brass face. He scrunched up his features, twisting his head this way and that, as if to discern intent on the unfamiliar countenance.

One of the younger Mongols, doing the same, dropped his gaze to the white stallion Qasar Khan rode. He brought this to the old man's attention by a hard poke in the ribs.

The old man's eyes fell on the stallion's face, then flicked to the striped feet.

"I have seen that horse on another day," he allowed.

"This horse is named Chino," Qasar intoned.

"The horse I knew was named Dog."

"Who would name his horse Dog?" Qasar asked thinly.

"Perhaps a man who was called Wolf," Dampildorj retorted.

Qasar Khan said nothing to that.

Bayar whispered, "You told me your true name was Dog."

"I am named Dog. Now," Qasar undertoned.

"And the horse was Wolf," Bayar added.

"The horse *is* Wolf. Now."

"You changed your name?"

"I traded my name to my horse in return for his. It was a good trade."

"It is an interesting trade," Bayar rejoined. "I think the horse got the better of you in that transaction, however."

The old man named Dampildorj called up with a quaver in his throat. "Whether you are Chino or Qasar, Skull-face, I ask what you want."

"I want every man of this clan to fall in behind my train. They will swear loyalty and fealty to Qasar Khan and obey the rules of the New Golden Horde. After that, the *gers* will be put to the torch and the women left weeping for the vanished menfolk, except for one."

"Will you accept the woman and leave the *gers*?" one of the young men asked.

"I am leaving the women, and burning the *gers*."

"We will fight for our *gers*," the other young man promised.

"You will lose, and I will have what I want in the climax. Minus the dead who will not follow me to glory."

"This is not my decision to make," Dampildorj said.

"All choice has fled from your miserable life," Qasar Khan said in a metallic voice.

At that, the old man flung his horse about and rode back to his life. The others followed, looking back in wonderment and fear.

"They are frightened," Ariunbold remarked.

"Frightened men are more obedient," Qasar Khan observed.

"It remains to be seen whether or not they will obey."

"They have no choice."

After a while a lone rider returned, wearing a cinnabar riding *del*.

"Is that not a woman?" Ariunbold asked.

"No. That is not any woman," Qasar growled.

The woman rode like the wind, leaning forward in the saddle, her cat eyes fixed on Qasar Khan like two arrowheads cut from some dead black metal, lit by deep fires.

"I see by the fierce expression of welcome on her face that she knows you," Ariunbold said dryly.

"Her name is Chulpan Goa."

"She does not much look like a Morning Doe."

"Her doe qualities are best experienced by moonlight," Qasar Khan said, watching the whipping of Morning Doe's long unbraided black hair.

Bayar laughed. But the grim expression of the oncoming rider made him swallow his mirth.

Qasar Khan dismounted and handed his reins to Ochinbal, who took them tightly in hand. Qasar walked ten paces to meet the oncoming rider.

The Mongol woman nearly trampled him into the steppe. Rearing back, her goaded mare lunged wildly. Qasar stood his ground until the last possible moment, then threw himself to one side. The woman hauled her horse down, brought it around and tried to trample him flat once more.

Qasar ducked under the horse's leading hooves and, rolling wildly, reemerged behind its dancing rump, untrampled.

He boomed out a great laugh, punctuating it with words. "Are you so angry you cannot see straight, Morning Doe?"

"I will kill you before I surrender to you!" the woman spat back, attempting to reorient the horse without success.

Qasar Khan made it easy for her by stepping into the mount's path. "Kill me if you can. I have already died and no longer fear death."

This time Morning Doe backed up her mount, then charged straight on. The horse galloped, its head low, and Qasar feinted left then right. As the horse surged past his position, he was suddenly in the saddle with the woman, pushing her away.

She tumbled off, landing on her back with an explosive grunt and whoof.

Laughing, Qasar walked the horse to her side and made it place its front hooves about her head. Then he jerked the reins about so the hooves broke and disturbed the steppe grass around her head, occasionally pinning her long lustrous hair. She ducked and dodged, but it was clear to any observer that if the big Mongol wished her head split open, he could have accomplished this at any time.

Tiring of his sport, Qasar drew the mare away.

Morning Doe rose up to meet him. Her eyes blazed even at a distance. Grinning, Qasar walked up to her— and she let fly with a mighty slap.

Qasar took it, shook it off, laughed, and accepted a second slap that rocked his head half around.

"You slap as you have always slapped, with more fire than anger," he remarked in an even tone.

Morning Doe spat on his armor. "I will die before I give myself to you again," she blazed.

"I died because you gave yourself to me. Why will you not return the compliment?"

The third slap was the hardest of all. It wiped the grin off Qasar's proud face, depositing the helmet of Genghis Khan into the dust.

His face stern, he slapped back. Morning Doe landed on her rump, dazed.

"I would not slap you for slapping me," he said, "but I now wear the armor of Lord Genghis. It must be respected."

Morning Doe lay on the ground, shaking her head as if to clear the stars from her eyes.

A man rode up, clutching a Kalashnikov rifle with a folding bayonet. A Chinese Kalashnikov, Qasar knew. The Russian version lacked the folding bayonet. Here, the bayonet was extended.

"I do not recognize this fool," Qasar said to Morning Doe.

"This is my new husband."

Qasar grunted. "I see you did not wait for me."

"You were dead."

"That is no reason not to wait for the man you love."

"Who said I ever loved you?"

"That night I laid you on my *kang*, and slew the man you said was only your brother, but who was in truth your husband, your body spoke of your passion."

"I could not live without a husband, so I took another."

"You should have waited. Now I have to slay another

of your inconvenient husbands. It is always very bothersome."

"If you spare him, I will go with you."

"If I spare him, he will follow me to the ruins of the Ishtar Gate. I know this, having tasted your charms once." Qasar shook his head. "No, he must die."

"Cut off his hands and let him live," Morning Doe pleaded.

"A Mongol without hands cannot ride and would prefer death. No, I will strike off his head. His spirit will thank me for it."

"He does not deserve death!"

"Nor does he deserve you," Qasar said, remounting and riding out to meet the oncoming threat.

Both riders stopped just yards short of one another. The husband of Morning Doe spoke first.

"I know why you are here. Go back. If you are the murderer called Wolf, you have paid for your drunken crimes and are free to ride on unmolested."

"Not without what I have come for," Qasar returned.

"That is your final word?"

"I am the New Khan. My word is law."

"Then your tongue will taste dust until it becomes dust, for you face Bato the Khalkha Mongol."

The rider flung his steed about, pounding out a tight circle. Qasar urged his own steed backward, drawing the curved sword of Temuchin. He waited for the man's first move.

It came at once. The horse lined up, then charged, tail thrashing. The Mongol came with his reins in his teeth, clutching his rifle, the bayonet point seeking Qasar's vitals.

Qasar waited until only yards separated them, then spurred his horse forward, one hand clutching the reins, the other lifting up the sword of Temuchin.

They clashed in a grunt of colliding horses. The bayonet skipped off the armor, while a quick chopping sword cut disconnected the Mongol's left ear.

Howling, Bato broke off, and came around again.

Qasar Khan met him with a laugh and another chopping cut and nicked his nose, turning it red.

"You fight the New Khan. How can you win with a blade made by Chinese factory workers?"

Bato howled anew, and came on.

This time he fired.

The bullet buried itself in the horse's armored shoulder. He reared, and Qasar, squeezing his mount's barrel chest with his mighty blue leathern legs, forced the horse down.

As the other Mongol swept past, Qasar casually relieved him of his head with a backhanded slice of the fine sword.

Catching the tumbling head by the hair, Qasar with a smooth maneuver brought horse and rider to Morning Doe's side, where he laid the head at her feet, the man's eyes rolling up in his head in death.

"Now you are free to wed anew," Qasar said simply.

Morning Doe kicked the head away. "I would sooner mate with a panda."

"We ride to China. I will bring you with me and arrange this interesting marriage personally."

"I will not go to China as your wife."

Qasar dismounted. He towered over her, slit eyes humorous. "Then you will come as my concubine."

Reaching down, he took hold of her by one ear and lifted Morning Doe off her feet. She slapped him twice, more gently than before so as not to upset his helmet.

Qasar grinned back. "I am pleased neither of your husbands has tamed you, for I need a good woman for the long trail ahead of me."

"You should have stayed dead."

Qasar smiled broadly. "How could I do that when your allures called to me from beyond the grave?"

"I will be your concubine, but not your wife, if you spare my clan."

"Your clan will ride with me. Except the women who must stay and tend the flocks and children in the event we return alive."

"You will not burn the *gers* out of spite?" Morning Doe asked.

"I will not burn the *gers* out of spite," Qasar Khan promised.

"Then I will go as your concubine."

"That is a wise decision."

Then turning his head to Ariunbold, he gave out an iron order that carried across the peaceful valley.

"Burn the *gers*!"

"You said you would not burn the *gers*!" Morning Doe flared.

"I said I would not burn the *gers* out of spite. I am keeping my word. The *gers* are being burned because my Golden Horde is sorely in need of practice at pillage and destruction."

"You will not have the women raped?"

"There will be no rape. But if some women give themselves to my men, rather than be left behind, I will accept their wise decision."

"You have not changed, Wolf."

"I am reborn," Qasar Khan said with great good humor. "Dying was the greatest thing that has ever happened to me. After loving you."

"If I am to be your concubine, then you must take me."

"I will take you, never fear."

"I will not be taken by you on the steppe like some

mare in heat. I will have a warm *kang* to sleep on and a *ger* of my own."

"We ride toward conquest. The weather is good. I cannot be burdened down by *gers* and useless possessions."

"I will have a *kang* or I will split your manhood with your own dagger at the first opportunity."

Qasar frowned darkly. "This is no way to speak to your khan and master."

"I have never been a concubine before tonight. Only a wife twice over. How am I to know how I may or may not speak?"

And seeing the steel in the eyes of the woman he desired more than any other, Qasar Khan thundered a new order.

"Spare one *ger*. The finest. Take it down and pack it for transport."

Morning Doe allowed her red lips to curl into a smile.

"If you continue to treat me with respect," she whispered, "I may let you be my third husband—if only because you would murder any other man I chance to marry."

"Why should a khan marry a concubine?"

"Because you have tasted my lips and desire no other," Morning Doe said, stepping close and turning up her radiant face.

There, on the site of his first military conquest, Qasar Khan drank deep of the lips of his first female conquest, while the men and women of his former clan cursed and howled as their *gers* were set alight and burned to unhappy ashes.

22

KOLYMA TOWER, FORMER SIBERIA

Komo Dath watched the video feed from the distant cluster of felt tents that burned and smoked until only scorched circles on the turf remained.

"Interesting," Dath rasped. "This Mongol slew only one man—and he not even the leader—yet this entire village surrendered to him without credible resistance."

Telian Piar nodded. "I have been scanning the histories of these Mongols. In years past, they would ride up to the gates of the cities they intended to sack and if the city surrendered without a battle, only the men would be slaughtered. If they resisted, all would be slaughtered."

"What is the purpose of such a choice? Of course the men will fight to the death."

"Not if they wish to preserve the lives of their wives and offspring."

"And see them handed over to brutal plunderers, to be enslaved and ravished? What kind of choice is that?"

"A terrifying one," Telian Piar intoned.

"It makes no tactical sense. Surrender and you live. Resist and you die. It is clear cut, and preserves one's own troops for further battles."

"True, but the Mongols had another talent evidently not recognized by you."

"And that is?"

"They were masters of the art of psychological warfare."

Komo Dath opened his fanged mouth as if to speak, hesitated, and shook his head savagely.

"You ascribe sophisticated thinking to dull bipeds who ride beasts of burden."

Telian Piar's single orb closed thoughtfully. His voice became mournful.

"Imagine you are the ruler of a city, and the thunder of pounding hoofbeats sounds over the next hill. The sky fills with their dust. They come howling, screaming, and promising death. There is no rescue, no retreat, no ultimate defense. As ruler, you, your chamberlains, your generals, and your soldiers all know that you are doomed. No matter what decision you make, what tactics you deploy, what weapons you possess, you are doomed."

"A doomed man still possesses the will to fight."

Telian Piar shook his enormous head. "The surety of death crushes the will to resist."

Komo Dath considered this. "Masterful."

"Brilliant."

"But this Mongol has only conquered a simple village of tents."

"Without taking a single casualty. Indeed, without a battle in the usual sense."

Komo Dath glanced sharply at the video feed. "We could learn from this Mongol."

"I trust you already have," Telian Piar said thinly.

23

THE BLACK GOBI, INNER MONGOLIA

Some two thousand strong, the New Golden Horde rode south to the border of the Free Mongolian Autonomous Region, otherwise known as Inner Mongolia.

It had been neither free nor autonomous even before the coming of the Martians. Its Chinese overlords had further fortified it as a buffer zone, with the absorption of Beijing by the conquerors from Mars.

The northernmost settlement of Inner Mongolia was called Paiyunopo, and it was to this place that Qasar Khan led his tireless forces. They made camp three *li* north of the city, where the personal *ger* of the khan was set up, and into this was led his concubine, Morning Doe.

"You will cook me mutton and tea," Qasar Khan instructed.

Morning Doe rested slim hands on her athletic hips. "That is the job of a wife. If you crave roast mutton, take yourself a wife. I am a concubine. My obligations and duties are restricted to the *kang*."

Qasar loomed over her. "I am khan. You will do as I say."

"And I am the khan's personal concubine. Make love to me or leave me to my mourning for my two cruelly murdered husbands."

Qasar Khan frowned, grinned, and frowned anew. His face became a thundercloud of warping brass.

"I have war to make."

Morning Doe presented her supple back to him. "Then make your war if love is not on your mind."

"That is on my mind, too."

"What will you give me in return for a hot meal?" Morning Doe asked suddenly.

"What pleases you?" Qasar asked carefully.

"I would like to be a captain of ten."

"Hah! A concubine cannot be a captain of ten."

"She can if her khan decrees it."

Qasar made a face. "This is true. My word is law. I can make the skies open with a frown."

Morning Doe turned, her dark eyes eager. "Then do this thing for me."

"You are worse than an old wife in your manipulations."

"But I am a perfect concubine in my other manipulations, and if you would enjoy any of these to the fullest extent possible, you will grant my wish."

"Why do you want to be a captain of ten?" Qasar wondered.

"So that I may ride at your side and not at the rear of the train, with the straggling sheep and the lone *ger* wagon."

"You could fall in battle."

"I could protect the back of my khan against treachery," Morning Doe countered.

"You could do that," Qasar admitted.

"So what is your decision?"

"Prepare the meal. I will be back for it—and for you."

With that, Qasar Khan flung himself out of his *ger*, grinning. "I rue the day I laid eyes on that hot-eyed wench, but she stirs my blood like no other."

Standing before the felt flap entrance, the nine-yak-tail

standard of Genghis Khan fluttering on one side, Qasar Khan surveyed the camp being made.

Night was falling. The horses were being hobbled, fires being made, sheep slaughtered, and weapons inspected for wear and future use. Qasar strode forward, bellowing exuberantly.

"No fires! No fires yet! We will organize our army before we eat."

Bayar came running up, his face long. "It is not better to organize on full bellies?"

"Mongols organize more efficiently when their bellies cry out for the rewards of organization."

This made sense to Bayar, so he said, "I will make arrows while you organize."

"Do so. But no mutton for you until we are fully organized. And see that you make horn bows and lesser bows, because I will first organize my forces into light cavalry and horse archers."

"Your word is my command."

Qasar Khan grunted. "That is a good response. Encourage the others to make it at every reasonable opportunity."

"Your word is my command."

Taking up a position on a low hump of land, Qasar Khan lifted his voice. "I command my loyal Mongols to assemble and attend to my words."

The Mongols who moved with alacrity, Qasar ordered to form a group on his right, those who were slow or who straggled were told to take the left wing. Then he spoke.

"You who straggled will straggle in war. You will be the dogs of the Dog Khan. You will be the first coins I expend and the last I will feed. You will be the last to receive war booty, and then only the leavings of those who obey my voice without hesitation."

Mutters of discontent came from the left wing.

"If any of you on the left object, I will hear your words."

A squat, bullet-headed Mongol stepped forward. "I swore fealty in return for an equal division of all spoils," he complained.

"And you swore also to obey me in every wise. You have failed me in this by your shameful straggling."

"A bargain is a bargain."

"True," Qasar Khan admitted.

"I, Durum, demand to stand on your right hand."

"If you insist. I will allow you to take a position on the right—assuming those on the right all agree you will receive a portion of their war spoils and other honors, though you do not deserve them."

"If you instruct them to do this, will they not obey?"

"It would violate their sacred oath if they failed in this."

Durum the Mongol blinked. "Then I will test their resolve." So saying, he strode toward the right flank with all eyes upon him.

Folding his arms defiantly, Durum took up a position unchallenged, and the eyes of Qasar Khan fell upon him without meaning or mercy.

"You are a brave man," Qasar said.

"I fear nothing. I am a Mongol."

"I fear a Mongol who fears nothing."

"A Mongol who fears nothing is a true instrument of your power."

"A Mongol who fears nothing does not fear his khan."

"I fear you."

"You said you fear nothing."

"Nothing except you, O Khan," Durum said nervously.

"That is not what you said."

"It is what I say now."

"What am I to believe? What you said before the sweat

broke on your brow or what you say now that your courage runs from you like urine from a sheep?"

"I swore an oath to serve you, Qasar Khan."

"Which you violated."

And without another word, Qasar Khan lifted his arm and said, "Slay the lying traitor."

It was done in a knot of violent activity. A sword slashed amid a rattle of gunfire. With the drawing of a dagger, the Mongol whose name history never recorded lay in a welter of his own sticky blood.

Qasar Khan looked again to those upon his left.

"Are there any others who do not fear their khan?"

No hand was raised, nor any voice lifted. Mongols lowered their heads. Some shivered.

"Next, I, being without heir, require a man who believes he could fill my boots, should I fall in a coming battle."

A ripple of surprise and interest ran through both flanks.

"Is there no Mongol who thinks he is my equal?" Qasar Khan demanded.

The ripple settled to a sound like the wave of tongues on a distant beach.

"None?"

No one spoke.

"Surely, one of you is willing to wear my armor and carry the redeemed sword of Lord Genghis?"

Finally, after much fidgeting and muttered discussion, a tall Mongol stepped forward. He wore a simple black *del*, belted about the waist with a scarlet sash.

"What name do you go by, O Khan to come?" Qasar Khan asked.

"Gerel. Of the Oirat Clan."

"You think you can take my place?"

"If you fall in battle, I am willing to do this."

"You will ride my horse Chino, after I fall from him?"

Gerel bowed his head respectfully. "If that is your command."

"If you are willing to ride my horse after I am dead, how do I know you will not plunge a dagger into my unprotected back in order to achieve this secret ambition you harbor?"

Gerel's face tightened. His mouth opened. His words held a quaver. "I desire nothing I do not already own."

"You ride with the New Golden Horde in search of plunder and women, and you say you have no desires?"

"I harbor no ambitions other than to serve you faithfully."

"How am I to know I can trust you in the heat of battle?" Qasar Khan thundered. "How do I know once we have conquered and you have a *ger* of your own you will not acquire adherents of your own and intrigue against me?"

"I was a simple herdsman before this hour. Now I am a horse Mongol like my greatest, oldest ancestors. All because of you. For this boon, I will lay down my very life."

"Those are silvery words. Speak more convincingly, for your naked ambition makes me fear for my own life."

Gerel the Mongol looked to the left flank and to the right. He saw only hardened faces and cold gazes. "Slay me if you will not trust me!" he exploded.

"I did not say that I do not trust you, Gerel. Only that I am in a quandary," Qasar Khan said evenly.

"You asked for an heir. I alone stepped forward. Reject me if you will. There is no shame in this."

"If I ask you to slice your own throat all the way to your backbone, will you do this?"

"My blood has sung for the two days I have ridden with you. If the choice is going back to the sluggish blood of my herdsman days or a swift death, I will accept death, for I have lived fully for two whole days."

Qasar Khan nodded. "Well spoken."

Gerel's face relaxed slightly.

And the silver dagger of Qasar Khan landed at the dusty toes of his boots.

"Now slice open your throat that I know you were trustworthy to the end of your days," Qasar intoned.

Sweating profusely, Gerel bent, took up the silver dagger, and laid it against his gulping throat.

He closed his eyes after taking a last look at the darkening Mongolian skies.

The tip of the blade touched his throat. He pressed it tight and began to draw a line across his own throat, his eyes squeezing out tears of bitterness. Blood trickled.

With a howl he dropped the dagger into the dirt. He screamed. Blood rilling down his throat, he hopped in place, as if stung by a scorpion.

"What! What!" he shrieked.

"You have an arrow in your arm," a man called out.

That and the burning sensation in his right bicep dragged his eyes to the red tufted shaft sticking out. His *del* sleeve was turning dark crimson.

He looked strange. Then he looked up to see Qasar Khan lowering his great bow silently.

"I trust you, Gerel the Mongol. You will be khan if I fall in battle. Until then you will ride at my back to protect my back."

And despite the hot burning sensation in his arm, Gerel knelt facing his khan and lowered his head with abject humility.

He was still kneeling when Qasar Khan stomped up to him and yanked the arrow from his pain-shocked arm with such force that he let out a howl of fresh pain.

"Let the hole in your arm remind you of the price of treachery."

His point made, Qasar Khan returned to the low hump of land and began barking out terse commands. In short order those with the lightest horses were designated light cavalry. Those with stout bows and the skills to use them became archers.

Others, armed with Kalashnikovs and other rifles, were made infantry. Still others became light horse-lancers. A small unit were called *ba'atur*, and these would be their elite guard of the khan.

When all had been organized, Qasar Khan looked them over.

"You make your khan's heart beat proudly. Now that you are organized, you may eat. Once you have eaten, you will train. Once you have trained to my satisfaction, you will lay siege to the city that lies but three *li* south of this camp, and subjugate it cruelly."

A roaring shout went up.

And with that Qasar Khan turned on his heel to march back to his *ger*, where he intended to fill his belly and exercise his concubine thoroughly. For with the dawn she would take her place as a captain of ten, and once that had been accomplished, her days of lovemaking would surely be numbered.

24

PAIYUNOPO, INNER MONGOLIA

The Military Governor of the People's Republic of China heard the first reports of campfires in the hills north of Paiyunopo and asked, "How many fires?"

"Six hundred," he was told.

The Military Governor lit a Panda cigarette, using the smoldering butt of another. "Six hundred fires. Nomads do not operate in units of that size."

"It has never been heard of before," the aide admitted.

"Six hundred suggests military numbers."

"The People's Liberation Army has ceded this area as a buffer zone."

"I know this, turtle's egg!"

"The beings said to be from Mars have not ventured south of their wall. This is by treaty."

"Treaties exist to be broken," the Military Governor snapped.

The aide was silent. The governor looked to the butter-yellow telephone that connected him to the Provisional People's Government in Hong Kong, far from the New Wall and its impenetrable mysteries.

"If they are Martians, we are helpless. If they are nomads, they must be refugees."

"Hungry refugees. Seeking food."

"I can't allow refugees to swell my population. There is little enough food as it is." The governor exhaled a smoky breath that was laden with dense blue cigarette smoke.

"Send a contingent of men to deal with these squatters. Have them move on. Tell them they are forbidden to enter Paiyunopo under any circumstances. Bring them old winter cabbage in case they are hungry. Bad cabbage that is spoiling. Maybe this will satisfy their hunger-gnawed bellies long enough for them to pull south."

"And if they refuse?"

"Do not attempt arrest. Retreat. I will contemplate how best to pacify them."

"Yes, comrade," the aide said, leaving the room and the Military Governor who silently recalled the days of stability before the Martians came and wrenched the heart out of the People's Republic, leaving men like him sitting behind desks of authority with no power to back up that authority.

Still, there was a positive side to things. With Beijing no more, and the leadership relocated to the far south, a man like him could become a potentate in his own right . . .

25

NORTH OF PAIYUNOPO, INNER MONGOLIA

PLA Captain Fung Yu led the intelligence probe to the nomadic encampment in the hills overlooking Paiyunopo.

He commanded a unit of twenty men, all armed with Chinese-manufactured AK-47s and Makarov sidearms. They sped through the hills with their safeties on. They wore the evergreen uniforms of the heroic People's Liberation Army, and their objective was to intimidate a band of ragtag Mongols who had come down from the old Russian Mongolian protectorate.

They did not expect trouble.

So they were not prepared for the thin whistle of an arrow high overhead.

The shaft arced high, and its whistling was shrill and very much unlike the normal flight of a loosed arrow into the air. It struck nothing that they could discern—certainly not any of them.

"Mongols of old used whistling arrows to signal an attack," a sergeant muttered.

"They know we are coming," Captain Fung said. "So what? The sound of our vehicles communicates this."

"Mongols were once very fierce."

"They drink sour fermented mare's milk. How fierce can they be?"

The convoy wound farther along, and the glinting red

eyes of campfires abruptly showed in the darkness. The air was so thick with horse dung smoke that their eyes began to smart. Before long the lead driver was complaining that he could not see the way, though it was illuminated by bouncing headlights.

"Keep driving," Captain Fung said. "I will guide you."

Pinching his eyes shut, the driver obeyed.

Captain Fung Yu experienced the first inkling of difficulty when a distinct crack like suddenly split wood reached his ears. It sounded very close.

"What was that?" he asked the sergeant driver.

The driver made no answer, except for a gurgle low in his throat. Then his hands slipped from the wheel and Captain Fung lunged to take it from him and steer the jeep into a ditch.

It turned out to be a very fortunate thing to do, for the trailing convoy vehicles began to crash and careen out of control.

The only other sounds were the soft *whisk-whisk* of arrows cleaving the air.

In the backglow of his upward pointing headlights, Captain Fung saw that the cracking sound had been made by a Mongol arrow splitting the driver's breastbone. The man had died with the rattle of death exhaling from his open mouth and his eyes showing as bloodshot whites.

Cursing, Captain Fung scrambled from the jeep to the ground.

Except the racing of motors and the futile whine of stuck tires, no more sounds came for several minutes.

"Call out!" Fung hissed.

No answer came.

"Speak! Who still lives?"

"I live," a voice groaned.

Came a whisper and a meaty thunk and the voice strangled off.

"Speak. Do you still live?"

A death sigh rewarded the question, and Captain Fung realized with a creeping coldness that he alone had survived the cowardly attack.

Mongols came slipping down toward his position not long after that, silent as panthers made of detached moon shadow fragments.

Captain Fung draped his Makarov from his sidearm holster and prepared to avenge his imminent death before it could be inflicted.

A loop of hemp caught his wrist from behind, yanking his gun hand back, also causing him to flip backward. The weapon clattered away uselessly, and he found himself looking down the bore of two AK-47s with extended bayonets.

"Surrender, Chinese," a voice hissed.

"I surrender."

"Hah! You speak our language. You are a smart Chinese."

They dragged him to his feet, bound his hands behind his bent back, and marched him into the hills.

Captain Fung walked stonily. These men were Mongols, yes, but some were dressed as if for a historic pageant. Beijing had attempted to stamp out all trace of Mongol ancestral pride, as had Soviet Russia when they controlled Outer Mongolia.

Except for the sprinkling of modern weapons, these men might have stepped out of time.

"You cannot take prisoner a captain of the PLA," Fung said bitterly, his face twisting with mixed rage and humiliation.

"Would you rather be slain?" a Mongol hurled back. "We are prepared to slay you."

Fung swallowed his rage but not his humiliation. "I would rather live."

"Then be silent."

Recognizing the reality of his situation, Captain Fung fell silent.

They escorted him to a *ger* where the hated nine-yak-tail standard of old waved proudly. Recognizing this from history books, Fung cursed in pungent Mandarin.

"What medieval madness is this?" he hissed.

He was cuffed to the ground for his pains.

A Mongol shouted into the closed tent flap, "A prisoner of war, Qasar Khan!"

"Hold him until I am finished with my concubine," came an impatient voice from within.

The slap of a hand against an unprotected face came sharply and the voice of Qasar Khan laughed boisterously.

"Slap my face again, cat-eyed wench, and I will return the favor double," he growled with more pleasure than anger.

A second slap came.

"Send them away until I am done with you," came a bowstring-tight female voice.

"You have it backward. We are done when I am done with you."

A third slap came.

"I am glad that I did not take you to wife," Qasar Khan growled. "If a khan's wife showed such disrespect, I would have her beheaded."

"What good would I be to you without lips or eyes to entice?"

"You possess other charms."

"Without my living head, I am without desire for you."

"That is a good point. I will remember that, if the desire to behead you overtakes me." Then, his voice hardening, Qasar Khan called out, "Interrogate your prisoner. Discover all you can of the defenses and weak points of this city."

"And when we are done?" a Mongol asked.

"Slay him for the food-growing Chinese he is."

"You cannot do this," Captain Fung sputtered. "Who do you Mongols think you are?"

"The Golden Horde of Qasar Khan," a Mongol said harshly as Fung was hauled by the hair toward a ring of campfires. There, he was made to squat in the circle until the overpowering heat sucked all moisture from his mouth and all resistance from his burning brain.

When he had given up every secret he possessed in return for a sprinkling of droplets of cooling water on his face and tongue, a Mongol crept up behind him, laid the curve of his blade against Captain Fung's unprotected throat, and jerked backward.

Fung's head rolled with its still-living brain into a campfire and sizzled like a shank of roast mutton.

26

KOLYMA TOWER, FORMER SIBERIA

"I have been scanning the historical intelligence digests," Komo Dath was saying.

"You find them interesting?" Telian Piar asked.

"Most interesting. These Mongols were very ingenious, in their crude way. Terran accounts all agree that they were the first tribe to engage in biological warfare, although on a massively primitive scale."

Telian Piar stood with his hands clasped within the joined sleeves of his violet robe. The two Martians stood in the spartan rectangle that was Komo Dath's office.

"I am not aware of this," he murmured reedily.

"They would catapult corpses infested with plague-ridden fleas over the walls of besieged cities, allowing the fleas to do their work for them while they waited patiently beyond the pest zone they themselves created. Once the population had sickened and was near death, they finished off the survivors and took what they wished."

"I am cognizant the Mongols brought what is called the Black Death to the western half of the hemisphere, thus changing the course of Terran history in incalculable ways."

"Yes. Many millions perished. The collection of city-states called Europe was decimated. Several Terran centuries passed before the indigenous population was reinvigorated. But this was not a military victory nor militarily significant, for the Mongols also suffered from this plague and their suzerainty soon collapsed under the sheer size of the unwieldy empire they had established."

"It is no wonder they were called the Scourge of God."

"We will see how they fare against modern Terran armies and weapons," Komo Dath rasped.

"I suspect they will fare very well," Telian Piar said.

"This remains to be seen," Komo Dath said, returning to his work.

"Considering how their leader dealt with Gnard forces, I am surprised at your skepticism," Telian Piar whispered, breezing from the room like a gliding lavender ghost.

Komo Dath threw a smoldering look at the Paeec's departing back. After the door hissed shut—and only then—he picked up a ceremonial dagger from his desk and bounced it off the portal in anger.

27

PAIYUNOPO, INNER MONGOLIA

The Military Governor of Paiyunopo was awakened a bit after midnight by an aide.

"What is it?" he asked sleepily as he fumbled the bed-side receiver to his sleepy face.

"The north quarter of the city is afire."

The words barely penetrated. But on the wall facing the window, the Military Governor saw the red glow. Turning in bed, he whipped aside the canvas shade. The north low skyline was backlit by leaping red flames.

"What measures have been taken?" he demanded.

"A cadre was sent to quench the flames, but they were slain to the last man."

"Slain! Slain by who?"

"The Mongols."

A brief chill touched the Military Governor's spine.

"Mongols," he spat. "What do they want?"

"They rode down and set several homes and buildings alight, after giving warning to the dwellers. They have slain all Chinese who they find and spare only their own people."

"This is madness! Why would they torch buildings?"

"It surpasses madness," the aide agreed. "But their purpose is unknown."

Throwing off the bedcovers, the Military Governor asked, "Did the intelligence unit ever return?"

"No. And they do not respond to their radio call sign."

"Could they have antagonized these animals, with bad result?"

"It is unlikely. Mongols are very high-spirited, but peaceful."

The Military Governor sat up and fumbled his feet into his shoes.

"I will assemble a special unit to deal with these madmen," he bit out, now fully awake.

Thirty minutes later the single aging PLA T-55 tank Hong Kong had allowed to remain in Paiyunopo for defense purposes was clanking and muttering down Thousand Flowers Street toward the conflagration that was now all that remained of the north quarter.

The fires had spread ferociously in the thirty minutes since the Military Governor had beheld it from his bedroom window. Paiyunopo was a simple city of woodframe homes, drab concrete office buildings, and even a sprinkling of the white felt yurts which the Mongol population called *gers*. Office buildings were few. Shops were modest, even by Chinese standards.

Now they were burning furiously, and as the Military Governor watched from his careening Land Rover, fresh fires started. Through the smoke and flames he could see mounted horsemen tossing blazing firebrands.

Whirling tornadoes of boiling gray-black smoke were befouling the sky, and through these streets of fire arced active dancing sparks.

"What are those?" he muttered.

The answer fell from the hazy sky.

A reed shaft struck a wood-frame home with a thunk. It burned. Soon the spot it had impaled darkened and blazed up, burning merrily.

"Mongol fire arrows," his aide muttered.

"Arrows are not proof against the armored might of the PLA. Advance," he ordered.

The T-55 began rumbling forward. Behind him three military trucks surged ahead, jammed with PLA regulars and a few civilian cadre volunteers mustered to fill out the depleted ranks.

They made their way through the burning avenues, amazed at the swiftness of the destruction, oblivious to the milling civilians fleeing with their meager possessions. Headless Chinese shopkeepers lay scattered here and there, their darkening blood bubbling and steaming in the streets.

The Military Governor had never believed in God before that moment, but now he felt he understood the old reactionary phrase Wrath of God.

Turning a corner, they stumbled upon a more wondrous sight.

A Mongol horseman sat on an armored charger, directing the destruction. Foot Mongols were sticking arrows against the burning sides of buildings until the wool-wrapped heads caught, nocking them, then letting fly at random.

Wherever their arrows fell, the Military Governor knew, a new fire would commence. It was wanton and senseless and mindless, and these nomads were going about it in high good spirits punctuated by boundless laughter.

"Cease this destruction!" the Military Governor roared.

The Mongols paid him no heed.

"I am Liu Xintong, Military Governor for this city. I demand explanations. Are you all drunk?"

As soon as the words were out of his mouth, Liu Xintong shrank inside. They sounded so foolish, so ineffectual under these surreal circumstances.

Turning to the waiting truck, he shouted, "Form a skirmish line!"

PLA regulars piled out of the backs of the trucks and formed a wide parade formation line.

Liu Xintong addressed them.

"You are directed to advance and fire at will. These lunatics are crazed with the lust to burn and destroy. Shoot them down like running dogs."

The line, straggling but formidable, started forward with AK-47s held at the hip, bayonets extended. Their boots made a ragged clopping under the growing roar of fire. All around were flames. Everything was fire. The soldiers' set faces might have been wax approaching intense heat, so much did they sweat and seem to melt.

In their eyes were the reflections of the conflagration, but there was fear there, too. Trained to fight foreign armies and local bandits, their skills were untested against arsonists and horse Mongols. And no Chinese who could read was ignorant of the historical terrors inflicted upon civilized China by the barbarian hordes of the khans.

Before a shot could be fired, the Mongol in the blue and gold armor turned, twisting his head about. His eyes were twin firebrands under the high medieval helmet. And on his metallic forehead lay the mark of a skull, white, outlined in red, over a bleached moon.

Seeing the skirmish line, he lifted a curved sword and shouted out in his native tongue.

The Military Governor stiffened. Now there would be a battle.

But there was not.

Instead the Mongol whirled on his charger and showed them its pale rump. He ran off into the blackest of ground smoke, his followers running and leaping after them.

Liu Xintong gestured as he shouted.

"Commence firing! Open fire!"

The skirmish line, almost as one, dropped to one knee, and the rattle of automatic weapons fire drummed over the fire's roar.

A few laggard Mongols twisted and fell. Only one returned fire and he only with his dying breath. The arrow barked a PLA kneecap and brought a howl of pain.

The marauders were quickly lost in the sea of smoke and flame.

"Advance! Advance! We are victorious."

The skirmish line broke into a run, the grumbling T-55 following after them like a humpbacked green beetle.

In the Land Rover the Military Governor grinned with pleasure. He had never directed a military campaign before. Paiyunopo was a quiet border town. This would of course mean a pay increase from the gray mandarins in Hong Kong. And possibly transfer to a more hospitable assignment.

A more fortunate turn of events could not have been orchestrated, Liu Xintong thought.

Entering the smoke was like driving into a realm populated by black life-clutching ghosts. The smoke robbed a man of his breath and stung the eyes. Yet it was possible to see things: homes alight, some already reduced to charred shells of alligator-skin frameworks, and leaping flames everywhere.

"They were fools to attack us," Liu Xintong shouted. "For this they will all die."

But a moment later he was fighting for air while straining to see through the billowing black smoke.

"Where are they? Where did they go?"

"I do not know," the aide choked out.

The road ahead was blocked by fire. They realized this when the skirmish line suddenly fell back in clots of coughing soldiers.

"Where? Which way?"

A stumbling soldier slipped on something and cursed.

"This way!" he said suddenly. "Come this way! I have slipped on horse dung."

"Yes? Where does the horse dung go? Call out!"

Compelled as much by the choking smoke as the need to discover the trail, everybody got down on the ground where the smoke was less dense and sought out horse dung cakes with their bare hands.

Lumps of it went down a side street, and Liu Xintong cried triumphantly, "Down this street! They have gone down Yong Street."

The tank rumbled around and the soldiers clustered to its green sides as if clinging to its armored protection. They walked low, coughing, choking, struggling to see, but determined to press on.

Back in the Land Rover, Military Governor Liu sat low in his seat, the better to breathe. The slipstream helped dispel the choking noxious stuff.

"I see horses ahead," a smoke-abraded voice called out.

"Lights!"

Headlights and tank searchlights came into play, roving briskly, looking pale against the leaping flames, and found a knot of nervous horses down a side street the flames had not yet touched.

"There!" Liu cried, standing up in his seat.

He was pointing toward the horses. It was a completely unnecessary gesture. The searchlights were doing all the pointing that was needed.

All saw that the horses stood hobbled, their high orange and scarlet saddles empty of men or their shadows.

Then something feathered his bicep.

He felt the shock before he did the pain. An arrow had

transfixed him. He could see the red feather tuft of the fletching. His eyes widened.

Then, as if he were sprouting quills, other shafts appeared almost magically in his legs, arms, and chest.

He was alive when he slipped back into his seat. Alive, but fully cognizant of his destruction. He hands were at once numb and hot. His head lolled over and he saw his aide, half out of the driver's seat, his backside bristling with arrows like a fat ridiculous green pincushion.

Somewhere beyond the range of his shrinking senses he heard the stuttering rattle of automatic weapons and heard the meaty *thuck* and *thunk* of other arrows feathering his PLA regulars as if they were but straw men set up for target practice.

In his dying moment Military Governor Liu Xintong had a flash of insight. Too late, it came to him that the Mongols of old had many cunning war tricks, a favorite of which was to feign retreat so as to lure an unsuspecting foe into ambush . . .

28

PAIYUNOPO, INNER MONGOLIA

From the roof of a house that had been left untouched for the purpose of ambush, on a slatternly street untouched for the same reason, Qasar Khan lay down his ram's horn bow and stood up.

Behind him the north quarter was ablaze, the sky aboil with sparks. The sparks themselves would carry more fire to other quarters. But Qasar had no stomach for patience. There were many campaigns between this first outpost and China proper.

Lifting a voice coarsened from inhaling smoke, he shouted, "Ariunbold! Lead your archers to the southern quarter and torch all you find. Spare no Chinese. Ochinbal, you have the west."

"Why burn when we can loot?" Ochinbal shouted back.

"We will loot Chinese cities. Not Mongolian ones."

"If we are to loot Chinese cities, why burn Mongol ones?"

"That you will learn as soon as this place is heaped with ashes," Qasar howled, the white skull on his forehead bristling.

It was done in short order. Ariunbold rode to the south, down the main street called Thousand Flowers, as Chinese and Mongols alike shrank before his company. They threw the occasional firebrands as they ran, but saved the bulk for their objective.

155

Back astride his charger, Qasar Khan piloted Chino down the main street, looking right and left as all over the town fire took root and grew into a lively creeper of orange and yellow flowers that ate and consumed all they touched.

Here and there resistance flowered. It was cut down mercilessly by snapping Kalashnikov rounds and whispering arrows. Soon, overwhelmed by the relentless destruction unleashed upon it, the town of Paiyunopo simply lost its will to fight.

"It is truly as Lord Genghis once said," Qasar muttered as he made his way through the town. "Resistance crumbles under the least merciful attack."

Bayar rode on his left. Morning Doe on the right.

"Why do you burn?" Bayar asked.

"He has a lust for burning," Morning Doe said.

"My lust is not for burning," Qasar returned. "Although it does burn."

"You are insatiable," Morning Doe murmured, not in complaint so much as admiration.

"To be insatiable is to live," Bayar said, eyeing the fleeing womenfolk.

"If you see one you like," Qasar said, "take her by the ear. It is the Mongol way with captured women slaves."

"I am a conquerer. Why should I take the first plump wife I chance to spy?"

"Because you may not live to see the sunrise." Qasar turned his gaze toward Morning Doe when he spoke.

Morning Doe said nothing. The heat was making her face perspire, and she shook her lustrous mane of black hair like a horse whips its tail.

The town of Paiyunopo burned all night. By the time the sunrise touched it, it was no longer red but black and gray. The air was pungent and scratchy and clogged the throat.

Qasar Khan assembled his horsemen on the plains to the south of the ruined town.

The inhabitants and survivors shivered before him. Qasar Khan addressed them.

"I have burned your town to the ground because for as long as I have lived and longer, it has been infested by Chinese. I could not root out these Chinese in a single night, so I resorted to purging by fire. Now the Chinese are all dead, but you survive. Be grateful. I know you not by sight or name or blood, and could have slain you as readily as I did the infesting Chinese."

Qasar Khan let his words sink in.

"But I refrained from putting you all to the sword, for which I expect gratitude unhesitating and everlasting."

No one spoke up in gratitude of any kind. Many cried. Others twisted their faces against the numbing shock and horror that had been visited upon them and their lives.

Qasar Khan continued his oratory.

"In return for your unexpressed gratitude, I ask that the men of the dead town follow me into China, where we will sack and loot and possibly take up residence in better cities than these."

The men among the survivors looked up in a kind of dazed interest. The women continued to weep bitter tears and comfort their shivering children.

"For too long have Mongols dwelt in inferior cities, breathing bad air and living like the accursed settled peoples of China. I offer any man who joins the Golden Horde of Qasar Khan his choice of residences once China lies broken and humbled under our boot heels. Become one of my war dogs and you will eat the greasiest food, drink the sourest mare's milk, and enjoy the comforts of unwilling Chinese concubines."

Red-rimmed eyes grew animated. Men whispered to one another.

"You will live as the sons of Genghis have lived. You will breathe open air, ride spirited horses, and rampage unburdened through life. And if it is your wish to dwell in Chinese cities when you have exhausted plunder and pleasure, I will ask only that you swear allegiance in the new empire I am welding together."

Murmuring interest swelled. Wives turned on husbands with slapping hands and kicking feet. This had the opposite intended effect, compelling the first recruits to step forward.

"I will join the New Golden Horde."

"So will I."

"All menfolk who can ride or fight are invited to ride south to spread the Mongol virtues of horsemanship and freedom," Qasar proclaimed.

"What about the women?" a man called out.

"They must stay behind, for women cannot fight."

Morning Doe's foot lashed out suddenly, and Qasar Khan caught it and twisted. She fell off her horse, then remounted, lavishly cursing his ancestry.

"The women may rebuild as they wish, in the event any Mongol desires to return to this accursed spot upon the completion of his service in the Golden Horde," Qasar Khan added, unperturbed by the momentary dissension in the ranks.

The man who had asked the question took one look at his red-cheeked wife and kissed her once. Then ran up to join the first recruits.

After that the menfolk came in slow but steady waves, some carrying rifles, others bare-handed. Horses that had been salvaged from the conflagration were brought out.

Qasar rode among them, his eyes busy. He was seeking Chinese spies—and one thing more.

He came upon a bald-headed Mongol and asked, "You. What is your name?"

"Ouji."

Qasar grunted. "I have heard better names."

"Guest suits me, for my mother was uncertain of my sire."

"You know these men, Guest?"

"Most."

"Then you know their minds and their strengths and their weaknesses."

"This is so."

"Thus I appoint you captain of a myriad. These men will be your myriad. And you will answer only to me."

The man swayed his shoulder. "But I wear rags. My face is a mask of soot."

"You will wear finery, and Chinese women will wash your face just to breathe the same air you do," Qasar Khan returned.

The man's warm brown eyes sparkled through his sooty visage.

"I am proud to captain a myriad," he said thickly.

"See that your pride does not poison your loyalty," Qasar Khan said, riding back to his position.

"We march at once. We march toward the town of Shenmu, which cries out to be purged of Chinese infestation."

Bayar blinked. "Does Shenmu not lie behind the Great Wall?"

"The Great Wall built to protect Shenmu will shield the horde from the populace's unsuspecting eyes," Qasar said.

"But how will we breach the barrier?"

"We are Mongols," Qasar cried, lifting his sword. "We are indomitable in our ways! *Ai-Yah*, war dogs! Fall in! Forward!"

And with that the Golden Horde began a slow, ponderous turn, like a disjointed wheel of horseflesh and Mongols, until it was under way again.

The new untrained myriad was slower to get going, but once organized, they rode like the wind until they caught up and were bringing up the rear.

At the head of the horde rode Qasar Khan, proud, stiff-backed, his knife-slit eyes fixed on the southern horizon. On his right rode Ariunbold, holding high the heavy standard of the Golden Horde. On his left Morning Doe bounced on her high saddle. Bayar bobbled just behind them, keeping a wary eye on Gerel the next khan— should misfortune overtake them.

"I know why you burned Paiyunopo," Morning Doe said after the day had begun.

"You are a smart woman."

"Men with no homes have no ties. Men with no ties ride toward freedom more readily."

"Men with hectoring wives yearn for freedom above all other things," Qasar remarked.

"I will never be your wife," Morning Doe hissed.

Qasar Khan grinned broadly. "Then possibly I may never tire of you."

29

KOLYMA TOWER,
FORMER SIBERIA

Komo Dath received the intelligence reports in his office.

They came in waves. They had come for five days, each more compelling than the previous one.

"Another town burnt to the ground," the Gnard factotum reported, his voice properly servile.

"Estimated size of the Golden Horde?" Komo Dath returned.

"Intel/Div reports they number some six thousand strong."

"A large force . . ."

"They train as they ride."

"Yes, yes, that pattern has been apparent for some time."

"Cities to the south are evacuating before them. These they burn with equal relish."

"This Qasar Khan is cunning. A standing city can be repopulated, its survivors coalescing into a revenge-bent military unit. A refugee population is more easily hunted down or recruited. The male Mongols will be forced to join the march south into China."

"He is unstoppable."

"He is our tool, nothing more. Once he fulfills his task, he and all his horde must be exterminated or sublimated to our will."

Komo Dath looked out his office window. The sky was hazy again today. The smoke from the south had drifted north. It would not penetrate the domed Martian colonies, but it was ominous to behold.

"Keep me updated hourly," he instructed.

"Your will," the Gnard said, withdrawing.

30

HONG KONG

In Hong Kong, China, in the newly built Great Hall of the People, the Premier of the surviving People's Republic of China faced his reconstituted cabinet in exile.

Outside, Hong Kong traffic blared and howled.

"We have lost the Autonomous Region," he said. "The capital of Sayn Shanda has fallen to this new scourge from the north."

"At least it was not lost to the Martian invader," the Defense Minister said resignedly.

"What does Intelligence say?" the Premier asked.

The Intelligence Minister looked uncomfortable. His face was like rehardened melted wax, soft to look at but hard of skin. His eyes were sleepy, but cunning. Like everyone else in this gray room of gray men, his words came spewing softly through blue tobacco smoke.

"Our surviving assets assure me that the Mongols, under pressure of having lost half of Outer Mongolia to the Martian invader, are naturally seeking fresh pastureland."

"They appear well-organized for houseless nomads."

"As organized as men on horseback can be," the Intelligence Minister allowed dismissively.

"Then why do they burn all they encounter?"

"They are Mongols reverting to their barbarian ways.

163

They burn for the same reason that a tiger pounces upon an antelope. It is their unbending nature."

This sounded reasonable to the Premier.

The Defense Minister, looking worried, said, "It is a serious thing to lose the Autonomous Region."

The Premier waved the concern aside in a cloud of cigarette smoke. "It was our buffer against Russian Mongolia. Russian Mongolia is no more. Therefore it is not important."

"It remained useful as a buffer against the Martian men-who-are-not-men."

"The New Wall serves that illustrious purpose," the Premier said.

"These Mongols will soon be at our gates," the Intelligence Minister warned.

"They would not dare. Horse cavalry against tanks! Bows and carbines against AKs and mortars! Nomads against crack PLA troops? Besides, the Great Wall still stands. They will not be able to ride over it unless their steeds sprout wings."

Polite laughter rippled about the great room.

"I recommend we prepare by creating a ring of steel about the northern cities of Yichwan and Yulin, as a precaution," the Defense Minister said. "For they lie exposed by fallen segments in the Great Wall."

"This is reasonable. Do it."

"These Mongols are ferocious as locusts, but the Great Wall will protect other towns from their wrath as it did in times past," the Defense Minister added.

"The Great Wall protected the Emperors of old only so long, and then not at all," the Intelligence Minister said slowly.

No one spoke for a long time.

"Is there other business?" the Premier asked.

Bland faces indicated not.

"Then we are adjourned. The world is changing about us, but we resist, impervious to change. We will also endure. And perhaps if these Mongol free riders grow sufficiently bold, they will seek to reclaim their lost territory from the Martians, and in doing so provide us with the wedge that will enable us to reclaim our capital."

The sadness on the faces around the great conference table spoke volumes—of how they all missed the comforts of faraway Beijing.

31

SHAANXI PROVINCE, FREE CHINA

Sixteen *li* north of the Chinese city of Shenmu, the Golden Horde of Qasar Khan lay camped. Their numbers exceeded the stars of the Silvery River in the overhead night sky. Their fires were brighter than the stars. The aroma of horse and human dung hung in the night air like a pungent perfume.

These were the smells that Qasar Khan loved. These were the odors that Genghis, whose armor he wore, had reveled in. He took a deep full breath and his heart swelled with a fierce pride that no Mongol in centuries had known.

"I am khan," he said in the smoky confines of his bed. He repeated it, with growing emotion. "I am Qasar, the first khan since Timur the Lame."

"Are you coming to bed, khan of my sleeping *kang*?" Morning Doe murmured, her half-closed cat eyes sleepy.

"Eventually."

"I will sleep if you do not come to bed soon."

"Then sleep."

"Have you tired of me already?"

"I will never tire of you, heart's delight. But my brain is afire and my heart seeks other delights."

A silken pillow came flying at his back.

"If you touch another woman, I will slit my own throat and leave you weeping."

"There are other concubines," Qasar said casually.

"None like me."

"Many like you. Sleep or slit your throat. That is up to you."

"Bastard! Defile your mother!"

"Defile her yourself if you are that lusty."

Morning Doe blinked. "Is she not dead?"

"If you are truly lusty, that will not dissuade you." Qasar Khan laughed, stealing off into the night.

He found Arrow Prince Bayar inspecting a wagonload of arrowheads, which had been poisoned with smeared yak dung.

"For a man in search of a desirable wife, you are very diligent in your princely duties," Qasar told him.

Bayar did not look up. "Now that I am Arrow Prince, I do not wish to lose the sublime honor. More women will ache to hold me if I am truly a prince."

"They will have no choice."

"I will enjoy them more if I do not have to fight so much for their favors."

"To each his own," Qasar Khan said. "I myself enjoy fighting with my women."

"You have more than one?"

"Morning Doe's moods are like the storms of the steppes. She is like many women to me."

"I would prefer many women to one that suffers moods. A woman's moods are incalculable."

Qasar's eyes crinkled up. "But fill the senses."

"I imagine concubines are different from other women I have enjoyed," Bayar said, tossing the arrowhead into the wagon.

Qasar Khan started off. "Walk with me, Bayar."

"Your word is my command." Falling in behind his khan, he asked, "Where do you go?"

"The where does not matter. It is what I do there."

Shrugging, Bayar spanked the dirt off his work *del* as he caught up to his khan. They walked past campfires and sprawled Mongols snoring under the stars like flocks of geese honking and snorting out of time.

Qasar grinned. "This is how a Mongol should live. Open and unfettered."

"I would prefer a *ger*," Bayar remarked.

"You will have *gers* in the days to come."

"I am tired of sleeping under a felt tent flap to ward off the summer rains and the biting lice."

"Lice will not harm you," Qasar Khan said, feeling an itch on his back. Reaching around behind him, he discovered a hairy brown insect, which he captured.

"You have lice?" Bayar asked.

"Lice are the lot of the free-riding Mongol. They harden his hide to adversity and remind him he is alive, where city sheets soften his skin until the dullest of arrows will wound him."

The six-legged brown louse squirmed in the pinch of Qasar's fingertips.

"I do not know this one," he muttered.

Eyeing it, Bayar said, "Nor do I. Obviously it is a Chinese louse."

Nodding, Qasar Khan lifted the insect to his mouth and killed it between his strong front teeth.

"We did not kill our lice in this fashion in Ulan Bator," Bayar said conversationally.

Qasar made a fist of one hand. His eyes were resolute as flint. "Ulan Bator is no more. But when I am done I will wrest it back from the Bone Heads and restore it to its former glory, where it will once again be called Urga, as in olden days."

"The Temple is a better name for a great Mongol city than Red Hero," Bayar agreed.

"The names of cities should not be changed unless they are conquered. When we subjugate the city that lies behind the Great Wall, I may call it Bayar in your honor."

"That is a very great honor."

"For the city, yes."

"For me, too."

"If you take it as such."

"I do."

"It is acceptable to your khan that you do, but not important."

Three *li* of walking brought them to low foothills beyond earshot of the most outlying Mongol sentry. Here, Qasar Khan reached into the front of his *del* and withdrew a small silver device.

Bayar eyed it curiously. "What is that?"

"The Bone Heads gave this to me."

"And you did not throw it away as accursed?"

"I can always throw it away when it is no longer of use to me," Qasar said, pressing a stud on one side. A red light glowed, bathing his adversity-hammered bronze features in an unholy glow.

A Bone Head voice rasped from the silver device. Komo Dath. "Speak."

Qasar lifted the device to his strong mouth. "Bone Heads do not command Qasar Khan to speak," he growled. "It is the other way around."

A strangled rasp came from the device.

"I ask for a desire to be fulfilled," Qasar Khan said.

"State this desire," said the raspy voice of Komo Dath.

"My horde lies camped sixteen *li* north of that city soon to be called Bayar but now called Shenmu. The Great Wall of the old Han Nation protects it. I wish the wall demolished at a suitable place so that my horde may pour through it freely."

The silver device vibrated alarmingly with the next words. "This is impossible!"

"You said that if it was possible, you would do whatever I desired."

"I did not. The Paeec, Telian Piar, made that promise."

"I care not whether these are Bone Head or Red Eye promises, only that they are kept."

"You don't understand. We cannot take overt action. You are on your own in this enterprise. There are political realities that must be respected."

"Political?" Qasar said to Bayar.

"It is another word for horse dung."

Qasar nodded. Into the silver device, he said, "Spare me your horse dung words. You have made a promise and must honor your word or it will be nothing and you will lose face."

"Face?" Dath rasped.

Bayar whispered. "He has no face. Remember?"

"Never mind," Qasar growled into the silver device.

"We can provide simple tools with which this can be accomplished," Komo Dath said tensely, "but that is all."

Bayar grinned widely. "Ask for Chof guns," he hissed.

"I therefore demand sufficient Chof guns to supply my horde, whose numbers exceed—"

"Exactly 6,798," Bayar said.

"You know the exact number?" Qasar asked Bayar.

Bayar looked indignantly glum. "I am prince in charge of arrow-making. I need to know such things."

Impressed, Qasar repeated the number into the silver talking device. "I desire 6,798 Chof guns."

"Martian technology cannot be supplied for the same reason," Dath bit out.

"That is two desires you have forbade. Are your words so hollow they cast no shadows?"

"You ask the politically impossible!" Komo Dath rasped harshly.

"I have raised an army and subjugated all of Inner Mongolia in a matter of weeks, and you speak of the impossible to me? I am Qasar Khan. The impossible is my daily exercise."

The silver device was silent for a very long while.

Bayar met Qasar Khan's unflappable gaze and shrugged.

Qasar shushed him with a curt gesture. They waited.

Before long, Komo Dath's voice rasped like a metal file against another metal file.

"Await my next transmission. I must confer with others."

"Do not keep the khan of all the Mongols waiting long, Bone Head," Qasar Khan growled.

Before the silent device went utterly silent, it emitted an unintelligible Martian curse.

"You treat the Bone Heads like Chinese," Bayar said with admiration.

"I treat them as inferior to Chinese. Are they not Bone Heads?"

"They are truly Bone Heads."

"But they will respect us deeply after we are done with them."

With that, Qasar Khan squatted down in the coarse grass and cast his sharp eyes heavenward. Here, he watched for luminous jade-green streaks, but saw none troubling the silver river of stars called in the West the Milky Way.

32

KOLYMA TOWER, FORMER SIBERIA

Komo Dath found Telian Piar kneeling in his quarters, tending to a tiny gnarled tree Dath at first mistook for a Martian *inko*.

"What is that?" he rasped.

"The Terrans call it a bonsai. My favorite canal lily has died and I have become interested in indigenous flora."

"It is like our *inko*."

"Just as these Mongols are like you, Gnard."

"I resist that comparison," Dath said stiffly.

"Which proves that it is more correct than not—otherwise it would not inflame your pride."

Laying aside a pruning tool, Telian Piar stood up. His gnarled hands clasped their opposite wrists as he shook the wide sleeves of his lavender robe. As the sleeve hems met, his fingers slid silently from sight.

Komo Dath met the round red gaze of the Paeec's single orb with narrow venom.

"What is wrong?" Piar asked thinly.

"The Mongols stand on the brink of invading China."

"All proceeds as it should."

"The abysmal Dog Khan is making demands," Dath spat. "Unreasonable demands. Demands we are obliged to fulfill because you promised him anything he desires."

"What does he desire?"

"Over six thousand KA-77s."

172

Telian Piar blinked once, roundly and thoughtfully.

"This is a difficult thing. I did not imagine a barbarian who preferred rude stringed catapults over noisy Terran rifles would ask this."

"He *has* asked, and if we do not fulfill this demand, his bonds to us are shattered by distrust."

Telian Piar turned to look out over the forbidding snow-swept Kolyma Mountain Range of the former Russia. He was several moments before speaking.

"His feet are firmly planted on the road to empire. He will not turn away from the invasion of China because we deny him superior technology."

"So we are to refuse?" Komo Dath asked.

"No," Telian Piar said thoughtfully. "It is time you take this matter to the Ruling Council."

Komo Dath fisted his hands tightly. "Is this wise?"

"Wiser than handing over the technological evidence that proves we have unleashed the scourge of scourges upon the nation of China."

"This dog awaits my answer."

"Then let us not keep him," Telian Piar murmured, moving forward like a wraith drawn by a string. Komo Dath fell in behind him, his boots clomping with ill-concealed impatience.

Soon they were walking on a higher level along the rust-red corridors of the Kolyma Command Center, and Telian Piar said, "Now we will reap the fruits of our well-meaning experiment or face the consequences of subterfuge."

"I do not fear the Council," Dath spat.

"Since you wield absolute military power, they fear you," Piar said, so softly that his words carried only to Dath's auris and to no other ears, living or electronic.

Komo Dath made no reply. None was necessary.

"Walk with me as we approach the Council chamber,"

Piar said as they turned the final corridor to the massive chamber portal.

"Why?"

"Because I request this," Piar said softly.

"You have some intellectual game in mind?"

"We will enter together, but I will speak first."

"Seeking all credit, Paeec?" Dath rasped.

"I do not seek all credit. I merely desire that the blame be shared equally in the event our punishment should be harsh."

"Hoping to lessen your own?"

"We have both known the thin joys of house arrest. I, now. You, in the past. Who is to say what the future holds for us once we broach this most difficult of subjects?"

"I comprehend your game. You desire reinstatement to the Council and a restoration of authority."

"As long as you remain Martian Military Commander, any seat on the Council is tantamount to a death sentence."

Without another word, Dath drew abreast and began walking in lockstep with the Paeec's silent tread. A Gnard guard stationed by the entrance shouted, "All Honor. The Council is convened."

The great double doors parted, the angular Martian skull symbol dividing itself before vanishing into the wall slots.

The hall was a multitiered gallery where the surviving Council sat on lofty perches, arrayed in their finest armor, a mixture of Gnard and Paeec.

In the beginning, there had been thirty-five Council members, divided equally. Now, sharp-toothed Gnards outnumbered the single-eyed Paeec members. All looked down, their red eyes intolerably hot with interest.

Council member Feep nodded as the two newcomers entered, the doors closing behind them.

"All Honor," Telian Piar said quietly.

"All Honor," Komo Dath echoed.

Nods of acknowledgment rippled through the Council.

"What matter calls us here?" Feep asked.

"A matter that has started small and insignificant but which grows in import by the hour."

"You have leave to speak."

"First," Telian Piar intoned, "I must tell you of a species of Terran that is called a Mongol. I am certain you will find my words compelling . . ."

33

SHAANXI PROVINCE, FREE CHINA

It was the reddest dawn Qasar Khan had ever seen. He squatted on the coarse grass, fingering the silver communications device the Bone Heads from the Red Eye planet had given him.

"See how the sun is like a burning caldron of blood, Bayar?"

Shielding his eyes with one hand, Bayar said, "It seems a very angry sunrise."

"It reflects my deep soul anger."

"You fear the Bone Heads have betrayed you?"

"I fear no betrayal from those I never trusted in the first place. Betrayal exists only between friends and allies, not between Mongols and hot-eyed monsters such as they. They have not our values or culture. They do not speak our tongue correctly. Nor do they love the horse." He shook his head from side to side. "No, there is no betrayal here. Only a shameful and insulting lack of respect."

Qasar Khan stood up, his legs unbending with a cartilage-crackling stiffness he refused to acknowledge by his expression.

"You will wait no more?"

Qasar nodded grimly. "Let the Bone Heads summon me when they will. It may be that I will not heed their entreaties, for whatever path they believed they had set me upon, I am a Khalkha Mongol. I ride to my own destiny, not theirs."

"How will we breach the Great Wall?"

"Possibly we will not."

"If we do not, how will we conquer Shenmu?"

"That, too, may not matter. For there are other walls and other cities ripe for subjugation."

"This is the city we have marched many *li* to oppress. The horde now lies dreaming of its wealth and its women."

"The Great Wall of the Han is a mighty wall," Qasar said, looking down upon its crenellated battlements.

"Yes, very mighty. But not proof against a good horde."

"It also functions as a road."

"Yes, sentries walk its paved ramparts."

"Horses may ride it safely over the soft earth that otherwise clutches at their hooves or harbors adders that bite."

"Yes, it is wide enough for six horses going abreast."

"It is a road suitable for the New Golden Horde."

"For short distances. Its paving stones give up little grass for the horses to pull at."

"Mongol horses understand privation. Empty bellies only spur them to greater feats of endurance."

"Yes," Bayar said, "the horde could ride this wall. But to what destination?"

"I hear that the Great Wall has been absorbed into another wall, farther east."

Bayar nodded. "The New Wall incorporates the Great Wall where the demarcation suits both sides. Many in the horde have attested to this."

"We ride the Great Wall the Han Nation built against us so long ago to the New Wall that will no more be proof against us than the old," Qasar said slowly, eyes tightening until only black gleams in bronze pockets showed.

"We ride against the Bone Heads, then?"

"Yes."

"Are they worthy of Mongol subjugation? Are their cities filled with treasure?"

"No, their cities are filled with Chof guns, with which we will rule over all Bone Heads and Chinese alike."

"I would rather subjugate the Chinese first, for Bone Head women do not appeal to me."

"You may put them to the sword if you do not covet their favors."

"Their mouths are filled with sharp teeth."

"Break their teeth if you fear their bite."

"It may be their lower mouths are also filled with teeth, as some say Chinese female demons are formed to unman the unwary when a man tries to make thunder and lightning with them."

"Then break their skulls and leave them to die in your wake," Qasar Khan said, squeezing the silent silver device. "For the time has come to deal with the Bone Heads as they must be dealt with."

"You are angry?"

"I am khan. They possess what I want, and they deny me my sworn desires. If word of this insult carries to the six directions of space, there will be no respect for my rule. My decrees will evoke no terror. We ride to ignite respect in their thinly beating hearts."

"I think we ride to ignite Bone Head towers."

"That, too," Qasar Khan said, and when his hard metallic fist opened, the silver device held the distinct indentations of his callused finger pads.

34

KOLYMA TOWER,
FORMER SIBERIA

Telian Piar finished his long discourse. His gesturing hands fell, dangled, then found one another, fingers grasping bony wrists. He waited as the Martian Ruling Council absorbed the full import of his words.

"You have presented us with interesting possibilities," Council member Feep said.

"But I trust no problems?" Piar returned.

Feep turned his hot gaze toward Komo Dath, who had remained mute through the entire proceeding. "You have stood there in an uncharacteristic silence, Commander Dath."

"Piar is more . . . eloquent than I."

"We are unclear on this matter. Is this Mongol experiment Telian Piar's doing, or yours?"

Dath hesitated only briefly. "His thought. My deed."

"A joint venture, then?"

"Equal and without division," Dath rasped, feeling Piar's monocular gaze resting upon him.

The multiform eyes of the Council flicked back and forth between the two supplicants. It chafed Dath to stand submissively under their burning gaze. His was the ultimate power during the present emergency, but decorum was decorum. At least until the Council was disbanded or dismembered and he ruled unchallenged.

"We will confer for some time. Await us in the holding room."

"Your will," Dath and Piar said in unison.

They bowed out of the room, not turning until the double doors parted to allow their escape.

In the adjacent holding room, Telian Piar was placid while Komo Dath paced.

"This was risky," Dath rasped.

"The Council will see the wisdom of the Mongol experiment."

"They will not strip me of my emergency powers for a program that so advances the conquest of this planet without cost in lives or material."

"You do not know this. There may be political repercussions."

"Politics. Bah. Better that we strangle those who would constrain us from achievable victory."

"Brute force is equally treacherous. Why do you not see this?"

"Because I am a conqueror. I conquer. I do not negotiate, nor will I stoop to beg, plead, or cajole."

"That is why I needed to speak to the Council. You would have frightened them from the useful and correct path."

Komo Dath shook an angry fist. "The only path to victory is a scorched road where nothing grows or walks," he rasped.

"I have not heard that Gnard saying in many years," Piar said thinly. "I had forgotten how vacuous it was."

"Better than the Paeec parables that say nothing unless unraveled—and even then are subject to broad interpretation."

An electronic chime pealed in the room and they exchanged sharp glances, then exited.

The Council members had resumed their seats when Telian Piar and Komo Dath stood before them anew.

Feep stood up before speaking. "We have conferred and have come to a majority, though not unanimity, on this matter."

A few low grumbles came from the tiers of members.

"First, we find this experiment good and useful.

"Second, we think it worthy of support.

"Third, we have communicated with the Chinese Terran government in Hong Kong to apprise them of the imminent Mongol threat."

"What!" Dath screamed. "What have you done?"

"We have taken control of your experiment," Feep returned.

"I have the power to effect my will!"

"You have backed an unauthorized project conceived by a Council member technically under house arrest."

Telian Piar felt hot gazes settling on him. He remained impassive, patient, waiting.

Dath continued to plead his case. "Weeks have gone into this project. There were no indicators pointing back toward us. Why—"

"Nor are they now," Feep returned smoothly. "We have as a gesture of goodwill informed the Chinese government of the imminent attack on their northern city of Shenmu. They will take countermeasures to crush the Mongol threat. Thus, we are washing our hands of this first Mongol feint."

"First?" Piar said.

"These Mongols are not under control and therefore are not controllable."

"That is the point!" Dath raged, fists shaking.

"After a suitable interval, we will initate the next phase of Project Mongol. That of capturing suitable specimens and implanting neural transmitters in their skulls."

"We rejected that approach," Piar pointed out. "I explained all this."

"Utilizing Mongols as surrogate conquerors is not feasible. For once we capture China from them, their usefulness will be at an end. Mongols are of no value in the opposite hemisphere, where they are not indigenous. Transporting a Mongol force to America would betray our hand."

"China is vast. It is worth taking in this manner."

Feep shook his one-eyed skull, his mouth tentacles fluttering fluidly. "That is not the Council's decision. We see these Mongols as surrogates in another, future phase of the conquest."

Both Telian Piar and Komo Dath waited in tense silence for the next words.

"The time will come when we control all of Earth. It is expected that surviving Terran populations will be of much value to us, but there remains the problem of control. We cannot hope to screen off all of Earth's hideously polluted atmosphere successfully. Nor is it feasible to station Gnards everywhere for long-term population control. Logistics and supply trains of such magnitude would be unsupportable."

"I fail to follow," Piar said.

"In that future time, we will require a controllable but effective Terran police and guard force. Terrans who can breathe the same sick air as our indigenous subjects. These Mongols subsist on limited diets of meat and milk supplied by animals as nomadic as they, require no housing, and possess certain hardy qualities that would seem to fit these requirements."

Komo Dath spat. "You are abandoning a supremely powerful surrogate conquering force, so as to create wardens for a future—yet you will not pursue that future with the ferocity needed to accomplish the mission! That hour will never come unless—"

"Dath," Piar said softly. "Accept defeat gracefully."

Teeth champing and clicking, Komo Dath subsided.

"This is the will of the Council," Feep said solicitously. "We are still the Council, Komo Dath. Our authority is enduring. Yours is but temporary. Do not force this issue, unless you would rather we issued KA-77s to these nomads and in doing so incur a possible nuclear counterstrike from the Chinese rulers."

Dath said nothing. His hunched shoulders trembled. Telian Piar stood in his robes, barely breathing.

"Your will," Dath said, turning to go.

Piar followed him a heartbeat later, sweeping the immaculate floor with his robes. His solitary eye was as expressionless as if blown of scarlet glass, the pupil squeezed down to an unreadable pinpoint.

35

SHAANXI PROVINCE, FREE CHINA

The camp of the Golden Horde was astir as Qasar Khan
strode toward his personal *ger*, the war boots of Genghis
Khan deliberately stamping on every pile of horse dung
in his path to awaken its stink and so awaken the fighting
souls of his followers.

Yak chip fires smoked. Men were pulling on their
battle *dels* and leather breeches, or squatting to fertilize
the spots where the horses did not tug at the tough
grasses. Various food odors from millet to green tea
mingled with the warming dawn.

"Find Ariunbold," Qasar Khan barked at a sentry.

"Your word is my command," the man returned
briskly.

"I have been telling all that it is your favorite
response," Bayar confided.

Qasar grunted. "I do not see Gerel. Or Ouji."

"Speak but their names loud enough and they will fly
to beg your favor."

"Fetch them. I must save my breath for the words they
need to hear."

"Your word is my command," Bayar said, racing off.

"Of course," Qasar Khan said, stamping into his *ger*.

Morning Doe was still sleeping on the brick bed plat-
form fed by the single stove built beside it. The smoke

was channeled up through the smoke hole after it had warmed the *kang*.

Drowsing, she turned over, her long raven hair disheveled. Reaching down, Qasar Khan pulled low her sheepskin sleeping cover to expose the fullness of her breasts.

"Wake up, tart," he bellowed. "You are naked."

Morning Doe murmured subvocally.

"Your khan keeps no lazy concubines."

"Mmmm?" Morning Doe said, tasting her own lips sleepily.

Seeing that, Qasar took a rubescent nipple between his fingers and pinched it hard, twisting until he got a satisfying yelp of pain.

Eyes snapping open, Morning Doe flared, hesitated, then kicked at his chest with both feet. "You come to me now to make thunder and lightning? With the dawn coming through the smoke hole?"

"Wake up, spitting cat. I care not for your charms by daylight. We have work to do. Fetch me tea and millet."

"Marry a wife."

"Then dress and assemble your ten. For you ride into battle this day."

Morning Doe's angry face softened in surprise. "Battle?"

"You are a captain of ten. I need every Mongol today."

"I am a concubine first."

"You are a concubine by night. It is dawn and now you are a captain of ten. Gather your forces."

"I must eat first."

"Cook for two. I will be back."

Qasar Khan left her crawling from the warmth of the *kang*, too shaken to dress.

* * *

Ariunbold and Gerel were waiting outside, their faces red, their chests pumping from their hard morning run.

"Your word is my command," they said in ragged unison. Behind them, Bayar grinned with ill-concealed satisfaction.

Qasar Khan barked out curt orders. "Assemble your myriads and companies all. I will address them as they eat their breakfast, for there is not time to wait, and I cannot deny them food on such a day as this."

"Your word is my command," they said, breaking ranks in three directions.

"They will take the news hard," Bayar told Qasar.

"But they will take it," Qasar Khan said, eyeing the vast sea of Mongol humanity. The air was more pungent than before.

"A new horde is no more easily broken of spirit than a horse," Bayar remarked.

"Without me they are but herdsmen and yakkers. They will go where I point my sword."

"If some revolt?"

"Their heads will fall when my sword falls."

Fingering his throat, Bayar said, "I have sworn an oath of fealty."

"And so your head squats on its proper pedestal. Spread the word. I must eat so that my voice carries."

Bayar departed. Qasar reentered his *ger* and found Morning Doe, still undressed, pouring tea mixed with millet.

"It is now done," she said thinly.

Squatting, Qasar Khan said, "It smells good. Now cover your womanly shame and assemble your ten."

"I have not yet eaten," Morning Doe pouted.

"There is only enough for one."

"I cannot go hungry."

"Then go naked, but go this moment or I will give your ten to another concubine."

"But I am the only woman in the horde."

"Today. Tomorrow it may be different."

"Tomorrow we may all be dead and rotting."

Qasar grunted. "All the more reason not to argue away the last precious minutes of your ill-spent life."

"I spit upon your morning meal," Morning Doe said, spitting into the tea.

Qasar Khan stirred it with an impervious finger and said, "Lacking sugar, I will accept your offering."

Morning Doe stamped from the *ger*, drawing on her leather battle armor. After the tent flap had resettled, Qasar Khan grinned pleasurably. It was the sweetest tea he had ever quaffed.

A short time later Mongols were stripping the *ger* of its felt panels until the willow framework was exposed for dismantling and packing in the waiting yak-drawn wagon.

Ariunbold had claimed the yak-tail standard and took a position behind and to the right of Qasar Khan.

Before him in a vast semicircle stretched the New Golden Horde, those in the forefront squatting on the grass like a million bright-eyed Buddhas, the middle ranks kneeling, and those in the back standing so all could see as well as hear their khan.

Their noise was as a murmuring breeze multiplied a thousandfold. Their smell was a rich mixture of perspiration-soaked leather and manure. Here and there came eruptions of venting bowel gas, adding to the heady aroma of conquest.

The lifting of Qasar's callused hand brought a profound silence.

"Attend my words," Qasar Khan barked loudly. He

waited. Those in the foremost ranks heard him clearly. A murmuring told him that those farther back were communicating the words to those far in the rear. Thus did the pronouncements of the Khan of the New Golden Horde filter back to the most distant sentry of his nomadic empire.

After the noise had abated, Qasar Khan spoke anew.

"During the night that has passed, I have communed with the holy spirit of Lord Genghis whose armor I proudly wear."

The words were carried back like sea salt by a receding surf.

"First, he bade me tell you these words of advice: 'In daylight watch with the vigilance of an old wolf, at night with the eyes of a raven, and in battle fall upon the enemy like a falcon.' "

Murmurs of quiet approval rolled back from the horde.

"Lord Genghis has asked that I spare the Chinese town of Shenmu as unimportant," Qasar said, sensing the ultimate moment to convey unwelcome news.

This time, the horde muttered darkly. No specific complaint reached Qasar's sharp ears, but discontent plainly mixed with puzzlement.

"To this I said, 'Your word is my command.' "

Bayar beamed widely as his own words rippled back through an infinity of round leathery faces.

"Thus, Shenmu will be spared my wrath," Qasar cried.

More murmuring. Some of it angry.

"This is not good," Bayar muttered in Qasar's cocked ear.

Qasar spoke through set teeth in a smiling mouth. "Tell Morning Doe to discover the import of their words. I will entertain them with temporizings and flattery."

Bayar took off, and in another moment Morning Doe,

dressed in her loose battle armor of red leather and gray felt, was filtering through the assembled horde.

"I look upon your faces, bathed in the red radiance of dawn, and I see Mongols who thirst for blood and battle," Qasar called out. "You shall have both. I see eyes that glint at the thought of soft gold and softer women. You shall have these things as well. But the cause of world Mongolism calls us to a higher purpose on this day of days."

Qasar Khan, sensing his words were sticking to the many mouths carrying them, let the thought hang in the heavy warm air.

"As I communed with my ancestor last night," he said after the last echoes died, "I saw visions. Jade falling stars in the sky. Ruby-eyed creatures who are not like us. To the north and to the east of this place where we are encamped, they have built great cities under *gers* of glass."

A hush fell. All recognized that these were portentous words they were hearing, though not all liked the ring of them.

"These cities lie behind the long blight that some call the New Wall. This New Wall cleaves to the Great Wall that was built to insult our ancestors and stands to this day. The New Wall, it is said, cannot be scaled. This was said of the old Great Wall, which was scaled many times and may be scaled again."

Qasar Khan searched the ocean of faces for one face in particular. He saw an unfamiliar Mongol race here, confer with another, who raced to Bayar's side. Then Bayar came pounding in his direction at a dead run, his long, mournful face flushed.

Reaching his side, Bayar panted, "There are those who say that they have ridden long and hard to a place of shame and cowardice. That if we turn away, the New

Golden Horde will show the rumps of its horses to the enemy, which the old Golden Horde of Genghis never did."

Qasar Khan frowned darkly. "Do these words fly far?"

"They fly noisily. I do not know about the far."

Qasar nodded. "Who launches such malcontented words?" he asked, fixing the horde with his slit eyes.

"Those on the left primarily. Some others."

"They yearn for battle this day?"

"They do."

Qasar nodded frankly. "I expected this."

"You did? Then why not have them put to the sword before they could sow discontent?"

"Because I am a wise leader who understands battle-craft and generalship as no one since Gyuk."

Bayar wrinkled up his features. "I do not know that name."

"A minor khan. I will tell you his story if we survive the morning."

Bayar stepped back to be better protected. He bent one knee, the better to drop to the ground ahead of assassins' arrows, should any fly.

Redirecting his attention to the New Golden Horde, Qasar spied certain men filtering up toward the front row. He recognized some hard faces. His expendable coins of war, stepping forward to their sublime destinies.

"We cannot scale the Great Wall here north of Shenmu," he continued. "Therefore we must go to a place where the wall is broken in order to penetrate China."

A stiff-faced Mongol folded his burly arms and shouted low defiance. "The wall can be scaled. For are we not true sons of our honorable fathers?"

His words were taken up by others. A few. Not many. Qasar Khan suppressed a thin smile of expectation.

"Men may scale a wall, but not horses," he said.

"Are we not men?"

"No, we are Mongols. That is better than being a mere man."

Grunts of acclimation greeted this pronouncement, and Qasar Khan filled his lungs deep to more powerfully deliver his next words.

"Are there those among us who would venture into Shenmu, unhorsed and bent upon pillage?"

The Mongol with the folded arms unfolded his arms and stepped forward. "I am one."

Three more stepped forward. And six others, emboldened by those who had acted.

Qasar Khan regarded them with clear untroubled eyes.

"I ask then that any Mongol so brave come to a place of honor in the front of my horde."

It took some time, but after five score Mongols stood with folded arms at the forefront of the horde, with others filtering up, Qasar Khan addressed them.

"I see among you many faces that I know. Faces who formerly stood upon my good left hand."

Nods of agreement.

Qasar Khan said, "You are Mongols among Mongols, you who would abandon your horses for the joy of sacking a Chinese city when there are other Chinese cities only six or seven days' ride lying beyond breaks in the Great Wall of the Han."

The men nodded more vigorously. These were honeyed words for men who ate the poorest meat and drank the bitterest water.

"I cannot deny the spirit of such men. Nor would Lord Genghis, who has whispered in my ear things I have not yet divulged. Among these things is that while the horde has more fruitful work elsewhere, that does not mean that a portion of the horde might not break away, to pursue its own objective freely and without bringing shame upon the horde, which remains to fulfill its singular destiny."

The men exchanged glances. They were not certain of their khan's meaning.

"I ask all who would break from the horde to come to the place of honor in front."

A few men actually stepped back, fearful of the shifting moods of their leader. But many more stepped forward.

"You who seek plunder and rapine on this day, I give you your freedom. I ask only that you leave your mounts with me, for they are useless to you. You may take whatever ammunition and arrows you can carry as a token of your khan's unsurpassed esteem."

Smiles of delight broke out. A few of those who had stepped backward now stepped forward again, their eyes alight, their hard fists clenching and unclenching in mounting excitement.

"You go with my blessing to sack Shenmu. And if it is your destiny to whelm that fat city, and you discover us on the march, you will be allowed to redeem your horses for gold and women as well once an agreeable price is arrived at."

This cheered the men of the left more than the words that came before. They loved their horses more than life. The prospect of seeing them again was a leaping joy in their fiery bellies.

"I ask as a final boon that you appoint one of your number khan, and that he swear eternal loyalty and submission to me," Qasar Khan added.

A momentary fistfight broke out among three men who saw themselves as the next khan. One's ambition was settled by a dagger in the heart. Another dropped with his kneecap shattered by a single Makarov bullet.

A flat-faced Mongol stood alone. He looked about the

knot of Mongols who clustered about him with surly regard.

"I, Mongke, am khan if no one challenges me," he cried.

No one did.

"Step forward," Qasar Khan said.

Mongke stepped forward, his boots churning soft earth and dung, his eyes proud, smoky brilliants.

"I accept you as Mongke Khan on the condition that you acknowledge me as your khakhan in turn."

Mongke Khan blinked like an astonished ape. "Khakhan?"

"If you are khan and defer to me, I can no longer be a khan. I must be the khakhan—khan of khans."

"But I am the only khan other than you," Mongke sputtered.

"Today. Tomorrow other khans will rise. But you will be the first to subjugate your will to my own."

Eyes shining, Mongke dropped to his knees and bumped his broad head against the ground in a full bow. "I am your servant," he said, voice thickening.

"Rise, for you are now Mongke Khan."

Flowing tears cutting through the dirt of his cheeks, Mongke Khan turned and took his place as the head of his horde.

His own face radiant, Qasar, Khan of Khans, thundered, "Go now, and fulfill your destinies! For you no longer stand on my left, but march off into Mongol history on your own unfettered feet and to your own rewards."

A whooping cheering and shouting welled up. Rifles of assorted vintages from old muzzle-loaders to Kalashnikovs lifted skyward, their bullets splitting the morning air. A few rounds dropped down to brain or kill the unfortunates who happened to stand beneath them, but this was hardly noticed among the din of celebration.

They were nearly an hour before they exhausted all joy, and then they started off, laughing, crying, and receiving hearty slaps on their backs from their former comrades.

As they drifted through, the horde gave before them like living water. Qasar Khan nodded to Morning Doe, who had taken up her rightful position at the head of her ten, then said in a loud voice:

"We ride east. East to the break in the wall and the glory that awaits us there!"

The shout that followed was like a great thunder, and it was heard in Shenmu, as Qasar Khan knew it would be.

When the dragonfly skyboats of the Chinese Army clattered overhead, peering down with curious, malevolent eyes, Qasar knew that the city had been alerted to the menace to the north. The numbers of the New Golden Horde would be reported to the city rulers, striking terror. This would help the cause of the splinter horde, although it would give warning of their intent, too.

Either way, Shenmu would fall or the splinter horde would be consumed in a paroxysm of fire and fury, while the New Golden Horde made its way to a better glory.

"I love being khan," Qasar said to Bayar.

"You mean khakhan."

"I am not accustomed to being khakhan yet. But I am certain I will enjoy that, too."

36

SHENMU, FREE CHINA

The siege of Shenmu lasted less than three hours, all told.

The foot soldiers of Mongke Khan went over the Great Wall like spiders scrambling over tumbled rock. They were unchallenged on the wall itself. They dropped off at the other side, losing only three men to broken legs, and in one case an unprotected skull that was dashed open when its owner slipped and fell head first from a crumbling merlon to the hard rocks below.

Overhead, Hind helicopter gunships clattered at a safe distance.

The forces of Mongke Khan moved in a ragged line, spaced well apart, knowing that the rockets of the helicopters could not crush their might with any but the most ferocious of multiple blows.

They moved through grass and trees and hills, initially encountering no resistance and presenting no definite target from air or land.

The city of Shenmu floated before them like a gleaming mirage of wealth and undreamt-of comfort, although it seemed very gray and lusterless at a distance.

Mongke Khan took the lead, creeping to a point where outlying farmer's huts came into view.

"We will burn the city," he told his second in command, hastily designated for the occasion.

"It is very big," Sambuu the Mongol returned.

195

"It will burn all the hotter for its great size."

"If it all burns, where will we live?"

"It will not all burn. We will burn it until the food growers abandon it, then we will save what we can and live in that portion. After all, it is a very large place and our numbers are modest."

"For a horde."

"For a horde, yes."

"Some of those buildings appear to be stone and metal," Sambuu pointed out.

"Yes."

"These do not burn easily."

"We will burn the wood structures. The sight of fire will empty the stone structures, for do they not harbor milk-livered Chinese, who will flee at any violence?"

Sambuu nodded vigorously. "This is true."

"Send back word that we are to wait until dusk, then infiltrate in ones and twos, burning as we advance."

"That will give us time to gather dry grass and other combustibles."

"These are my first war commands as khan. Carry them out."

"Your will is my instruction."

And the two Mongols withdrew from the forward observation position, never suspecting that they would not see dusk, never mind the burning of Shenmu.

Colonel Chan, of the PLA rapid deployment force called the Fist Platoon, walked the length of the transport plane as it thundered north toward Shenmu. His orders were clear: drop onto the advance probe of Mongol barbarians and butcher them without mercy.

The static line checked, he took his place at the rear of the aircraft.

From the cockpit came the call. "Approaching drop zone. Three minutes."

"Ready!" Colonel Chan barked.

The Fist Platoon stood up, clutching their AKs, their green-uniformed bodies pregnant with main and reserve chutes. Under their helmets their faces were stern as soapstones cut to similar expressions.

The rear ramp began dropping and cool air rushed in like a flood of dry water.

Another call came from the cockpit—the signal that they were now directly over the drop zone.

"Go! Go! Go!" Colonel Chan screamed. He screamed it over and over again and the two lines of PLA special forces soldiers jumped out the back and into the slip-stream, to tumble and fall away.

Green parachutes the exact color of the surrounding countryside sprouted like so many dull flowers.

When the final man jumped, propelled by the colonel's hard back slap, Chan followed them down, the last to go but the first in command.

The operation began badly.

Rifle fire greeted them. A shroud collapsed. Then another.

A man hanging in his chute was fumbling to bring his AK into return-fire position when one leg kicked the wrong way and began dripping blood. The man lost his assault rifle and so was helpless as two arrows sought him, with disastrous consequences to his vital organs.

Here and there the rattle of return fire gave encouragement.

Colonel Chan had his own AK pointing downward. These Mongols were surprisingly good guerrilla fighters. They hunkered down under grass stands and in the shadows of stunted trees, firing with casual precision. They appeared fearless. They possessed overwhelming numbers, but skill—not numbers—would prove decisive on this day.

When his boots struck the ground, Colonel Chan rolled, shook off his shroud lines, and let the wind carry his chute away. It would not hurt, he thought, to have the great silken bells carry downwind, where they might entrap and confuse the wily enemy.

The colonel reached a low hill and oversaw the action. The Mongols were giving a good account of themselves, but their weapons were unquestionably inferior. Their Kalashnikovs were a mixture of Chinese- and Soviet-made versions. Yet their ammunition was limited.

The arrows, however, proved the most fearsome. These impaled and intimidated. More than one heroic PLA soldier was knocked out of action when his arm was transfixed by a quivering shaft of reed. They were impossible to extract in the field, Colonel Chan soon learned. He learned it the hard way when he was coming off the hill, firing at a wide-spaced knot of Mongols. They were loosing arrow after arrow with tireless precision at several of his men, and he felt his left calf muscle tighten up as if cramping severely.

He sought to take two more steps. But his leg refused his mind.

Stumbling, he felt new pain—searing pain. And he was not surprised when he saw the broken shaft jutting from his calf.

Colonel Chan had taken a bullet wound once and lived. A flesh wound. The bullet had burrowed through his forearm, leaving a tunnel through muscle that had soon healed into a livid pucker on either end.

But this was different. The bullet had passed clean through; an arrow had to be extracted. Sitting down, he tried to pull his legs back and get at the hateful shaft.

This proved difficult. Then, when he at last got hold of it, he faced a quandary.

Which way to pull? To pull by the feather quills would be to tear the muscle worse. But to pull by the arrowhead meant to pull the longer part of the shaft through the meat of his leg, with the risk of leaving splinters in the meat.

He tried to cut off the arrowhead with his survival knife. That way he had only to pull the shortest part of the shaft. This was a good plan. The only problem was that it was battlefield surgery, and was being done on an *active* battlefield.

With a hurried sawing motion, he attacked the shaft just behind the arrowhead, one eye on the conflict raging about him.

At that point the hot muzzle of an AK-47 was placed to the back of his skull.

His head jerked up. He mouthed the word *no*. The breath that would make the word was never exhaled up through his larynx.

Colonel Chan saw the smoke of battle, tasted it in his mouth and nostrils, and then all his senses were obliterated by the burst of AK fire that scooped out his brains, eyes, and sinuses, depositing them on his legs and lap like a vomited-up meal.

The history of the siege of Shenmu records that the Fist Platoon gave an excellent account of itself—under the circumstances. Only three Chinese died for every Mongol casualty. Historically, this was considered an equal exchange of casualties. In the end, the Fist Platoon was forced to retreat to the outskirts of Shenmu and dig in.

The Mongols were beaten back by defensive enfilading fire and simply retreated into other hills and melted into them.

By the third hour the gun smoke and blood and bowel

stink had largely been carried away by the prevailing wind, and higher military authorities, assessing the tactical reality of the situation, ordered the hills napalmed.

The work was done by helicopters out of Dong Sheng Feng Air Base. They bombarded the hills until all were scorched black and the dead on both sides had been reduced to carbonized bones and charred meat.

No accurate casualty count emerged from that day. And the PLA lost only one helicopter gunship to opposing fire, that only due to engine failure. The crew was butchered on the ground following a hard but survivable landing.

By noon, aerial reconnaissance was brought to the local military commander, who scanned the still-wet photos, fresh from their developing tank. He exulted, "We have beaten them. They retreat to the east. This is proof that the Mongol threat so feared by Hong Kong is hollow. They run without giving battle."

"Mongols sometimes retreat as a ruse," an intelligence officer suggested.

"If this is a ruse, we will not be enticed to disaster. Let them retreat. If they continue, we will know they retreat in truth. If they return, then we will meet that threat easily. For they are only barbarians and we are a modern nation possessing superior military might."

No one doubted that, so they sat back and awaited developments.

37

THE GREAT WALL OF
FREE CHINA

Evil black smoke smudged the eastern horizon beyond
the razor-backed undulating stone dragon that was the
Great Wall of China.

It was first seen by the rearmost train of the Golden
Horde, and word carried from lip to lip up the line to
Qasar Khan, who looked back with interest.

Bouncing alongside in his saddle, Bayar copied the
gesture.

"Shenmu burns."

Qasar shook his massive head slowly. "No. That is not
the smoke of wood, but of grass and flesh."

"How can you tell?"

"I am khan. I can tell these things."

Shading his eyes with one hand, Bayar tried to see the
low city of Shenmu more clearly.

"The smoke rises before Shenmu, not from it," he said.

"That is another way to tell," Qasar said, redirecting
his attention to the way ahead.

"The splinter horde is no more."

"Doubtless they have cost the Chinese many steel-
hatted soldiers, just as they have bequeathed extra
mounts for their former comrades. Mounts that will
prove useful in the long pull before us."

"They will not be missed, except by themselves,"
Bayar said.

The wind was blowing their way and carried the smoke to their nostrils. Qasar sniffed it like his namesake.

"Scorched flesh," he murmured.

"Mongol flesh."

"And Chinese both."

"Good. The horde of Mongke Khan did not die in vain."

Several *li* along, a noisy clattering overtook them. The horses whinnied nervously, but squeezing thighs and soothing words quieted them down.

"Skyboats," Ariunbold said.

"Helicopters," Bayar corrected.

"I have never seen such," Qasar remarked.

"They fly lower and slower than the winged skyboats and hold fewer men."

Qasar nodded.

"They also fire metal arrows of great destruction," Bayar added darkly.

"They will not fire upon us."

"Why do you say that? They are plainly searching for us."

"Because they see how our numbers stretch, and now they have insufficient arrows to slay us all. Therefore, to strike is to incur our wrath."

"This is wisdom. But the markings I see are PLA markings. Soldiers obey orders. They do not think. They are forbidden to think. If their orders are to slay Mongols, they will slay Mongols without regard to the consequences."

"It may be that some of us will die, then."

But the helicopters continued orbiting like impotent dragonflies, neither threatening nor withdrawing.

And the New Golden Horde pushed on.

38

KOLYMA TOWER, FORMER SIBERIA

In the spartan headquarters office of Martian Military Commander Komo Dath, Telian Piar stood contemplatively.

"I should have known better than to have listened to you," Dath rasped.

"No harm was done, and perhaps some good," Piar said softly.

"In the Council's eyes, I have exceeded my authority."

"The Council is not unaware of your lust for absolute power. They defer to you because you are their only hope during the present crisis."

"So we are done with our Mongols?"

"The Council has issued its decision. We are done. There remains but one small matter."

"What is that?" Dath asked impatiently.

"The secure communications link we provided Qasar Khan."

Dath's angry red eyes flared. "Yes. Of course. It is the only link between us and the barbarian and his horde."

"The self-destruct code sequence is the first three bars of the Paeec hymn to tranquility."

Dath hissed, "I believe I can whistle it manageably."

And taking up a communicator, he brought it to his lips.

Teeth half parted, he began to suck air through them. The sound was strange, like a keening wind through thin stalactites, but it had a melodiousness to it that made Telian Piar's black pupil widen with unexpected pleasure.

The last note hung in the air for a very long breath, then Dath snapped off the communicator and pressed the self-destruct switch on the side.

The unit sizzled into slag in a metal desk tray. Dath let it slide into a floor disposal unit and, replacing the now-immaculate tray on the desk, turned to Telian Piar and rasped, "Our business is concluded. You may leave at your will."

Bowing his head curtly, Telian Piar glided from the room like something ethereal.

39

THE GREAT WALL OF
FREE CHINA

"We could have conquered Shenmu," Ariunbold was saying.

"Perhaps," Qasar Khan returned.

"But there are fatter cities elsewhere," Ariunbold added.

The New Golden Horde jingled and clopped and grunted behind them, their sounds blending into a low mutter like that of an unknown thousand-legged creature.

"We ride to the Bone Head Barrens," Qasar growled.

"Is that their true name?" Bayar wondered.

"It is the name given by the khakhan. Therefore it is the true name."

"The Bone Head Barrens is a good name."

Qasar nodded. "We will fertilize it with blood and brain—Bone Head blood and brain."

Bayar shivered so hard his sheepskin *dacha* seemed to come to life.

"Red Eye skulls, too. As much as I detest Bone Heads, the Red Eyes are more terrible still. They are like fish who stand up and speak. Fish should not stand up or speak. It is contrary to reason."

"I have never beheld a Bone Head or a Red Eye," Ariunbold commented. "Why are they so terrible?"

Bayar replied, "They have worms for mouths, and the scarlet eyes of a fish seen from its side."

Ariunbold shook at the thought. The nine white yak tails, now yellow from Gobi dust, shook as well.

"I fear no man nor Mongol, but these Bone Heads are terrible to contemplate," he muttered.

Behind and to the south, green helicopter gunships clattered as they patrolled. They made no advance nor showed menacing intent.

"The voice of the Bone Heads is like dry sheep's bones rubbing together," Bayar said.

"Truly?"

"They speak to us through a silver device."

"No more," Qasar Khan said.

"You have the device still?" Bayar wondered.

"Yes."

"Why do you not communicate with the Bone Heads and ask for a new desire?"

"Because I am a proud man who has lost face to his horde, and besides, all that I desire now is to pulp Bone Head skulls."

"A simple talk would provide amusement on the long pull."

Qasar Khan seemed to contemplate this for a time. Then reaching into his armor, he extracted the silver device. It seemed more dented than Bayar recalled it having been from the hard squeeze Qasar had given it the night before.

"I spit on the red-eyed Bone Heads who came down from the Red Eye planet, and on all they possess," he said tightly.

With that, Qasar threw the silver device over his shoulder carelessly.

Twisting in his saddle, Bayar followed its arc. A hand jumped up, capturing it.

"What is this that has fallen from the sky?" came the excited voice of little, bald-headed Ouji.

"A Bone Head device that your khan has discarded as accursed," Bayar warned.

"Am I forbidden to hold it?"

Bayar looked to Qasar Khan. The khan nodded, saying, "I give my permission."

Calling back, Bayar said, "It is on your head." Then, to Qasar, he said in a hurt voice, "I would have liked to hold it."

Qasar made no reply. His eyes were on the way ahead.

After a while there came a violent popping back among the horses. All eyes went to it. Up popped a bubble of black smoke and flame. And a voice began screaming, shrill and frightened.

"It is Ouji!" someone shouted. "He burns!"

Back in the horde they could see him jumping on his saddle, enveloped in a halo of gaseous blue flame. Under the flame, his skin blackened and shriveled. Horses took up his screaming.

Wheeling his mount, Qasar Khan shouted, "Clear the way!"

A milling confusion of men and mounts melted aside.

Qasar fought his way back through the column, Chino's nuzzle pushing lesser horses aside, until he reached the place where Ouji writhed in his death throes on a burning saddle.

Qasar crowded Ouji's rearing steed against the battlements. With a hard kick, he knocked the man from his saddle. The burning Mongol tumbled over the wall. He made no sound until he struck hard earth. Death had been on his black face at the last.

Features harsh, Qasar Khan returned to the head of his horde.

"Ouji died the death the Bone Heads meant for you," Bayar told him as the horde re-formed itself.

Qasar's only reply was a baring of teeth and a low growl that made his nose wrinkle.

Bayar called back. "Let that be a lesson to all loyal Mongols! When your khan calls a thing accursed, believe it. For you all saw the device of the Bone Heads consumed by its own accursedness, taking Ouji with it."

A low mutter of superstitious fear traveled back from rider to rider. It was as Bayar had said, they knew.

"But never fear," Bayar added. "Qasar Khan will mete out harsh punishments for what has just happened. Is that not true, my khan?"

"My wrath will be a thing to behold," Qasar Khan promised, the knuckles of his bronze fists turning to bloodless ivory as they gripped the reins.

"I look forward to beholding it," Bayar said in a small voice. "Although I fear it, too."

"You are a wise Mongol to fear my wrath," Qasar growled.

And the New Golden Horde continued its long pull.

40

HONG KONG

The Premier of China studied the intelligence reports at length, his coarse features thick with worry.

"The Mongol invader continues to ride east," he muttered.

"They are in retreat," his Defense Minister said.

"I steeped myself in their histories when I was young. I shivered at the tales I read, and learned certain subtle arts of statecraft from the cleverer khans," the Premier said. "They are not retreating."

"They are not attempting to lure our forces into ambush."

"Or if they were, by now they would understand that the old ruses of the khanates will not work against modern men who have read *The Secret History of the Mongols* and have learned their ways."

"Our analysts suggest certain alternatives."

The Premier waved the words away. "Spare me. I can read maps. They follow the undulations of the Great Wall. They intend to cross at the first break they encounter. While you marshal tank cavalry and supporting ground forces at the breach at Six Dragons, direct your air assets to harass them from the skies. That should give you time enough to plug the hole."

"It is strange that after all these centuries, the Great Wall should once again defend us from the barbarians."

"It is not strange. It is an example of our ancestor's wisdom, industry, and foresight. Would only they had been communists, I would have the builders of the wall made into people's heroes for the edification of the populace today."

All nodded at this regrettable state of affairs. But political realities were political realities. The old dynasties and their glories could not be rehabilitated, lest they cast cold shadows of shame over those who had taken their place in these unfortunately interesting times.

41

SHAANXI PROVINCE, FREE CHINA

As the day darkened to dusk, the New Golden Horde rode and rode, a shimmering serpent of horseflesh and stiff-backed men that clanked and clinked and creaked of iron and hardened leather. They ate and drank as they rode, untiring as their mounts. When a man had to relieve himself, he broke from his place, did his business by the side of the road, half obscured by yellow trail dust, then rejoined the train in a spurt of hard riding.

The horses dropped their dung on the move, as horses do.

The mighty procession ate up *li* and swallowed saffron trail dust. "This is how a horde rides," Qasar remarked to no one in particular, his golden ear loops dancing.

Eyeing the helicopter gunships that were still dogging them, Bayar remarked, "Genghis never contended with such birds of disreputable omen."

"They are harmless."

"They hound us like fleas."

"I would prefer fleas," Qasar said. "Fleas I can scrounge for amid the hairs of my body. Their bodies are tiny. And they make no noise known to man or Mongol."

After a while the helicopter gunships clattered away and Bayar began to relax. He also began to sneeze.

"Alkalai dust," he said, looking for something to wipe

his nose on. Finding nothing, he hung back a little and employed the sleeve of his *dacha*.

"I saw that," Qasar said when Bayar caught up again.

"Saw what?" Bayar asked, innocence silvering his voice.

"You are accursed for wiping your nose on Lord Genghis's sleeve."

"I will not do it again."

"You have done it once. You must ride a horse's length behind me now, for you have dishonored the sheepskin *dacha* of the First Khakhan."

"You jest."

"A horse length back or it will be three when next I speak."

"Very well. Just remember that I knew you before you were khan."

"I am khakhan now," Qasar said, unmoved.

And tears starting from his wise eyes, Bayar dropped back, his head hanging in shame. After that every sneeze that rose in his nose was stifled mercilessly.

"Have you a cloth?" Bayar whispered to Morning Doe.

"Use your sleeve," she hissed.

"I cannot."

"Then use the sleeve of another."

Bayar eyed her red leather and gray felt raiment.

"But not mine. I am a concubine and a captain of ten."

"I am Arrow Prince. I outrank you."

"You outrank no one but your own nameless horse."

Bayar frowned. Feeling dejected, he dropped back farther.

It saved his life.

The helicopters came out of the south horizon. Some from the west. A pair circled around and swooped down from the forbidden north. Their sounds bounced off the Great Wall like the frenzy of airborne demons about in the sky.

They came in low, and when they began loosing their air-to-ground rockets, it was as if the sky bloomed bright, noisy flowers.

The rockets struck the New Golden Horde at several points, front, rear, and places in between. The detonations came in a string like firecrackers. Men screamed. Horses shrieked, stumbling. The mingling of their cries was unearthly to the ears. Here and there it rained crimson as partially vaporized bodies precipitated as blood and bits of reddish flesh.

Ochinbal the Mongol took a direct hit, horse and rider absorbing the blow that would a moment before have claimed Arrow Prince Bayar, who had dropped back, only to lash his pony into a dead run.

At the head, Qasar Khan lashed his own charger, shouting, "Break ranks! Break ranks! Scatter to the winds, dogs of war, if you would preserve your lives."

The horde obeyed. Captains of ten or a hundred or a thousand mustered their charges in different directions, just as they had been drilled. Where a moment before a train of rippling hair-sheathed muscle had wended along in a single purposeful direction, now they were like the independent fragments of an explosion speeding off in a million directions.

Once the various components mustered themselves, they, too, exploded into smaller components, and almost as quickly as it takes to record it, the arid plains north of the Great Wall of China were busy with horsemen the way a disturbed anthill becomes busy with ants.

The gunships came back for their second pass, crisscrossing the skies, but were instantly confounded. Where they had enjoyed one continuous target, they now faced teeming knots and clusters of riders. No single target was worth the expenditure of a rocket.

A few rockets arrowed to earth, to throw up clods of dirt and rock dust and the occasional unbalanced horse and rider. But nothing useful was accomplished by this action.

Strafing runs began. These proved more effective, but after a half dozen, the multitudes continued to swarm like ants moving in a million directions.

Soon, the hot, smoking Gatling guns fell silent, their ammunition stores exhausted.

That left the helicopter gunships of the PLA impotent once more. As they settled into a south-flying line of clattery steel dragonflies, Qasar Khan watched them from a point of low vantage. He was alone but for Ariunbold, who sat on his mount, tirelessly holding aloft the nine-yak-tail standard of the Golden Horde.

Qasar spoke up. "We are victorious."

"They will return."

"They will kill a few more Mongols, perhaps, but they will understand that they cannot defeat the Golden Horde."

So saying, Qasar Khan called for Ariunbold to follow him to the highest point of land so that all could see the proud standard that followed the khakhan wherever he rode, like a shadow cast by a living god.

Qasar himself shot a whistling signal arrow into the air. It arced high, shrill and penetrating. Before it split the skull of a grazing rabbit, he had turned his mount around and was resuming the course to his new objective, Ariunbold behind him.

The New Golden Horde, led by captains of ten, and one hundred, and one thousand, pulled back into formation, reconstituting itself like a dragon whose interred dust had been miraculously summoned up from its desert grave.

Qasar Khan never looked back. He knew his Mongols.

The sound of their hooves falling into line and cadence told him all he needed to know.

42

HONG KONG

The Premier of China received the news from his Defense Minister without his bland expression changing a particle.

"The first air assault has failed utterly."

"What is meant by utterly?" the Premier asked.

"Successive rocket attacks dispersed the Mongol forces, killing an undetermined number."

"That sounds like success to these ears," the Premier said, thin-voiced.

"Numbers of Mongol dead are negligible, and now the column is reconstituting."

The Premier blinked. He lit a cigarette from the butt of a half-smoked one. "If they were tanks, would they not be crushed?"

"If they were a tank column, the lead and trail tank would have been rocketed, immobilizing the column long enough to take out the center vehicles in the confusion. But these are men riding horses. They operate as one, horses and riders reacting to danger in the way a slow-moving, insensate, man-driven tank cannot."

"So, strike again and again until they have scattered to the four quarters."

"It is not so simple. A single rocket can take out a tank or a position. But there are six thousand riders. One rocket may take out one enemy or three or five, but that is the best ratio achievable. We do not possess a helicopter force with three thousand rockets available for battle."

The Premier paused, his cigarette poised before his thinning lips. The hand dropped. He looked out his main office window and said after a pause: "You are saying a modern air force cannot humble cavalry?"

The Defense Minister made no direct reply. Instead, he said: "There is an option."

"I would like to hear this option," the Premier said, bringing his smoking cigarette back to his waiting lips.

"It is nuclear," the Defense Minister said in a bland voice.

Somewhere on the way to his mouth the Premier's cigarette got turned the wrong way and, when the glowing hot tip entered his mouth, it seared the tip of his tongue.

When he finished spitting out wet ash and foul pre-Revolutionary curses, he whirled on his Defense Minister and roared, "Are you mad?"

The Defense Minister kept his face impassive. "It is presented as an option."

"It is unthinkable. Besides, we may need our lone surviving Long March missile in the event the Martian occupiers make a grab for additional territory."

"There is that," the Defense Minister said.

Facing the window again, the Premier murmured, "How goes the blockage of the Great Wall?"

"Ahead of the timetable. The breach at Six Dragons will be fully armored by the time the horse column reaches it."

"Then let us see what their intent is," the Premier said, stubbing out his cigarette in an onyx ashtray that was already overflowing with half-smoked Blue Swallow butts. For these were nervous times, as well as interesting ones.

43

SHAANXI PROVINCE, FREE CHINA

The day after, the purple shadows lengthened and the New Golden Horde trotted on, hammering the yellow soil of China as if they had already conquered it.

They were not challenged from the air again, and this brought a thoughtful expression to Qasar Khan's immutable face.

"We are riding into trouble," he said quietly.

To his left, Morning Doe spoke up.

"We always ride into trouble. Unless we are riding from it. Are we not Mongols?"

"I am a Mongol. You are a woman."

"I am a Mongol woman."

"You speak of a technicality. You are a woman before you are a Mongol. I am a Mongol before I am a man."

"Do I not ride high in my saddle like a Mongol?"

"You do. But you are still a woman."

"Do I not wear armor?"

"Which fits loosely about your womanly shape."

"Perhaps you will respect me all the more if I offer some of my womanly charms to your sword for hacking?"

"I would no more whittle you down into the shape of a man than I would trim my own manhood to make our lovemaking more pleasurable to you."

"It is already pleasurable."

"You complain about my girth," Qasar remarked dryly.

"I cry out. I shriek. That is not complaint."

"You curse me."

"I curse your manhood, not you," Morning Doe spat back. "I accept you as you are. Why do you not accept me as I am?"

"I do."

"I am no longer satisfied with being a captain of ten."

"I will make you a captain of one hundred, then."

"That is gracious," Morning Doe allowed softly.

"You are gracious."

"But I prefer a greater honor."

Qasar's lifting eyebrows made the red-edged skull on his face frown. "Yes?"

"I wish my own horde."

Qasar Khan made his lips tight and released a rude noise that might have come from under his saddle.

"Are you ill?" Morning Doe wondered.

"I am stupefied. It is more uncomfortable than being ill. You wish a horde?"

"Yes."

"Therefore you wish to be a khan."

"You are khakhan now. You have khans beneath you."

"One khan, and that one is smoke and black bone now."

"Therefore you are in need of new khans. Otherwise, you cannot be khakhan. It is simple logic."

Qasar Khan frowned darkly, the metal of his facial skin warping and twisting into deep lines of concentration, the white moon on his forehead turning to water.

"Ariunbold?" he barked.

"Yes, my khan?"

"I hereby appoint you khan."

Ariunbold bowed his head deeply. "Your word is my command."

"Of course. Gerel?"

"Khakhan?"

"I hereby appoint you khan as well."

"I am honored, lord."

"That is your concern. Mine is that I am sorely in need of khans." Raising his voice, Qasar Khan barked over his shoulder, "Bayar?"

From three horse lengths back Bayar trotted up expectantly.

"Is your sleeve clean?" Qasar asked.

"Absolutely."

"Therefore I appoint you khan."

Bayar's eyebrows shot up and his jaw hung slack, making his long face longer. "I am a khan?" he sputtered.

"As are Gerel and Ariunbold."

"They are khans, too?"

"Yes. Did I just not say this?"

"I was still becoming accustomed to being a prince."

"If you wish to remain a prince, I will find another khan. For I require three."

Behind Qasar's back Morning Doe lashed out a felt-sheathed foot at Bayar's shaggy knee. Her face was fierce as she shook her head no.

"Do you wish me to decline the honor?" Bayar whispered, rubbing his knee with difficulty because his mount was throwing him about in his saddle.

Morning Doe shook her head yes, her narrow cat eyes flashing. For good measure she made a cutting gesture with one finger across her own throat.

Clearing his throat, Bayar directed his voice to his khan. "I decline this honor and wish to remain Arrow Prince," he gulped.

"That is your privilege. Now you may ride at the end of my train."

"The end?"

"You have displeased me."

"I have changed my mind," Bayar said hastily.

Qasar shook his helmeted head. "I cannot accept this. You may change it again."

"Then I go to the end of the train," Bayar said meekly.

Flinging his steed around, Arrow Prince Bayar cut back along the eight-hundred-foot column of hammering horses.

Morning Doe spoke up again. "He is loyal to you."

"But he listens to the whispery wiles of women when he should submit to the will of his khan."

Morning Doe said nothing to that, allowing time for the vaguely accusing words to be carried away on the wind.

"If Bayar can be khan, why can I not be khan also?" she asked pointedly.

"Bayar declined the honor. If you wished to be khan, you should not have pursuaded him otherwise. For how could I make my concubine khan before my first adherent?"

"Liar! You had no intention of making a khan of me."

"You do not know this for a fact. Therefore you cannot prove or disprove this as truth."

"You make my blood boil with your cruel ways."

"As long as it boils," Qasar Khan said flatly. "For it is a long pull to the Bone Head Barrens, and the night will pass more satisfyingly in your hot arms."

"I hate you, Qasar Khan."

"I am khakhan again, now that I am surrounded by loyal khans."

"Make me a khan or I will open up my wrists and throat and let all the hot blood flow freely."

"Do this and I will drink it all and find another concubine."

Morning Doe fumed in her saddle, her cat eyes tight slits.

"What does my lord require of me in return?" she asked in a supplicant tone of voice after a long fume.

"I will think on this conundrum, for no woman has ever before been a khan."

"I deserve to be the first."

"We will see."

The *li* passed by with a monotonous drumming of hoofbeats. Night fell. The moon rose. Stars came out in abundant profusion, and Qasar Khan looked often skyward for streaks of fiery jade.

He saw none among the windy star webs.

44

SIX DRAGONS PLUG

General Shai Shang wore only two stars on his shoulder boards but looked forward to the fortunate day when a third would appear as he inspected what was being called the Six Dragons Plug.

Three lines of T-64 and T-72 tanks, green as turtle shells, the red star of the PLA on either side of their turrets, sat track-to-track in the tumbledown rubble between two of the surviving segments of the thousand-mile-long Great Wall of China.

The order of battle was exceedingly simple.

The first line of defense sat with 115mm Smoothbore guns and machine guns trained on the approach to the breach. If the order was given, they could advance to attack. They could not pull back. This had been the direct order of the Defense Minister himself. No retreat under any circumstances. Burning tanks could be abandoned, but not moved.

The second line of defense was poised to leap into the breach should the first line advance to attack. Like the first line, the second line could not retreat, for it, too, was blocked by a line of tanks. These were top-of-the-line T-75s acquired from the old Soviet empire as it had crumbled in the handful of years before the Men of Mars came down from their now-fallen mother ships to swallow up Russia the way a dragon swallows a lesser serpent.

Behind the tanks stood self-propelled howitzers and their crews. Mi-24 Hind helicopter gunships sat on hastily poured concrete landing pads for close air support operations.

The nearby Dong Feng Sheng Air Base stood in the highest possible state of alert, its pilots sitting in the cockpits of waiting PLA Air Force Jian-7 III attack fighters, which were bristling with PL-7 air-to-air missiles and twin-barreled 23mm nose guns.

Although an advancing force greater than any Chinese had faced since the days of the original khans marched upon their position, General Shang was confident that his position was impregnable. The heroic tanks of the PLA would not budge, except to attack. They would never retreat. It was ridiculous to think otherwise, especially as dawn now approached. In the distance a yellow haze showed.

"What is that haze?"

"The dust of the horse column," a major reported.

"It looks like the smoke of a fire from some demonic realm."

"Demons and Mongols share the same hot blood, my grandmother once told me."

"I do not fear either Mongols or demons, for I have sat across the negotiation table from the bloody-eyed beings from Mars. *They* are devils to be feared."

Then the earth under their boots began to hum and vibrate.

General Shang looked down in growing alarm.

"Earthquake!" the general said.

"No, Mongols. You feel the low, unquiet thunder of their approach."

It was true. Earthquakes troubled the Sino-Mongolian

border area, but they were always of short duration. This went on and on, building in intensity until it made the steel helmets on their heads shimmy and quiver, and the skull bones in their heads grew distressed.

"Now I know how the old Emperors felt when the Mongol hordes drew near . . ." Shang said thinly.

The major tried to reply, but settled for swallowing his fear-cracked words rather than shaming himself.

Together they shared a shiver neither acknowledged to the other. It was a shiver that vibrated in sympathy with the growing trembling of the earth under their boots.

45

SIX DRAGONS

The New Golden Horde rode into the east, their faces bathed in the bloodred light of the dawn.

At the head of the column, tall on his horse, Qasar Khan's windburned face was the first to meet the rising sun, and was the reddest of all. His slit eyes burned like coals, his firm lips were set. Beside him shook the nine white yak tails the world had last seen eight centuries ago, when the East was new and nothing made by man or Old Man God could hinder the expansion of Mongol culture.

"I smell Chinese," he muttered after a while.

"They sweat, though the night was passed coolly," Ariunbold Khan remarked after tasting the air himself.

"They sweat with reason. They sweat as their ancestors sweated. From Peking to Baghdad, Genghis's very own nose enjoyed this scent on the wind."

"I relish the thought of reducing Baghdad to rubble one day."

"Time enough for that once we accomplish our ends— and assuming our survival."

"Beside you, I always assume surviving, my khan."

Qasar nodded. He eased his charger to a slower gait.

The entire column dropped into the same ambling cadence, row upon row moving so smoothly the entire transformation took less than twenty minutes. It was as if a ripple of magic ran along the back of a dragon that was sheathed in motley horsehair, iron, and leather.

They rode on, fearless and unminding of the green helicopter gunships that lifted into view to stir and trouble the low-hanging yellow road dust.

"They will not attack," Qasar said.

"They have learned a great lesson."

"No. They will not attack because they have been ordered not to attack. If a second attack was forthcoming, it would have transpired long before this hour."

"This is a wise assessment."

"I am khakhan. All my pronouncements are wise. If they were not, I would not be fit to be khakhan."

"That, too, is a very wise thing to say."

Riding on, Qasar Khan looked to Ariunbold and said, "Ride ahead with me. Let the Chinese see the proud standard that caused their ancestors to tremble and wail."

"Ai-Yah!" Qasar Khan said, spurring his mount onward.

They soon came to the top of a rise. Below, the Great Wall lay like a broken-backed dragon of stone whose weather-worn spine had sunken into the earth. In the gap sat lines of armored battle tanks, like steely teeth in a mouth of stone.

"The way into China is blocked," Ariunbold commented.

"There are ways to unblock it."

"We can ride into the teeth of their tank fire and then under it. Many will die. But most will live."

"And after that?" Qasar asked.

"You are khakhan. I do not know."

"The horses cannot vault those machines. They lie too thick."

"Perhaps the first two lines can be drawn out after a feinting attack."

"A good plan, but the horses cannot vault a single line either, for they sit in a row as if welded side-to-side."

"Can they not be made to retreat?"

"Not easily. If at all. For if we attack the front line, what will compel the second line or the third to withdraw?" Qasar shook his head. "A very wise general devised this blockade. It is worthy of Kublai."

"Then what course of action remains? We are Mongols and our horses are Mongol horses. If this were a river, we could ford it. Ice, we could pass over it. Soldiers on foot, we could trample them without mercy."

"Our numbers are too great for those things," Qasar Khan said thoughtfully. "Possibly the key lies in applying the least force to the greatest link in the chain."

"Do you not mean the greatest force to the weakest link?"

"No," said Qasar Khan. "I mean what I mean."

Pulling back, he turned his horse around. Chino responded as if part of him, sharing the same nervous system and connective tissue.

Holding the shaking standard in one iron hand, Ariunbold followed his khakhan, his face awarp in puzzlement. His last look at the Chinese defensive position made him think even being a Mongol might not be sufficient to win the day.

It was not a good thought to have when one rode at the head of an invading army.

46

SIX DRAGONS PLUG

The saffron smoke was an obscuring haze through which two figures appeared at the crest of a hill.

General Shai Shang had retreated to the relative security of his command Land Rover. It was not armored. Nor was it in a place of safety. But it did sit on rubber tires, and these absorbed some of the steady hammering thunder of the approach of the Mongol invasion force. This quieted the general's nerves sufficiently that he recovered some of his steel.

But when an aide shouted that Mongols had been sighted, Shang half jumped out of his seat, whipping his Makarov from its belt holster.

Running to the other side of the Great Wall, he looked up at the thin cloud of saffron. His eyes narrowed, then widened as through the haze a vision resolved itself.

Two riders. On horseback. One wore armor that gleamed blue and gold even at this significant distance.

The other wore armor of lesser opulence, but he held aloft a thing that General Shang had seen only in books and propaganda films, and never imagined he would behold in the course of his duty to his homeland.

It was a standard, thick as a sailing ship's mast and unwieldy as a crow's nest, topped by a brass and silver trident and hung with white yak tails.

Yet one Mongol of good size held it one-handed, balancing it as he himself balanced on his high wooden saddle.

In the westerly breeze the nine yak tails blew and fell, blew and fell, like breathing lungs.

"They have arrived. There is no turning back for either side now," Shang muttered to himself.

And though he was a good communist and believed in neither Buddha nor Mohammed nor Christ, General Shang muttered a subvocal prayer to whatever gods might or might not exist, because suddenly he lost all confidence in the Great Wall of his ancestors and the armored might of his nation . . .

47

SIX DRAGONS

Returning to the head of his Golden Horde, Qasar Khan rode up to Morning Doe, who flung her horse about and presented both her rump and the steed's to her khan.

"If you are offering yourself in a new way, this is not the appropriate moment," Qasar growled.

"I am showing you my rump," she hissed. "Make of this what you will."

"Another time. The horse's rump is also magnificent, but I have no use for it either."

Morning Doe shook her lustrous black mane angrily. "If the view does not please you, face another direction, for I will not face you."

"Not even if I offer you the opportunity to become khan?"

Morning Doe wrestled her horse around so swiftly she almost broke its neck.

Her eyes blazed. "You trifle with me?"

"I offer you a fair bargain."

Eyes slitting until her face most resembled a cat mask, Morning Doe asked guardedly, "What is it?"

"Go down to the armies of the Han and treat with the highest general you find there. Speak to him in my name. Tell him of my terms."

"They will butcher me like a bleating lamb."

"They may. But your chances are certainly better than any other Mongol I could send."

Morning Doe regarded him with no expression. Her voice became arid and thin as the Gobi.

"You offer me a difficult choice."

"You cannot expect to ascend to the exalted rank of khan without incurring risk or sacrifice."

"And what will I be to you if I accept this challenge and survive it?" she flung back.

"You will be one of my khans, of course," Qasar said.

"And by moonlight?"

"You will not lose your rank if the moon shines favorably upon your face."

"You are toying with me."

"This is not a new thing. I have toyed with you ever since I looked upon your round moonlit face long ago, when I was known as Wolf."

Under her leathern armor, Morning Doe relaxed her tense shoulders.

"I do not think I can trade the strong warmth of you by night even for the sublime honor of being the first woman khan in history," she said grudgingly.

"Well spoken. But you have no choice. I have no Mongol capable of performing this exacting duty."

"You think the Chinese will not kill a woman?"

"I do not know. I must discover their intentions."

"Am I a coin to be expended?"

"When you became a captain of ten, you took on the likeness of a coin, not a concubine," Qasar said frankly.

Morning Doe's eyes became knife wounds full of black blood.

Qasar Khan returned the venomous glare with eyes like the seams in old walnuts.

"Then if these are the burdens of being khan, I will

accept any challenge," Morning Doe said at last, her tone proud.

Qasar Khan nodded. His voice rang out. "Ariunbold!"

Ariunbold Khan drew near on his strutting Appaloosa.

"Ride with Morning Doe down to the position of the Chinese Army as the sign of my power and my protection. Speak no words. It is Morning Doe who speaks for me."

"A woman?"

"Nay. A khan, if she comes back with her head balanced upon her shoulders."

"I will not allow her head to be removed, my lord," Ariunbold vowed with a curt bow of his head.

"This is not your responsibility but hers. Preserve your own life, and above that, the symbol of my power. Morning Doe will preserve her own life or forfeit it as Fate decrees."

"I am ready," Ariunbold said.

Qasar Khan urged his mount closer to Morning Doe's gray mare. Their flanks rubbed skittishly, then they nuzzled.

Face-to-face, Qasar and Morning Doe looked into one another's eyes with sparks like blades clashing.

"I will return," Morning Doe said, her voice smoldering.

"Whether you return or you do not return, I do not know. I only know that I must taste your wine lips before you go."

Their faces fell together. Their lips met, exploring, then withdrawing with a sudden part that pulled them momentarily out of shape.

Morning Doe ran her tongue around her supple lips, the better to taste her khakhan's lingering kiss.

"Go now," he said, turning the rump of his charger

toward her. "And let your last sight of me be my back, for I must return the favor of a few moments ago."

Without another word, Morning Doe lashed her mount and raced hard, her leather bottom out of the saddle, her cheek tucked into her mare's neck. Their manes flowed and swirled together in the whipping wind, as if one.

Ariunbold, clinging to the standard of the Golden Horde, was hard pressed to catch up to her. But he did, shouting and cursing all the way.

After a suitable interval, Qasar Khan piloted his stallion after them so as to watch the proceedings from a vantage point where all would be revealed to his inscrutable eyes.

And where the slayers of his woman would be marked for a future reckoning, if Fate so decreed.

48

SIX DRAGONS PLUG

"Two riders!" an aide to General Shai Shang called up.

"I have eyes," Shang returned, bringing field glasses to his face. He trained them on the riders.

One he recognized. It was the mighty Mongol who had borne the hated standard of the terror khans of medieval China.

The other was a warrior, riding low on his mount. As he came, he shed portions of his armor as if to urge the greatest speed from his mount.

It was a while before General Shang understood that this lead rider was female. The whipping of her long black hair suggested the first glimmering thought, but some Mongols wore their hair longish.

Her bouncing breasts under a thin garment confirmed the suspicion.

"Why would they send a woman?" he muttered to himself.

His aide thought it a question and said, "It is most passing strange."

"Order the men to stand down," he said.

The aide ran off, stumbling.

The two riders drew to a halt a quarter *li* short of the Great Wall and its temporary fortification. They stood in their saddles, resolutely fearless, utterly without concern for the hopelessness of their position.

The aide came back panting. "The order has been communicated."

"Good."

The aide looked out over the saw-toothed rampart. "They wait."

"Yes. They want something."

"To talk."

General Shang nodded. "Go to them and find out."

"Alone?"

"They came alone. Unarmed. I see no clear danger."

"I do not speak Mongol and they do not look as if they understand Mandarin or Cantonese."

The general frowned. This was an excellent point.

"I speak Mongol," he said quietly, taking another peek at the woman rider's slowly heaving bosom.

The aide started. "You?"

"Why do you think I was given this assignment?" he said, unbuckling his gun belt.

General Shang walked out on the grass, alone, hands raised slightly, thinking of the extra stars his bravery would earn. He would become a people's hero. His face would be known from Shanghai to Hong Kong and to the farthest western provinces that only God knew.

And he would be treated to an excellent up-close view of the most magnificent female chest he had beheld in years.

General Shang walked under the scornful gaze of the two Mongols. Had there been any remaining question of the unencumbered rider's sex, it would have been dispelled by the steady rising and falling of her breasts, whose dark nipples were visible through the thin undergarments that had cushioned her discarded leather and felt armor.

"I am General Shang," he said in careful Mongolian.

"I am called Morning Doe, in service to Qasar Khan."

"Khan?"

"He is khakhan now."

The general blinked. The tales were true; wonderfully, amazingly, paralyzingly true.

"Your forces attacked Shenmu," Shang accused.

"No. That was a splinter horde." ·

"Horde?"

"We ride with the New Golden Horde."

Hearing those words, the moisture in General Shang's mouth died like urine on a flat rock in midsummer.

"You think you can attack Chinese with impunity?"

"We have no interest in China. We seek a direct route to the New Wall."

"What would you do there?"

"In the name of Qasar Khan, khan of khans, I am obliged to inform you that no enmity exists between us. We have mustered our forces and seek to recapture our territory from the Bone Heads."

General Shang blinked. "What are these Bone Heads you speak of?"

"Those who it is said came down from the Red Eye star that is not a star."

"Oh, you mean the Brain Skulls?"

"We call them Bone Heads."

"They are called Brain Skulls in Chinese. They are men of Mars."

"They are occupiers and must be cast out. I am directed by my khan to command you to withdraw your steel mounts from the wall that the true horses of liberation may ride its high ramparts to victory."

"You cannot command anything!" Shang sputtered.

The woman's eyes fell on his star-sewn shoulder boards. "You are a general."

"Yes."

"My lord Qasar is khakhan. He outranks you."

"Mongols do not outrank generals!" Shang exploded.

"Shall I take your insulting words back to Qasar Khan or will you swallow them silently and fully?" Morning Doe asked.

General Shang fell silent. After a moment he swallowed reflexively.

Morning Doe lifted her proud chin in victory. "Take to your highest general this offer. If you allow us to ride your Great Wall, we will bring down the New Wall. Mongolia will be restored to Mongolia. Perhaps Beijing will be restored to China."

"Perhaps. But how do I know this is not a trick?"

"You do not. But the next break in the Great Wall lies only forty *li* east of this position. Riding hard, the Golden Horde will reach it before your slow and clumsy engines of war."

"That breach, too, has been barricaded," General Shang said, knowing his words were a lie.

"And beyond that another breach."

"That breach is far distant," Shang pointed out.

"But reachable. You cannot fortify them all."

"I must take this to my superiors."

"I will wait here for word. Do not dare keep me waiting long, for in keeping me waiting, you keep Qasar Khan waiting. He and his horde do not enjoy standing still. They yearn for the thunder of hoofbeats and the pounding of their own pulses."

"I am not used to being addressed in that tone. What rank do you hold, woman?"

She met his eyes unflinchingly. "I am the personal concubine of Qasar Khan."

"A whore?"

"I will not make you eat that insult only because it will

cost my lord time and you your worthless life. But do not tempt me, food grower."

General Shang flinched from the lash of the warrior woman's cutting words.

But he turned on his heel and walked back, his face smoldering and his neck very, very red.

The offer went up the line to the Defense Minister himself, who read the decoded communiqué personally.

He pounded the desk with his fist and roared, "It is a naked bluff! Do they think we are fools?"

The Premier of China took the call from the Defense Minister without the intermediary of a secretary. He listened. He smoked throughout and let the Defense Minister exhaust his anger and frustration until a more receptive frame of mind showed in his tone of voice.

At length the Premier said, "Pull back the tanks just enough to allow them to take the high road they crave."

"But there are breaches along the way," the Defense Minister warned.

"We will plug those, too."

"To what purpose, Comrade Premier?"

"To this purpose, Comrade Defense Minister. These Mongols have waxed too great in numbers to be suppressed easily and without price. Let them ride on their mad quest. Who knows? Perhaps they will succeed."

"And if they do not succeed?"

The Premier smiled thinly, a smile lost on the Defense Minister on the other end of the line, but one that flavored his voice agreeably.

"If they do not succeed, it will be because the Brain Skull Martians have vanquished them utterly. A task they are welcome to, for it comes at too dear a price in people's heroes."

"Put in that way, this is reasonable."

"It is not without risk, but I authorize this step to be taken."

"I will notify you of the result."

The better portion of an hour later, the decision from Hong Kong was conveyed to General Shang through a coded field telegram.

He tore it open, read it, wrestled with the coding, and then tore it to tiny pieces which the westerly wind carried away.

Neck once again very red, he trudged back toward the waiting Mongol riders. They looked down on him with disinterest bordering on contempt. The expressions on their faces were unreadable but suggested to Shang's active imagination that the decision mattered to them only to the degree it inconvenienced them. The outcome was preordained.

Suppressing a shiver and the bile in his throat, Shang spoke to the woman while the standard bearer looked on in stony silence.

"The tanks of the People's Army will be withdrawn only to the position that allows your column to mount the Great Wall."

"Do not delay," she shot back. "You have already cost us an hour."

And with that the woman piloted her mount around and spurred it so it kicked clods of yellow earth that stung General Shang's face.

He was picking grit out of his half-blind eyes all the way back to his forward position. It would have been worse, but his tears of shame and rage helped clear them.

His tanks would pull back. Though the command came

down from the highest military authority, the shame fell squarely on his shoulders.

It was unbearable, unthinkable, but now irreversable.

49

SIX DRAGONS

Qasar Khan occupied the identical position he had when they left him.

"What news?" he asked in a neutral tone of voice.

"I am khan!" Morning Doe cried. "You cannot deny me!"

"You have lost your armor," Qasar said, eyeing her lack of helmet and armor as she pulled to a halt beside him.

"The food growers needed to see my womanly charms and my alluring features in order that I might sway them with my honeyed words."

"You used honeyed words?"

"Do you think otherwise?"

Behind Morning Doe, Ariunbold Khan met Qasar Khan's questioning gaze and carefully shook his head from side to side.

"You are a good liar for a woman, therefore I decree you khan."

"I will accept this honor if you will kiss me full on the mouth."

"There is no time to kiss you full on the mouth. We have *li* to cover. Besides," he called back as his charger high-stepped around, "I do not kiss mere khans. Especially those who flaunt themselves so shamefully before other khans and display their fleshy bounty to the soul-less Chinese."

Morning Doe dragged her peaked leather helmet off her head and sent it flying in Qasar Khan's direction.

It made a swish, and that alone alerted the Dog Khan. He weaved to the right in his saddle. The helmet went sailing past his own and a grunting laugh floated out after him.

The New Golden Horde started off almost instantly. They had ridden three abreast, but under the direction of Qasar Khan, they re-formed smoothly into a six abreast horde.

Coming down off the hill, they heard the rumble and mutter of diesel engines as the tank line—first the rear T-75s, then the T-72s, and finally the expendable cannon fodder T-64s—pulled back from their defensive positions.

The Mongols of Qasar Khan looked neither right nor left as they wended their way toward the reopened breach. Coming to the place where the eastern portion of the wall had sunk in ruins, the horses began climbing the rubble until they were clopping along the elevated roadway that was the Great Wall of China, built to keep their ancestors at bay and now facilitating their eastern advance.

Two hours passed before the trailing *ger* wagon creaked and clambered up onto smooth paving stones. By this time the horses had dropped so much dung that the sound of their progress softened to a mushy kneading, like bread dough in a strong woman's hands.

General Shang stood on the opposite side of the broken wall, saw the mashed horse manure and said, "Those damned Mongols are ruining a national treasure."

But at least no lives had been lost, although the PLA

had lost face. And General Shai Shang's military career was surely as dead as Mao Zedong in his crypt in the crushed ruins of lost Beijing.

50

THE GREAT WALL OF FREE CHINA

Morning Doe, having selected from the Golden Horde her choice in uncaptained Mongols, now rode directly behind Qasar Khan.

She caught occasional glimpses of his profile as they moved easterly on the undulating saw-toothed road of the New Wall.

"You look unhappy, my lord," Morning Doe remarked. "I was certain that you would come back without your head."

"That I did not causes you unhappiness?"

Qasar shook his head. "I regret that I must postpone my predestined conquest of China merely to punish the Bone Heads who have twice angered me," he said. "But I would not be worthy of Lord Genghis's armor if I did not smash those who tried to make of me a fool and a dead man."

"You can always conquer China," Morning Doe assured him. "China lies waiting to be ravished like a sleeping concubine."

"China will not wait long," Qasar vowed. "For Bone Head necks are easily snapped. We will pile their unclean corpses like cordwood and set them alight so that their death smoke ascends back to the red world that spawned them."

Morning Doe cast her cool catlike gaze in the direction of the placid Chinese countryside.

To the south lay mountains darkened with evergreens. The Yellow River wound its sinuous way to the sea, blue here, brown there. Rice paddies lay like pools of chocolate and manure amid the lowlands. The day was warm as a baby's breath.

"The Chinese do not regret their decision, it appears," she murmured.

"They will," Qasar said. "For once we have chased the Bone Heads back into the sky, we will use their Chof guns and sky pavilions to conquer all of China."

"I have heard that all that protects China from the Bone Heads is a treaty," Gerel Khan chimed in.

"I have signed no treaty with any man or race. Nor will I, except for the sake of expediency, and then with a careful eye to its terms so that I am not constrained from conquest. It is a bad thing to be constrained from conquest. It is a bad thing to be constrained from anything. Especially for a horse Mongol like myself."

"Mongols should never be constrained," Gerel agreed.

"And never again will we be," Qasar Khan vowed as he led his horde eastward, ever eastward, toward the New Wall that had been built by man and monster alike to preserve an untenable truce that Qasar Khan intended to abolish by sword and rifle.

51

HONG KONG

The Premier of China met with his Defense and Intelligence ministers in private, in a room which the Politburo had not bugged, nor had the National Assembly planted spies.

"The so-called New Golden Horde continues its eastern march?" he asked coolly.

"They show no sign of leaving the wall," the Intelligence Minister replied.

"They are exceedingly wise," the Defense Minister noted. "The man who leads them understands full well we will not attack them so long as they enjoy the protection of the national treasure that is the Great Wall."

"Perhaps," the Premier allowed. "But perhaps their intentions are honest, as well."

"As honest as naked conquest can be," the Defense Minister said aridly.

"What nation has not conquered? Including our own. We still press our boots into the unprotected neck of Tibet."

"I would trade all of Tibet for Beijing," the Defense Minister grumbled.

"That is a trade we are not privileged to make."

"Still, I would make it."

All agreed. The Premier moved on to other concerns.

"We have a dilemma," he said.

"Which is?" the Intelligence Minister wondered.

"To allow matters to unfold as they will, or to take certain measures."

"Measures?"

"Political measures."

"Such as?"

"Whether to alert the Brain Skull Martians of the Mongol intent."

"Why would we do that?" the Defense Minister wondered.

"On the face of it, because they alerted us to the Mongol threat."

"We are not obliged to reciprocate with oppressors," the Intelligence Minister spat.

"The face of the oppressor depends on who is being oppressed," the Premier said blandly.

The two ministers nodded sagely. It was a quotation they had never heard, but no doubt it was from Mao. Unless the Premier thought himself the next Mao, and was trying out uncirculated slogans on his ministers.

"What would China receive in return for this intelligence? Goodwill?" the Intelligence Minister wondered.

The Premier shook his head. "Perhaps land. Territory."

"Would the Martians consider the Mongols a serious threat?" the Defense Minister asked.

The Premier thought long and hard. "If their brains are not made of rice, yes. For is not the Great Wall our ancestors built to fend off Mongol depredations visible from Mars? Would Martians therefore not know what horrors Mongols are capable of?"

"The Great Wall is visible from the *moon*," the Intelligence Minister said dubiously. "I do not know if it is visible from the red planet."

The Premier waved the comment away.

"No matter. I have decided. We will lay this matter

before the Brain Skulls without precondition. If they later show gratitude, good. If not, the Mongol menace will at least be obliterated."

All agreed that this was a good thing in and of itself. For Free China had enough problems with Martian invaders, never mind resurgent Mongols.

52

KOLYMA TOWER, FORMER SIBERIA

Council member Feep placed the matter of the approaching Mongol force before the Martian Ruling Council.

"The Chinese leadership offers this intelligence without asking for concessions," he concluded.

An excited murmur rippled through Paeec and Gnard alike. And the inevitable arguments began.

"It must be a trick," Council member Ole'o, a Gnard, snapped.

"They seek to curry favor," rejoined the reasonable voice of Yuia Riq, a Paeec.

"If we attack these Mongols on Chinese soil, we will be in violation of the treaty," snapped another Gnard, Edd Sol. "This is clearly a pretext to draw us into conflict on the ground."

"Which we would win," Riq returned.

Feep let the arguments run their course. Then he addressed the quieting Council.

"We all know that in any battle, our Martian might will prevail. But this is not the hour for might, but for subtlety."

The Council stared down at him in burning expectant silence.

"Let the horse column come to our gates. Once on Martian soil, we may bend them to our will or destroy them at will. But their leader must be dealt with. He has shown unforgivable arrogance and temerity, which makes us look weak to the Chinese Terrans."

"What do you suggest?" Ole'o asked suspiciously.

"This appears to be a stealthwraith situation," Feep said.

The discussion that followed was heated, but ultimately produced more noise than dissent. The stealthwraith was sanctioned. Not that there was any surprise in that. Even the Gnard understood that there were certain delicate tasks only Paeec guile could accomplish.

53

INFILTRATOR
MOON'S SHADOW

Killerghost captain Vie Dio guided his skimming infiltrator low over the dusty yellow soil of China, his eyes on the viewscreen, trying to ignore the four silent Paeec standing behind him. Their indistinct forms reflected eerily on the screen glass.

It was not that they were Paeec, or even that they stood stark naked trilling some unknowable mantra. Hideous as naked Paeecs were, it was the disquieting fact that they belonged to the ancient, infallible guild of the stealth-wraiths that compelled Dio to keep his eyes averted at all times. It was profoundly chilling to be in their presence.

As Dio tried not to watch the reflections, the four silent trillers took up their light-bending hooded cloaks, drawing them on until only the assassins' light-sensitive monocular orbs showed. From a shared chest they drew various weapons, stowing them under their cloaks. It looked as if the weapons were levitating themselves, only to disappear into folds that could not possibly contain them.

Captain Dio recognized an ancient blinding fork, various needle blades designed to leave no traceable wound, and a very modern Tech/Div antipersonnel insect grenade. All vanished from sight.

As he dropped the *Moon's Shadow* to landing speed and called out, "Approaching drop zone," he wondered if the stealthwraiths' secret mission might not require his own ignominious disposal.

For it was said the stealthwraith guild despised the very thought of Gnard eyes on their prepenetration rituals.

54

THE GREAT WALL OF FREE CHINA

At each breach in the Great Wall, some very great, the Mongols descended to the soft earth, and the horses of the New Golden Horde had opportunities for rest and grazing. All this was done under watchful Chinese eyes. They buzzed by in PLA helicopters, and at every break there were the ubiquitous dome-turreted tanks with their observant soldiers in green, looking like olive-drab beetles and servant ants.

Qasar Khan and Bayar were standing apart from the horde, stretching their limbs beside their grazing mounts. Qasar's bow hung at his side in an open felt sheath, the red-fletched arrows handy in a box saddle quiver. He looked over the dusty *dacha* rifled from the tomb of Genghis Khan. "Have you been sneezing?"

"Some," Bayar admitted.

"I see some snot on your sleeve."

"I have not wiped my nose once. But snot flies. Some flies upon my *dacha* by chance."

"I will accept that explanation."

"Good. Because I do not wish to ride at the end of the train, where my horse is liable to slip on manure. Manure and paving stones do not go together. Especially at the end of the train."

"I will allow you to ride in front with me, but only upon one condition," Qasar Khan said.

"What is that?"

"That you ride wherever Morning Doe goes, and should arrows or bullets or other missiles of death seek her, you will willingly and without hesitation throw yourself before them, to preserve her life at the expense of your own."

"That was not in the oath I swore."

"The oath you swore called for you to obey my every whim," Qasar reminded.

"I do not specifically recall the word *whim*."

"Whatever the words, you swore the oath. Ride beside Morning Doe or ride over heaps of dung at your peril."

"Dung can be as deadly as an arrow at times," Bayar said, relenting.

Qasar Khan's eyes went to Morning Doe, who was bathing in a rice paddy, oblivious to the avid gazes of Mongols and Han soldiers alike.

"But nothing is as dangerous as the fear of losing all you hold dear," he said softly.

Bayar stared at his khan with a look of growing incredulity upon his face. Without warning, his eyes flew wide. He started to lift a pointed finger, then caught himself.

"Behind you," he hissed. "A Red Eye."

"In my camp?" Qasar growled.

"Lurking amid boulders. I see only its burning orb. It is staring at us."

"Have you a mirror?" Qasar asked, not moving.

Bayar fumbled a broken shard of mirror from his *dacha* and slipped it to his khan.

Qasar pretended to examine his own weathered reflection, and the white skull outlined in red against an ivory moon set on his sweat-shiny brow.

"I see no Red Eye," he said.

"It peers just above the rim of rock," Bayar warned.

Eyes narrowing, Qasar grunted, "Why do I see its unholy eye but not the head it is set in?"

"I do not know," Bayar admitted. "My eyes are not as keen as yours."

Unholstering his bow, Qasar Khan whirled, simultaneously grabbing and nocking a barbed arrow in one smooth motion.

He let fly, then dropped to one knee ahead of possible return fire.

The arrow flew true. It made the sound an arrow makes impaling meat. As Qasar lifted to his feet, he saw his shaft standing up behind the rock, quivering like a struck gong.

"Mongols! Surround that tumble of rock and kill anything you find there!" he shouted, starting forward.

When Qasar reached the spot, he pushed through a circle of jostling Mongols and found the arrow standing vertically, seemingly embedded in stone.

"Your arrow missed, O Khan," a Mongol said.

"I never miss," Qasar growled, kneeling beside his arrow whose red fletches quivered in the breeze.

Feeling about with his hands, he encountered something.

"What is it?" Bayar asked.

"A body."

"I see nothing."

"But I feel the cooling corpse of a foe." Questing about, Qasar's hands made sudden clutching fists. Abruptly, he pulled back, as if uncovering a sheeted object. But there was no visible sheet.

There was, however, an object. It simply sprang into view.

The circle of Mongols fell back with gasps of horror as a dead Red Eye Martian suddenly appeared at their feet— the arrow of Qasar Khan transfixing his half-dissolved, bloodred single orb. Its pink mouth tentacles lay flaccid like dead worms.

"Sorcery!" Bayar hissed.

Ignoring the dead thing, Qasar struggled with the unseen cloth he felt in his hands. Experimenting, he let it drape over one arm. The arm vanished at the elbow. He tossed it over Bayar's head, and Bayar became a Mongol without a head. Part of his shoulder evaporated.

The circle of Mongols jumped back in slack-jawed horror.

"I can't see!" Bayar complained.

"That is because you have no head," Qasar pointed out.

Struggling, Bayar got the sight-confounding cloth turned around so that one very round eye suddenly appeared in a circle of flesh. "I can see now. Is my head back?"

"Only one eye."

Bayar dragged the cloth that no one could see off his head and flung it on the ground.

"It is accursed," he spat.

Qasar retrieved it, saying, "The Red Eyes have tricks that would shame even the crafty Chinese." He stuffed the unseeable cloth into his bow quiver, adding, "I will keep this magical cloth, accursed as it is."

Addressing his forces, Qasar Khan spoke angrily.

"The Bone Heads have sent a Red Eye to assassinate your khan. But they have failed. As they will always fail. Henceforth look into the shadows for their disembodied red eyes. If you see one, shoot it without hesitation. I will make any Mongol who slays a Red Eye one of my khans on the spot. Spread the word down the horde. Now, regain your saddles, for my lust to slay my enemies makes my pulse pound more fiercely than anything else in life."

"More fiercely than I?" Morning Doe asked, stroking his arm. She had materialized at his side, her long black hair dripping, draped in a lambskin that was not sufficient to conceal her rounded contours.

"On this day, yes," Qasar said, shrugging off her touch and vaulting into his silver-chased saddle. Chino took off as if shot.

Fuming, Morning Doe mounted her mare and lashed it around in angry circles until she fell in place behind her khan. She dressed as she rode, her catlike eyes hot opals.

55

KOLYMA TOWER, FORMER SIBERIA

Telian Piar was tending his bonsai tree when the door to his private quarters emitted a thin *breep*.

"Enter."

A Gnard stepped through the hissing door. He stopped, then said, stiff-voiced: "Elder, I have the information requested by you."

Piar nodded without turning. "Proceed."

"Intel/Div provides the following: the Terran Mongol horse army attacked the Chinese city called Shenmu without success. The Mongol aggressors were repelled in the engagement, suffering absolute casualties."

Piar froze in the middle of pruning a branch. "Is Intel/Div certain of its facts?"

"Yes, Elder."

"Interesting." Piar moved the pruning tool back slightly, snipped, then laid the dead branch and tool aside. "All that I understood about Mongols indicated they could not be defeated except by overwhelming force or technological overkill."

The Gnard said nothing to that.

"It may be that I overestimated their prowess. Or that the Mongols of this era suffer in comparison to the Mongols of old."

The Gnard remained silent.

"Is it Intel/Div's understanding that the Mongol leader, Qasar Khan, also perished during this engagement?"

"Absolute casualties suggest this strongly."

Piar let the emptiness of the reply hang in the scrubbed Martian-grade air.

"Tell me," Piar intoned, filling the awkward silence, "is it still the intent of the Council to create a Mongol occupying police force?"

"That is my understanding, Elder."

"Interesting," Piar said softly after absorbing this information in the quiet contemplation of his bonsai tree.

"You may go," he added after a while.

"Your will," the Gnard said, withdrawing.

After the door hissed closed, Telian Piar whispered a single damning word: "Liar."

56

THE GREAT WALL OF FREE CHINA

Gerel Khan rode up from inspecting the New Golden Horde as it drummed along the Great Wall of China. It was the third day of this stage of their march. The horses had grazed, but the men were living off dried mutton, and by sucking the marrow from the sheep bones. Some, low on rations, opened wounds in the necks of their horses and drew sustenance from their veins, as did the Mongols of the original Golden Horde. In their saddlebags some carried dried milk curd. When water was poured in, the relentless jostling of the horses' cadence churned the curd and water into a grayish porridge that sustained their strength—but did not appease their stomachs' yearnings for mutton.

"The men grow weary," Gerel Khan reported.

Qasar Khan accepted the news with an impassive expression.

"I care not about the men. They will endure because my will is their will. What of the horses?"

"They do not flag so much."

"But they flag?"

"They show signs of flagging," Gerel Khan admitted.

"Should the horses flag," Qasar said thoughtfully, "it will not matter how strong my will is, for it cannot keep

Mongols in the stirrups if their mounts lay down to rest or die."

"There is no break in the Great Wall for a half day's march, and no way off the wall otherwise," Ariunbold Khan pointed out.

"Then it is imperative that we make it to the next break in the wall of the old Han Nation."

Qasar Khan fell silent. The drumming of hoofbeats assaulted the very air. The Great Wall seemed to vibrate to the unending drumroll. Here and there ancient brick and mortar fell away, as if invaders were assaulting the wall itself. Absently, he scratched himself.

"We will sing," he announced.

"We will?" Bayar said.

"We will," Qasar Khan said. "For a song will lift the spirits of both horses and Mongols. It will fall on their ears more sweetly than upbraiding them."

"They need upbraiding, too."

"If the song fails, I will upbraid them as necessary," Qasar said, shifting his scratching hand from the small of his back to his abdomen.

Skeptically raised eyebrows passed behind the back of Qasar Khan. Even Morning Doe seemed dubious of mien.

"We will sing 'Uncle Namsan,' " Qasar announced.

"I know that song," said Morning Doe Khan, who immediately began humming the melody.

"It is a very good song," Bayar added.

"Yes. Very good," Gerel Khan added. "But I do not think the horses know this song."

"They need not understand the words, only the beauty of the sound of the words," Qasar said.

At that, Qasar Khan lifted his deep throaty voice to render the first stanza of "Uncle Namsan."

"Riding on his bay horse,
Leaving her kinsman weeping,
Here comes Uncle Namsan
With a young girl he has taken from her home."

As he sang, Qasar squirmed in his lamellar cuirass as if it were suddenly lined with scratchy mohair. His face twisted this way and that.

With the second stanza the horde of Morning Doe joined in—having been prompted by repeated kicks of her felt boots as she rode up and down the line.

"Wearing my lambskin robe
Do you feel like—"

Without warning, Qasar Khan jerked in his saddle like a man impaled by an arrow.

Morning Doe reacted first, riding up to his side, crying, "My lord, are you wounded?"

Qasar clung to his saddle, head down, eyes searching his blue and gold armor with the expression of a man who thinks he is about to die and is looking for confirmation of that awful truth.

"Qasar!" Morning Doe shrieked. "Where is the shaft?"

"I do not know," Qasar returned tightly. "Do you see blood?"

"I see no blood. Bayar?"

"I see no blood," Bayar said, eyes wide.

"Nor I," Ariunbold chimed in.

It was Gerel Khan, crowding up, who spied the round black object.

"Under your right arm, Khakhan!" he cried.

Carefully, staying in the saddle so his white stallion would not break stride, Qasar Khan lifted his arm and looked down. He saw a dull black egg no larger than a

child's fist. It bristled on the rounded end, with tiny
ebony hooks surrounding a single penetrating needle.
The needle was embedded in the hardened leather of the
cuirass of Genghis Khan.

"How deep?" Gerel asked.

"I feel no pain," Qasar said, reaching down to tear the
black egg from his body. The moment his fingers
wrapped around the object, it emitted a sharp click and
vented a coil of hissing white gas.

Fighting the barbs, Qasar wrested it free. With an
angry effort, he threw it ahead of him. It struck, rolled,
and came to a spinning stop, still releasing fumes. When
it stopped spinning, an angular white skull Qasar Khan
knew all too well was revealed. An identical skull burned
on his furrowing brow.

"The mark of the Bone Heads!" Bayar breathed.

Checking the puncture in his side, and finding no
blood, Qasar barked, "I am not wounded. Ride on."

The horde continued apace. The black egg broke hollowly under the first hooves to stamp it.

"Sing," Qasar commanded. He resumed his absent
scratching.

Morning Doe took up the female chorus of "Uncle
Namsan."

"In the gown of heavy lambskin I feel shivery.
The Chinese brocade rubs my—"

With a sudden howl, Qasar Khan suddenly began
clawing at his armor.

"What is it?" Bayar said.

Howling anew, his face contorted in a mixture of fear
and consternation, Qasar began pulling at his cuirass. He
tore at it wildly, flinging off sections of leather and steel.

"Column halt!" Ariunbold Khan shouted. The column

jerked to a halt, segment by segment, as the word passed down the line.

Throwing himself off his saddle, Qasar wrestled with his armor. It was bowing in front, bulging and buckling as if the man inside were growing new and strange muscles where muscles should not be.

"Stay back!" Qasar cried as Morning Doe reached down to wrench at the holding straps.

"When I am done," she hissed, yanking a strap free. "And not before."

Jerking at side straps, Qasar pulled away. And the cuirass, contorting weirdly, sprang apart to disgorge an eyeless brown head whose sucking insectoid beak quested about thirstily.

Morning Doe screamed in horror. Others jumped off their saddles to come to the aid of their khakhan.

Two hands wrapped about the thing's narrow head. Qasar's hands. Holding tight, he pulled the thing from his half-open cuirass. With a chittering complaint, out came a hairy grayish-brown armored body ringed by six segmented legs.

"It is a louse!" Bayar gasped.

"No louse grows so large!" Morning Doe said, kicking him.

"A louse. Definitely."

The hairy legs ended in hooked black claws. Scampering and digging wildly, some found purchase in Qasar's undergarments.

Angry, his face turning red, Qasar wrestled the unclean thing, squeezing and twisting it. Its claws scratched along his armored arms, catching here and there.

"Back! I will deal with this abomination!" Qasar thundered.

All hung back.

A swiping claw sliced a red line along one cheek.

Qasar didn't flinch. His muscles knotting, he compressed the head tighter and tighter. But the beak remained menacingly free. The veins in the Mongol leader's neck swelled and turned blue under the reddening skin as the thing chittered in an accelerating distressed pitch.

"Defile you!" Qasar snarled at the blind thing in his unshakable clutch. "Defile all of your accursed kind."

Clinging legs pulled spasmodically, bringing the beak closer and closer. Qasar pushed back with all his might, his hands bearing down with single-minded ferocity.

The head made a loud pop. Blood squirted, reddening Qasar's fingers. The legs quivered, then froze, one dropping free where its purchase was weak.

Exhaling a gusty breath, Qasar Khan let the dead thing fall from his shaking grasp. It hung off his body as if reluctant to surrender its prey. Qasar pulled the hairy legs loose one by one, cursing with every exertion, until it landed with the sound a shelled crab makes when discarded.

The thing lay there on its back, its legs slowly curling together. When Qasar Khan regained his breath, his eyes were ablaze with a smoldering rage that had no voice.

"Lice grow very large in this part of China," Bayar said uneasily.

"No louse achieves such size," Morning Doe insisted.

Bayar toed it over, exposing a dark spot on its carapace. "See? That is the spot found on a louse that has just fed."

"It was no louse," Morning Doe snapped.

"It was Red Eye sorcery," Qasar snapped back, eyeing the terrain on either side of the Great Wall. "Pass the word. All eyes will stay sharp for lurking Red Eyes. But do not kill."

"Why not?" Gerel Khan asked.

"That is the privilege to be reserved for your angry

khakhan," Qasar growled, recovering his scattered armor.

When he had once again donned the armor of Genghis Khan, Qasar Khan regained his mount and gave the order to continue. The hooves of the New Golden Horde passed over the dead thing in the roadway. Its carapace cracked, split, and oozed blood. By the time the last clicking hoof had passed over it, all that remained was a thin rust-brown smear embedded in the well-worn paving stones. The New Golden Horde again rode with one purpose, followed one leader, and sang with one voice:

> "In the morning when I get up and look at you,
> Uncle Namsan, you are all drained of color;
> When I sit leaning against your knee,
> Uncle Namsan, I know you've had your day."

In the lead, Qasar Khan's enraged eyes raked the way before him, his glowering visage like an approaching storm cloud carrying a death's-head before it.

Behind him, his Mongols sang themselves and their mounts to greater effort.

Not one day's march away stood the spot where the Great Wall and the New Wall conjoined. It would be there that they would pour over the ramparts of the invader from the Red Eye planet, despoiling and looting and taking all of value.

With every sinew in his tireless frame, Qasar Khan ached for that hour, his gripping knuckles the exact whiteness of naked bone.

57

KOLYMA TOWER, FORMER SIBERIA

Komo Dath received the message from Telian Piar, read it once, twice, then tore it apart and rushed past the servile Gnard factotum who had delivered it. He proceeded to the lower level of Kolyma Tower, where the Paeec's private quarters were.

The Paeec greeted him at the door.

"I do not believe what you have told me," Dath rasped.

"Intel/Div assures me it is true."

"These Mongols are more Gnard than Terran. They could not have been wiped out so easily."

"Intel/Div says otherwise."

"Intel/Div is composed of blind guessers and prevaricators. I believe half of what they report and none of what they predict."

"It would be a simple thing to discover the truth."

Komo Dath closed his wicked needle teeth slowly. "Are you attempting to lure me into another one of your misadventures, Paeec?"

"A cavalry of six thousand Mongols, even if scorched into the dirt, would leave undeniable traces."

"True. . ."

"Just as survivors of any consequence would leave spoor."

"I do not believe the Dog Khan could be so easily exterminated," Dath said slowly.

"Burning fuel was dropped from the sky. What Terran or Martian could survive such a conflagration if it descended upon his head?"

"The Dog Khan impressed me greatly."

"He offended you deeply," Piar reminded.

"That, too." Komo Dath scissored his teeth thoughtfully for several moments. Finally, he lowered his raspy voice and said, "I have reason to overfly the World Wall."

Telian Piar fixed him with his singular eye. "Yes?"

"An inspection flight. Where it intersects the Great Wall of China, it may be that I might persuade the Killerghost pilot to follow its course."

"I would like to see the portion of the Great Wall that lies in the Profane Zone," Piar said, his mouth tentacles fluttering.

"I have no objection to you acting as observer," Dath said.

"Then it is settled. I am ready to leave when you are."

"And I am ready now," said Telian Piar.

The door gave before their moving presences and closed after them with a hasty hissing.

58

THE GREAT WALL OF FREE CHINA

After 334 choruses of "Uncle Namsan"— many created anew out of sheer boredom—the New Golden Horde reached the long breach at the Yellow River, where the horde fed and relieved itself along the muddy banks until the air over their heads was a vast cloud of methane gas.

They were not in pasture long when Qasar Khan ordered them to form up and push on.

Morning Doe Khan objected. "We are without remounts. The horses require more rest."

"And they will get it when we reach the joining of the two walls, for horses cannot jump from these ramparts into the accursed barrens where the Bone Heads dwell. At the conjunction we will leave them to their devices, and we will seek treasure and carnage on foot."

"Is this wise?"

"Wise or not wise, it is the only plan that will work. We need the wall to carry the horses, and we need the horses to sustain our horde. Once in the Bone Head Barrens, men—not mounts—will win or lose the day."

"Your word is my command."

Qasar's eyes crinkled up in good humor. "You have been learning generalship, I see."

"I am a khan. I will be a khan while I ride this horse.

But when you ride me, I will be your consort. I do not confuse the two, nor should you."

"I would consort with you now, but it would be unseemly, and we must be on our way."

"The horses need more rest, and I perhaps need you," Morning Doe said simply, her eyes growing dark and hot.

Pounding boots presaged an excited hollering.

"Qasar Khan! Qasar Khan! Hear Gargal the Mongol!"

Qasar turned. A panting Mongol archer threw himself on one knee before him, his head bowed.

"I give you leave to speak," Qasar said.

Gargal shot out a pointing arm. "A Red Eye. To the east!"

"Lead the way," Qasar said, turning away from Morning Doe as if she no longer existed.

Gargal the Mongol took him to a hump of tufted grass overlooking the Yellow River. Shadows were very long now, for dusk lay upon the land.

"By that ugly Chinese willow. I saw it with my own eyes."

"A Red Eye?" Qasar demanded.

"Three Red Eyes. Winking like fireflies, and advancing with careful stealth. One always visible. When one closed, another would appear near it. Never more than one visible at a time."

"Three. You are certain of the number?"

Gargal nodded. "Three Red Eyes."

Turning, Qasar Khan lifted his voice. "Mongols. Attend me!"

Heads turned. Eyes narrowed.

"Form a skirmish line with bow and rifles."

The nearest Mongols fell into action. There were too many to muster the entire horde, and it was impractical to do so.

Soon, a double line of Mongols was arrayed on either side of their khakhan, weapons at the ready, their faces collecting shadows.

"I see no Red Eye."

"But they see us," Gargal said. "They do not reveal their red eyes lest they invite your wrath."

"My wrath cannot be denied," Qasar said tightly, scanning the banks of the Yellow River, his head rotating on his thick neck like a machine with the head of a man.

"I spy footprints," he said at last.

"I see none," Gargal said.

"That is one reason I am khan and you are a mere archer," Qasar said, taking up his bow and nocking an arrow. He drew back, using his leather thumb pad to derive the greatest tension possible. Without the protective pad, the tight gut would have split his thumb in two.

"Do not fire until I have," Qasar warned, sweeping the riverbank with his gleaming arrowhead.

Time passed. Nothing moved. Qasar let the arrowhead fall on an empty space, paused, then moved on with methodical patience.

A faint puff of dust where there was no wind told him what his eyes could not. Something had moved. He let fly into the gathering murk.

The arrow flew across the yellow soil and suddenly stopped, hung in the air. A red eye popped open, staring with a red resentment.

Both floating eye and arrow retreated erratically until the eye simply fell back, to vanish from sight. The shaft nosedived into the ground in a cloud of saffron dust greater than a falling arrow would naturally stir.

The meaty thud of a falling body confirmed what their own blinking eyes failed to see. And on either side, two new hellish red orbs appeared, disembodied as dying stars.

Nocking another arrow, Qasar shouted, "Fire! All fire at those spots!"

A cascade of arrows whispered into the air. Some shattered to kindling, struck by rattling automatic and small arms fire. The surviving arrows converged on a patch of soil. Many impaled seeming emptiness, but began twisting and spinning in midair. The floating red orbs flared in recognizable but alien horror. Shrill trilling cries welled up. They were brief.

A single red pencil of light came back, and a nameless Mongol fell with a smoking hole in the exact center of his face. The light collapsed without inflicting more death.

On the riverbank, flowers of blood began blooming. Under relentless bullet strikes they turned into a red rain that sprinkled the bullet-churned riverbank until all was gory mud.

When the firing ceased, Qasar Khan strode confidently forward.

He found nothing living in the red riverbank. Only morsels of strange flesh mixed with chips and splinters of raw bone and unfamiliar metal shards.

Qasar Khan spat into the stew.

"You have tasted my wrath, Red Eyes from Red Eye, but may count yourselves fortunate because you do not live to see the carnage I yearn to inflict upon your fellow demon spawn," he said in a low and venomous voice.

Turning on his heel, Qasar Khan marched back to his horde, which gave silently before him—and before the fierce expression on his smoldering bronze countenance.

No one dared ask which of them would become khan

for having slain a Red Eye. For no one knew which of them had accomplished this great thing.

Other than their khakhan himself, of course, who had taken only the meagerest portion of his planned revenge.

59

KILLERGHOST
RED SANDS

At the exact moment the sun went down, a full moon crept over the horizon line, impregnating the Gobi Desert with soft maroon light. It presaged what Mongols called a Red Circle day.

The Killerghost saucer *Red Sands* was skimming low through the spectral atmospheric effects, Komo Dath watching the monitor screen, Telian Piar at his side, his face and posture in quiet repose.

They had traced the course of the World Wall from a point south of Lake Baikal to the area west of Beijing, China, where a section of the Great Wall of China had been incorporated into the concrete and steel World Wall, by mutual agreement between the Martian Ruling Council and the People's Republic of China.

"Strange how similar these walls are," Telian Piar said softly as the rust-red wall became one of old stone and mortar.

"Coincidence," Dath rasped.

"Coincidence is the creator's way of keeping his existence invisible," Piar intoned.

"I share none of your beliefs and little of your philosophy," Dath returned. But his teeth continued to scissor rhythmically, betraying a subtle nervousness not lost on the quiet Paeec.

Responding to a sharp order, *Red Sands* captain Lhyso

vectored his ship away from the World Wall to follow the long serpentine traverse of the Great Wall of China.

"It is quite long," Dath said as the terrain shifted, rose, and dipped, the Great Wall rising and falling with it like a long living thing that had collapsed, died, and been petrified by time.

"For Terrans, it is a magnificent feat of engineering."

"For anyone," Dath replied grudgingly. Addressing the captain, he said, "Scan both sides of this wall for significant concentrations of men and animals."

"Your will."

The saucer sped on through the shifting landscape. It ran without lights, inasmuch as its flight path took it over Chinese airspace, which was by treaty forbidden to uncleared Martian spacecraft.

Dath turned to the Gnard at the sensor nest. "Readings, technician."

"Large concentration of airborne methane."

"Source?"

"Unknown. No obvious source on either side of the stone wall."

A moment later the technician spoke again.

"Sir. There appears to be an unusual concentration of Terrans, several Terran land units along our track."

"Identify."

"Terrans riding beasts of burden."

"Numbers?"

"In excess of six thousand of each."

Dath eyed Telian Piar pointedly. "Could this be . . . ?"

"Could it be otherwise?" Piar retorted softly.

The two Martians moved to the main monitor screen, their bodies tensing with interest.

"Approaching concentration in question," Captain Lhyso called out.

"Slow to observation speed," Dath said.

The Killerghost decelerated without any onboard shift in motion or inertia.

"Switching to night-vision scanners," the technician announced.

The screen became gray, then red, and soon the landscape resolved into a clarity of deep shadows and muted red hues.

The crenellated Great Wall of China stood out distinctly. But nothing else immediately revealed itself.

"Where is this concentration?" Dath bit out.

"On the Terran wall itself," the technician said, pointing with a gnarled finger.

Dath and Piar leaned in, gaped, then reacted with different outward expressions of startlement—Dath clenching teeth and fists, while Telian Piar's single black pupil squeezed down to a pinpoint of intense concern.

"They ride the Great Wall," Piar said, vague awe softening his tone even further.

"To what purpose?" Dath spat. "Why would they do this?"

"We have just traced the course of the wall," Piar pointed out. "It follows only one clear trajectory."

"To the World Wall," Komo Dath said.

"To Martian Holdings," Piar echoed.

"They would not dare! They cannot possibly—"

Telian Piar cut Komo Dath's raspy sputterings off with a graceful wave of his hand. "You attempt to glean meaning without possessing sufficient verified data factors."

"They are on an elevated roadway. It goes where it goes. They are not hiding from the Chinese military machine. Not riding on the most obvious landmark in the hemisphere."

"I do not question your conclusion, Dath. I only warn that it is arrived at imperfectly."

Komo Dath faced the monitor again. "Technician, locate for me a White Card Terran among that company."

Hunched over his control board, the technician began keying expertly, and the screen pulled back, crisscross electronic lines dividing it into a glowing green grid. As each red grid was scanned, it turned blue. After a dozen blue grids, the in-progress scanning exploded a single grid and targeting arrows locked onto a single horseman, whose face expanded exponentially until both Telian Piar and Komo Dath saw the familiar hammered features of Qasar Khan riding at the head of his seemingly endless horse column.

His eyes were like knives, his black hair hanging over his forehead, the White Card tattoo—a pale skull, outlined in red, against a white circle—showed clearly through Qasar Khan's stringy black bangs.

"He lives. . ." Dath rasped.

"He lives to conquer. And we have offended his sense of pride and honor very deeply," Piar mouthed softly.

Dath banged the console with his fist. "This is a matter to be brought before the Council."

"I will allow you that honor," Piar told Dath.

Dath flung a hot glance in Piar's direction. "Seeking to avoid responsibility this time, Paeec?"

"No. Merely acceding to your obvious experience and vested authority. For if the Council issues the order to exterminate this Mongol and his force, clearly the responsibility for this operation will fall on the broad shoulders of the all-powerful Martian Military Commander . . . Komo Dath."

Dath regarded his rival and ally with grudging respect, then, as the ship once again crossed the boundary of the World Wall, he turned to do his duty.

60

THE GREAT WALL OF FREE CHINA

Night fell.

A quietude settled over the New Golden Horde, making even the relentless drumming of naked hooves on paving stone a muted, otherworldly sound. Their leather armor, still drying after the fording of the Yellow River, squeaked like hungry, complaining mice.

Qasar Khan looked skyward, his eye attracted by an unfamiliar gleam.

"What star is that?" he asked Bayar, pointing to the skies over Martian occupied lands.

"Which star?"

"The jade."

Bayar squirmed his features as his eyes tightened.

"I know no jade star of that size or color so near Ulan Nud," he said carefully.

"Perhaps it hovers near Ulan Nud because it hails from Ulan Nud."

"You suspect it is a sky pavilion of the Bone Heads?"

"It is reasonable to suppose, if the stories are true."

"I do not know if the stories are true, Khakhan. But if you suspect a thing is so, then that is the first proof of it being so."

"Of course. Am I not khakhan of all the Mongols under the Everlasting Blue Sky?"

"The sky is black tonight, my lord," Morning Doe

280

Khan offered. Until that point she had been steadily humming "Uncle Namsan." No one had ever heard her hum before.

"It is black now, but with the sun it will be transformed to blue. I live for that hour, as do you."

"I savor every hour under the living sky, whether blue or black," Morning Doe Khan intoned.

And hearing the somber tone of her voice, Qasar glanced backward. Her face was in shadow, as if the caul that had covered it at birth had reappeared and blackened forbiddingly.

"As do I," Qasar Khan said softly. "As do I."

Above their heads, the jade star burned, cool and unwinking. As he rode, Qasar Khan never let it out of his sight.

After a while Morning Doe fell to humming again—a melancholy tune this time. Its cadences fell upon their souls like a cool beating of vulture wings.

61

KILLERGHOST
<u>RED SANDS</u>

Komo Dath faced the comm screen that linked him to the Martian Ruling Council at Kolyma Tower.

"A routine patrol has discovered the horde of the White Card Mongol," he reported. "He lives."

"Our intelligence indicates otherwise."

"Intel/Div has lived up to its reputation," Dath said acidly. "The Dog Khan leads his pack. And all indications are he leads them toward the World Wall."

"What would be his purpose in that?"

"He has turned away from his intended conquest of China. It may be that he seeks to regain the portion of eastern Mongolia now designated Martian Holdings."

"This violates the treaty."

"No treaty exists between the Council and Mongolia. Their government was crushed utterly, leaving only nomads and herdsmen. No flowery communiqué or piece of parchment constrains this Dog Khan."

"We will consider this possibility."

The screen winked out.

Only then did Telian Piar glide into view.

"You heard?" Dath rasped.

"You told them what they already know," Piar murmured.

"Their decision will reveal the truth of your words, or the craftiness of the Council."

A ruby light signaled an incoming transmission, and Piar stepped back out of viewing range as Council member Feep reappeared on the screen, his sole eye placid and beguiling.

"It is the decision of the Council to allow the Dog Khan to continue his journey unchallenged."

Komo Dath stiffened in voice and posture. "This is wrong! He comes to invade our territory."

"You do not know this, Dath."

"I suspect it strongly. We must take precautions."

"If the White Card Mongol Terran reaches the World Wall, he and his force will be more easily captured for Personal Modification by Tech/Div."

Dath blinked. Once. Twice. His needle teeth froze like a bear trap. "You seek to tame him?"

"He is intent upon delivering his horde into our hands," Feep returned coolly. "Why should we not take advantage of his foolhardiness?"

"He will not be so easily bent to the Council's will," Dath warned.

"You say this because you could not bend him to yours."

Behind his back, Dath's fists tightened to knots of bone and lean flesh. "I say this because I know this Mongol. His psychology is of the Gnard type."

Feep's voice became dry. "I am a Paeec. I cannot speak to this point. The Council's decision has been rendered. Your advice and counsel is appreciated, Komo Dath."

The screen blanked out, and Dath spat at it with a ferocity that caused Telian Piar to halt in mid-stride.

Noticing him, Dath said, "You heard all that?"

Hovering at a respectful distance, Piar nodded quietly. "Your hands are tied."

Dath shook his huge head savagely. "As Martian

Military Commander, I cannot allow the Dog Khan to violate our holdings. I am duty bound to stop him—an obligation that supercedes the Council's will."

"The Council has stated its wishes. They desire to control the Golden Horde."

"And they will. But as much as I have come to respect him, I cannot allow the Dog Khan to live. Without him, the horde are merely nomads without direction. With him at their head, they will fight to the last Mongol."

"I make no comment."

"Politically wise. But I must take action. And I will."

Whirling on a technician hovering over his station, Komo Dath rasped, "Acquire the White Card's homing signal. Follow it until I give the command to terminate. Single beam. No overkill. Just the White Card. Spare the others."

"Your will," the technician returned, fingers going to his control console.

62

THE GREAT WALL OF FREE CHINA

Deep in the night, Qasar Khan stood swaying on his stirrups, the nine-yak-tail standard shifting and waving on his right. Morning Doe Khan followed a half horse length behind and to the left, with Bayar bobbling beside her, sneezing occasionally but not violently.

"The jade star is not a star," Qasar muttered.

Hearing this, Bayar said, "You know this for a fact?"

"See how it follows us?"

"The moon appears to follow us," Bayar said.

"The moon rises in the sky as it appears to follow us. This jade star neither rises nor falls. It simply follows us."

"If you say this, it must be true."

"Your own eyes should tell you this."

"They do. But I prefer to accept the word of my khakhan to the evidence of my eyes, which are not always trustworthy."

Qasar Khan grunted. "You have been loyal to me since I first set out along the Winding Road to my exalted new existence."

"It was a happy day I found you," Bayar said amiably.

"I found *you*," Qasar amended.

"I forgive you for slaying the sheep I coveted."

"Your forgiveness is accepted with this token of my esteem."

And reaching into his saddlebag, Qasar flipped a white object back over his shoulder. Bayar caught it in one hand, raised it to the moonlight, and saw that it looked back at him cloudily.

"A sheep's eye?"

"The mate to the one you spurned. I have been saving it."

Bayar squinted at it. It stared blindly in return. "It is a delicacy, you say?"

"I say this, therefore it must be true."

"Then I accept this gift from you." And Bayar popped it into his mouth and began rolling it around on his tongue.

"Taste, but do not chew," Qasar warned.

After he had swallowed it, Bayar said, "It is very good."

Qasar grunted. His eyes were on the unshakable jade star. All at once, it changed position.

"It moves," he said suddenly.

Bayar looked up. "All stars do."

"It is approaching," Ariunbold said.

The jade star swelled in size, becoming a sphere, then a vast plate showing tiny lights of colors that were not jade, but gold and silver instead. Suddenly all the lights winked out.

"I do not like that way it is behaving," Qasar said.

"What do we do? There is no place to run. We are prisoners of the Great Wall."

Doubt touched Qasar Khan's tone. "The Bone Heads perhaps suspect our intent."

"How could they? They are but Bone Heads."

Qasar growled, "Bayar, remember your vow."

Slapping his gelding, Bayar spurred it to Morning Doe Khan's side. Seeing this, Morning Doe shot him a look and demanded, "Why do you crowd me?"

"I am protecting you."

"I need no protection," she spat. "I am a khan and you are but Arrow Prince."

"Without me, your quiver would be empty," Bayar said defensively.

Whipping her horse, Morning Doe Khan trotted up to Qasar's right. Seeing this, Qasar forked his mount closer to the ramparts, cutting her off. She twisted her horse around, coming between her khan and Ariunbold. Finding himself crowded, Ariunbold was forced to drop back lest the standard of Genghis Khan be damaged by the ramparts of the Great Wall.

"I command you to return to your position," Qasar barked.

"Command Bayar to defer to me as first khan," Morning Doe flung back, her eyes scornful.

"I never designated you my first khan."

Morning Doe frowned. "Then what is my designation?"

"I do not favor one khan over another," Qasar growled. "It would be unseemly."

"Not even the khan who makes your pulse pound?"

"My loyal horse makes my pulse pound," Qasar said, eyes flicking between Morning Doe and the jade object still seen dimly in the sky.

"I set your blood afire," Morning Doe reminded.

"You do. Sometimes."

"Therefore I deserve respect."

"Respect your khan, and his respect will shower down upon your head like a cool soothing rain."

"I will do as you command, but only because you command it."

"Just so long as you do what I command," Qasar Khan growled, his eye falling from the jade-green object to the catlike features of Morning Doe Khan.

That instant proved fatal.

From the jade eye, a lance of white light streamed. It crossed the night sky in a heartbeat.

Morning Doe saw it and a chill overtook her arched spine.

Bayar saw it as well.

Digging her boot heels into the ribs of her mare, Morning Doe lunged to intercept the beam. And seeing this, Bayar gave out a howl and flung himself from his saddle.

The beam of white light seared through space like an arrow. Intended for Qasar Khan, it sought Morning Doe Khan, but in truth pierced Bayar in mid-leap.

The sound it made was like sheep meat sizzling over hot coals. The sound was brief and was lost in the screaming and rearing of horses frightened by the unknown and the unexpected.

Qasar Khan reached over and yanked Morning Doe from her saddle. Under his spurring, *"Ai-yah-yah-yah!"* his charger leapt ahead. He carried her nearly a full *li* along the Great Wall, wheeled and looked back.

The horses were bunching up. Some stumbled badly. Caught before an inexorable tide of hooves, Mongols and mounts succumbed as their bones were snapped and their vitals crushed in their helpless bodies. Very quickly their cries were silenced by death.

Confusion overtook the first horde.

And in the sky the jade object tracked toward them in a sweeping, purposeful arc.

63

KILLERGHOST
RED SANDS

"You missed!" Komo Dath hissed, striking a panel with his fist.

"Permission to fire again!" the gunner-technician responded.

"Do it."

A lance of light seared the night sky again. On one screen the face of Qasar Khan was as a blur of darkness. Then it was gone.

The ray touched the spot and melted a section of rampart, which sublimed into rock smoke, leaving a smooth bite mark in the ancient stone.

"How could you miss twice?" Dath screamed.

"He moves like an animal, not a Terran."

"Seek him. Find him. Slay him!"

The Killerghost saucer dipped as it scanned the Great Wall of China, where two advance guard horses reared in confusion. Reared without mounts.

Soon the Golden Horde caught up and pushed the confused animals ahead of it like a torrent of brown water churning along a flume.

Komo Dath watched the horses pass, rank after rank,

until the spot where Qasar Khan had been stood exposed again.

"He may have fallen over the side," he warned. "Scan for a body."

The *Red Sands* overflew the wall, coming up on its opposite side. Technicians busily read sensor feeds. At a monitor, Telian Piar watched intently.

"There is no sign of the White Card," Piar murmured without emotion.

"He is somewhere. Technician!"

"The sensors do read him, Commander."

"Where?"

"Amid the mass of Terran men and beasts."

"Has he been trampled?"

The technician shook his big head. "No, he is moving with them."

"His body is being carried along?" Dath suggested.

"It is possible, but doubtful," Telian Piar said, shaking his head. He was staring at the screen with his single red orb, which possessed greater night-vision properties than enjoyed by the binocular Gnard, as if to pick out one man in a fast-moving mass of thousands.

"I have never seen anything like this, Commander," the technician was babbling.

Hissing with rage, Komo Dath cuffed the technician who had dared to suggest a low-skilled Terran nomad had outwitted Martian technology.

"Follow the horde, then."

"Your will."

64

THE GREAT WALL OF FREE CHINA

A pinpoint of searing white light warned Qasar Khan of the stabbing beam of death, and he flung himself off his mount, kicking Morning Doe Khan from hers.

He slipped over the rampart, felt empty spaces behind him and, strong fingers snapping out, arrested his death fall.

The horny knuckles of his fingers grew hot as the white ray burned past.

"Morning Doe," he gasped. "Speak!"

Her voice shook with emotion. "I live, my lord."

"The horde comes. Leave your mount to run free. Climb into the saddle of the first horse that seeks to trample you."

"What if the rider will not allow this?"

"Knock him under the hooves of his own steed and take it. You are a khan. He is but a dog of war and lives to die."

"What about you?"

"I will see you alive or not see you at all. Prepare now!"

The thunder of hooves drew near. The stones under Qasar's hooked fingers trembled agitatedly.

Qasar let rank upon rank thunder past, then hauled himself up by dint of his muscular forearms, his peaked helmet, already askew, tumbling down into space.

The unfortunate rider he happened to dislodge fell screaming from his stirrups, was dragged, but saved himself by taking an offered hand from another rider.

Digging his booted feet into the jumping stirrups, Qasar Khan took control of the lathering horse and lashed it through the ranks, cutting in and out, shouting at the top of his lungs, "Make way! Make way for your khakhan, dogs of the Golden Horde!"

Not a Mongol refused him. In this way Qasar Khan came to the head of the horde, but hung back three ranks, one eye on the elusive jade star.

"Ariunbold! What of Bayar?" he called through the darkness.

"I have him, my lord."

"He lives?"

"No, he dies."

Qasar Khan's face turned metallic in the moonlight.

Then he spurred his mount to overtake the shaking, agitated nine-yak-tail standard of his temporal might.

"Give him to me," he growled.

Ariunbold Khan was riding with the reins between his teeth, the tall standard unrelinquished, his other hand clenching Bayar's sheepskin *dacha*. Bayar was all but falling out of it, his boot heels nearly grazing cracked paving stones.

Without discernible effort, Qasar took him up and laid him across the pommel of his saddle. Bayar smelled of roast pig. His *dacha* smoked foully.

"You have served me well, Bayar Khan."

Bayar spoke with difficulty. "I am a khan?"

"You did not hesitate to do the will of your khakhan, therefore I decree you khan."

Bayar smiled through his pain. "It is good not to hesitate. Sometimes." He coughed once, very painfully. "Sometimes not."

"Sometimes to hesitate or not to hesitate is the choice between being shot or strangled. You made the honorable choice. Thus, I declare I am proud to have known you."

"I am proud to die a khan. It is more than I ever dreamed of in Ulan Bator, in my old life."

"When I rule Ulan Bator, I will name it after you, for it will be a happy place under my heel."

"It will be a great honor to have the capital of your khanate named after me."

"Not for you," Qasar shot back. "My capital will be Genghis's old seat, Karakorum."

"Still, I die fulfilled, even if I do not die in the arms of my plump wife, whom Fate has decreed I am not to meet in this life," Bayar said, his smile relaxing, then his face. Finally his eyes closed halfway.

Qasar Khan held his loyal companion in one strong hand until he was completely limp. Feeling about the loose sheepskin, he found the spot on his chest where the heart beat. Qasar felt three beats, a pause, and then one more. After that, nothing.

A tear started in Ariunbold's eye. Seeing it, Qasar barked, "I forbid you to weep."

"I have dust in my eye."

"I forbid you from watering it then," he said thickly. "I have spoken."

His face tight, Qasar stripped the body of the scorched *dacha* of Genghis Khan and let it fall under the merciless hooves of the New Golden Horde, who, for the better portion of the next hour, pounded it out of the shape of anything remotely human.

Whipping the *dacha* over his shoulder, Qasar Khan cried, "The *dacha* of Bayar Khan will confer great power and responsibility upon the man who catches it."

"I have caught it, O Khan!" a voice whooped.

"Good. Now put it on and ride beside Morning Doe Khan, and should death seek her, let it take you instead."

"I hear and obey!"

65

KILLERGHOST
RED SANDS

"I have a lock!" the gunner-technician called out.

"Show me," Komo Dath hissed.

"This grid, Commander."

Dath leaned into the tracking monitor. The targeting arrows had a fix, but in the mass of men and horses on the leading edge of the Golden Horde, it kept shifting, the lock cutting out and reacquiring the target fitfully.

"Which rider?" Dath demanded impatiently, seeing the arrows embracing a clump of shadowy heads.

"This is the optimum lock under these conditions."

Telian Piar hovered close. "I see him," he announced.

Komo Dath whirled. "There are days when I wish I possessed the Paeec overeye, odious as it is to contemplate," he said. "No dishonor intended," he added quickly.

Piar ignored the comment. Laying a thin finger to the screen, he touched a jumping head, saying, "There. That is the Dog Khan."

"Fire!" Komo Dath screamed.

66

THE GREAT WALL OF
FREE CHINA

Qasar Khan rode low in his saddle, just behind the lead horses. It was difficult to see the sky and control his mount both. All was confusion now.

Here, within a short ride of the conjunction of the two accursed walls, the first taste of fear crept up from his stomach. He forced it back down.

A lance of the searing death-light bisected the horse and rider beside him. They had no time to scream. One moment they were a single unified entity of conjoined muscle and brains, the next they were a tumbling ball of disconnected meat that was soon swallowed up by the ranks behind them. Two additional horses stumbled in the encounter.

But Qasar Khan rode on.

Keeping low, he barked, "All of you! Ride low in your saddles."

"It is not the Mongol way!" someone shouted.

"Obey me or die!" Qasar shouted.

Another searing ray vaporized the head of a nearby man. The rest of him continued bouncing in his saddle until the dead hands were separated from the shaking reins and the felt seat of the dead man bounced too high off his blue wood saddle so that his boots came free of the dancing stirrups. Already dead, he made no complaint when his limp body fell beneath remorseless hooves.

Qasar raised his voice over the hoof thunder. "Morning Doe!"

"Here!"

"The jade star of death follows on the right. Hang your body over the left side of your mount, if you would live!"

"I would sooner eat horse than cower."

"I would sooner eat Chino than lose you to the Bone Heads. Cower as I say or I will strip you of all your honors and titles."

"Your word is my command, but I protest."

"My word ensures your survival," Qasar muttered to himself. His face was all but buried in his mount's shaking mane. It was difficult to ride in this manner. A Mongol horse demanded attention and strict posture, lest the rider be thrown. Qasar detested poor riding posture, but this was a matter of life and death. His.

A sudden stink of burned horseflesh coming with a white-hot sear against his eyes told of another death strike. Stealing a glance, he saw a horse in mid-stride— with only a smoking stump of a neck where its head should be.

The rider looked at his headless steed with stunned incredulity and threw himself clear. He went over the rampart and screamed his way to an abrupt death below.

"The Bone Heads seek you, my lord!" Morning Doe cried, her eyes tearing.

"I forbid you to weep," Qasar shouted back.

"I do not weep for myself. I weep for you."

"Stay down."

"They will find you. They know where you ride. You can see this."

"The accursed Bone Heads must have the eyes of cats," Qasar barked.

"Perhaps they know you by the mark upon your brow, my lord."

Qasar's hand went to his forehead and the skull brand there. His slit eyes narrowed in thought.

"Perhaps they do . . ." he said to himself.

Then another flash of white warned of death arrowing toward him . . .

67

KILLERGHOST
RED SANDS

"Keep firing! Keep firing!" Komo Dath was screaming. "They are within sight of the World Wall!"

"Your will," came the servile voice of the technician as he launched another microbeam death-ray.

In a twinkling, a horse lost its head, stumbled, and both horse and rider were lost in the pounding confusion.

"Status!" Dath rasped excitedly.

"The homing signal indicates the White Card Terran lives," the gunner-technician said fearfully.

Whirling, Komo Dath fell upon him, plucked him roughly from his control seat and dropped into it himself. "I will finish what obviously no Gnard on board is capable of finishing!" he raged. "Piar! Aid me! I need your eye!"

Telian Piar, his red orb fixed on the jumpy monitor screen, laid his finger on the grid where his light-sensitive organ detected Qasar Khan. "There."

And Komo Dath triggered another microbeam death-ray.

68

THE GREAT WALL OF FREE CHINA

Fumbling in his saddlebag, Qasar Khan found an antique tinder box. He sparked it to light a scrap of sash, also pulled from the saddlebag, and got it smoldering.

Taking the free end between his strong teeth, he set the burning end to his forehead and, though hot tears started from his pain-squeezed eyes, held it there until the flesh screamed and smoked and he could smell himself burning.

"My lord! What do you do?" Morning Doe Khan cried, fear in her voice and in her dark eyes.

Qasar Khan made no reply. His teeth gripped the silk sash agonizingly.

Only when he could take no more, and the creeping fire started to lick at his dry lips, did he fling that last flaming rag away and rear up in his saddle.

Standing tall, he looked to the jade star in the onyx sky.

"Do your worst, Bone Heads!" he screamed.

A pinpoint of white-hot light warned him of the coming of death.

The beam cut a dazzling line before his fierce face, not a sheep bone's distance from his nose, turning the Mongol beside him into a pair of smoking legs that quickly separated and went tumbling out of the stirrups. The lathered horse continued pounding on, and seeking to confuse the Bone Heads, Qasar got out of his own stirrups and jumped across to claim it.

A new beam caught the horse he had abandoned, wringing from it a short, strangled, nearly human scream before it lurched to one side, colliding with the horse next to it. One stumbled, the other nearly so. The wounded horse collapsed into a bag of suddenly snapping bones without another sound emerging from its great throat.

"My Khan! Do you live?" Morning Doe Khan wailed.

"I live. For nothing can harm the khan of khans!" Qasar cried, sensing that he had outwitted the Bone Heads.

Then a new beam sizzled over his head, and he felt the heat so keenly he slapped at his hot hair in case it had caught fire.

Looking ahead, Qasar saw Ariunbold Khan and Gerel Khan in the lead, his free-riding horse, Chino, pounding away a nose span before them. He called out.

"Ariunbold, let drop the standard of Genghis!"

"It will be lost!"

"Do this!"

"I would rather eat horse."

"I will feed your living balls to your ball-less steed if you do not obey your khakhan! For the Bone Heads know that where it rears, I am not far away! They seek my life!"

It took a long moment, but at last Ariunbold lifted the standard so high Qasar could feel his strong shoulder pop out of its socket, then flung it away.

It went over the toothlike merlons of the Great Wall to vanish from sight. If it made a sound upon landing, this was lost in the thunder of horses and the cries of the men.

But a vagrant wind did carry back a choking sob.

"I forbid you to weep, Ariunbold Khan!" Qasar shouted.

"Go to hell, my khakhan," came the racking voice of Ariunbold the loyal.

A lance of light extinguished him in the next instant, as if he were never there.

The stink of his consumed body burned into Qasar Khan's laboring lungs. He coughed it out, his face a mask of sweat and determination.

69

KILLERGHOST
<u>RED SANDS</u>

"We have lost the microtransmitter signal," Komo Dath said, his voice shaking with disbelief. "The Dog Khan is no more."

"You do not say this in a tone of acceptance," Telian Piar rejoined.

"I killed a horse, not a man. Yet the signal has vanished."

"Do you question your own technology?"

"Of course not. He should be dead many times over."

"That he has at last died is all that matters," Piar suggested.

Komo Dath lifted out of the control chair, his body tense with a mixture of anger and nervous tension. He flung a scarlet glance at the hovering Paeec.

"You saw him die?"

"No," Piar said, thin of voice.

"But he is dead?"

"I see him no more. How can he be otherwise than dead?"

Dath nodded. "The horde approaches the World Wall. It will be interesting to see how the Council deals with the problem of the Golden Horde."

"They are trapped upon the confines of the Great Wall, with no place to turn," Piar observed.

"But they ride like madmen, unstoppable and uncontrollable."

"The ending of the Council's charade is ordained in advance."

"But it will be interesting to watch nevertheless," Komo Dath said, his hot red eyes fixing on the monitor screen.

70

THE GREAT WALL/WORLD WALL CONJUNCTION

Once again standing in his stirrups, Qasar Khan laid his eyes on the roadway ahead. The Great Wall of China jogged left, where it abruptly became a massive bulwark of dark red concrete that had nothing of the grandeur of the Great Wall, but looked infinitely more formidable. The two walls fused imperfectly, for the New Wall stood higher than the old wall, except for a span of the New Wall that sloped down to meet the old.

Qasar lashed his Mongols with his tongue. "We approach our goal! Forward! Forward!"

And the Golden Horde, as if spurred on by the voice of a single man, redoubled its speed. Their controlled hoof thunder seemed to shake the very stars—including the lone low-hanging jade one that seemed to have exhausted its will to destroy.

All at once luminous green shapes began rising from the dark moonlit fortification of the New Wall. They rose like a dozen cold moons of jade, lit from within.

"Sky pavilions," Qasar grunted.

The skyboats of the Bone Heads were soon hovering overhead, and on their lowermost hulls, ports opened and down showered the silver-green locusts of the Flying Bone Heads.

Bellowing at the top of his lungs, knowing his orders would be carried down the line, Qasar gave cry.

"Archers! Fire! Fire! Fire!"

Almost with one voice, the twanging of suddenly released bowstrings reverberated in the night. A cloud of shafts rose like darting needles. Many struck. Some wounded, but most killed.

Bone Head bodies began dropping down.

And in response, the emerald-green fire of their Chof guns rained down with vicious intent.

"Aim for their Chof flashes!" Qasar howled.

And another leaping cloud of arrows lifted with deceptive slowness, popping Kalashnikovs and other small arms joining in.

Soon the skies rained more dead, as well as their Chof guns.

"Capture any weapons that fall!" Qasar cried. "Do you hear? Any!"

"The abysmal fools!" Komo Dath was saying. "What manner of pacification operation is this?"

Telian Piar stood resolute, his tone unperturbed. "The Council has underestimated the Mongol will to fight."

"This is folly. They are almost to the World Wall."

"This can have but one ending," Telian Piar intoned.

"Yes, absolute destruction for the Golden Horde. So much for the Council's Personal Modification plan," Dath said acidly.

Piar shook his oversized head slowly. "They should have heeded us."

"I should never have heeded *you*. This resolution reflects well on no one. Not even you."

"I would accept any ending at this juncture," Telian Piar said quietly, his red eye on the monitor, where he could see what escaped the Gnard crew.

He saw KA-77s fall from the heavens—some landing in Mongol hands—and suddenly a chill crept up along his sagittal crest and his facial tentacles became very still.

He began to regret his words of a moment ago. For another possible ending began presenting itself.

Morning Doe Khan lifted her voice and a Chof gun simultaneously. "I caught one, my lord! What shall I do with it?"

"Throw it here!" Qasar cried.

Morning Doe set herself, her body jumping with each touch and go of her mount's hooves, and flung the gleaming silver device.

Qasar caught it handily, inserted his finger into the trigger guard, and pointed the weapon skyward.

He fired an experimental shot.

A fragment of emerald flame ascended, melted the glass globe on a Bone Head shoulder, and when the smoke cleared, the body fell head first—without head or helmet.

Then Qasar began triggering steadily and remorselessly at every moon-burnished silver figure.

Along the Golden Horde other emerald flashes began spurting.

In falling, the dead exacted their own toll, often landing on horse and rider with catastrophic results. The Golden Horde pounded on unflinching, an unstoppable force with no mind but Qasar Khan's, no will but Qasar Khan's—and no fear at all.

Rags of greenish flame claimed Mongol lives, but the numbers in the sky were comparatively few. The numbers of the horde were by contrast boundless. Many Mongols fell dying. But the horde poured on, having no retreat, no exit, no luxury but to race on and on toward their nearing goal:

The looming World Wall that marked the beginning of Martian Holdings.

Aboard the *Red Sands*, Komo Dath watched the raging green-lit tide of battle.

"The Council is making a gift of Martian technology to these barbarians!" he fumed.

"I see," Telian Piar murmured.

"Don't the blind fools see that they are arming them with the very tools the Mongols need to resist capture completely?"

"Obviously not."

As they watched, support Killerghosts swept down to disgorge reinforcing Air Death Squads. Almost instantly their numbers began to dwindle under the amazingly effective return fire, which consisted of nearly invisible arrows, supersonic bullets, and intermittent KA-77 fire.

Dath lifted two shaking fists before his naked face. "Reinforcements! What is wrong with the Council? They cannot hope to capture sufficient numbers for their needs. This operation cries out for the overkill option. They should have called down Shatterforce fighters and Death-clouds instead."

Piar, ever the voice of reason, intoned, "This is happening in Free Chinese territory. To destroy the wall would have political consequences."

"Better an incident than Mongols pouring into our side of the World Wall."

"The Council has issued its instructions. They will relent when failure is unavoidable and undeniable, not before."

"Politicians!" Dath spat. "I must contact them myself before they waste more Gnard lives."

Striding over to a comm monitor, he opened the line personally, his posture that of a caged animal.

* * *

Two Chof guns had fallen into Qasar Khan's hands, and he had the reins in his mouth now, while he triggered both weapons into the busy vaulting sky. Every shot counted. Every burst of electric-green fire sent a foe plummeting from the night skies. That many of these smoking dead became in themselves missiles of death falling on his own horde mattered not in the least to Qasar Khan. He was driven by blood lust and a fierce will to survive.

The front ranks held. For some reason, no attempt was made to take down Gerel Khan and Morning Doe Khan, who rode in the lead. It was a strange thing, Qasar thought. For to bring them down would surely stagger the horde, trapped as they were on the road that was also the Great Wall.

A suspicion flowered in Qasar's cunning mind. It blossomed, and he knew.

The Bone Heads seek to capture us living!

As soon as the thought coalesced, another followed on its heels.

They will not take Qasar Khan alive.

Calling over his shoulder, he cried, "Those with Chof guns! Concentrate your fire on the sky pavilion your khan targets!"

Selecting a sky pavilion up ahead, Qasar trained his weapons upon it. The first flashes licked its underside harmlessly.

Then, as if it were a magnet for green fire, volley after volley of the iridescent flashes chased it as many of Qasar's followers joined his attack. The underside quickly began shimmering, glowing green, then reddish. The red overwhelmed the green, and the object abruptly pulled back, its port closing with frightened alacrity.

Green fire continued to follow without letup, splashing

against its wobbling sides. Ripples of electric-blue began spitting from its windows, and Qasar howled, "Show no mercy! Show no mercy!" But his Mongols, concentrating on the wounded sky pavilion, began succumbing to attacking fire. This they ignored in order to carry out their khakhan's will.

The retreating sky pavilion broke apart without warning. It fell from the sky, crashing into the New Wall not half a *li* ahead. The wall exploded. Large chunks of steel and concrete flew in all directions, landing with thunderous reports.

As the fiery slag heap that had been a Bone Head sky pavilion melted into the newly excavated gap, Qasar peered through the leaping flames, seeing the gigantic glass domes of the enemy he lusted to despoil. Reflecting the fires of war, the structures looked as if they burned already. His heart leapt, and a cry of mixed rage and triumph exploded from his chest.

"Ride for the glass *gers*, my war dogs! Victory lies within your merciless grasp! Pillage undreamed of calls to our hot blood! This is the hour! This is the day! Victory! Victory! Victory! *Ride!*"

On the *Red Sands*, Komo Dath was addressing Council member Feep in a tight, barely controlled voice.

"You are squandering my troops!"

"The operation is almost over," Feep replied without umbrage.

"If any more KA-77s fall into Mongol hands, it will be over. Decisively. And we will be the losers."

"These are but Terrans."

"You utterly fail to understand, Feep! They were bred in red sand deserts like our own. They subsist on raw protein. They are on a road with no return or retreat. They will never surrender. They can only fight and die. It is all they know. This is exactly why they were selected for this experiment. They are Gnard! Do you understand? They wear the soft pink flesh of Terrans, but they are Gnard!"

Council member Feep stared long and hard at Komo Dath's raw working face.

At length, his voice lost its unctuous surety. "What would you suggest, Commander?"

"Transfer control of this operation to this ship. And to me."

"You have just assured me that the Mongols cannot be delivered into our hands alive."

"They cannot. They will be exterminated. It is the only way. And there must be no further delay. They near our wall. I must have your answer instantly."

Feep hesitated only a moment. "This will not sit well with the other Council members."

"Leave them to me," Dath rasped. "And leave the Mongols to me, too. There are other Mongols."

"Not trained as these are."

"These are dead men—of no use to the Council. And soon they will be spilling over the World Wall."

"Do what is necessary. I will inform the Council."

The screen winked out.

Telian Piar drifted up, curious of eye. "Interesting. You stampeded Feep into making a unilateral decision."

"A decision he will deeply regret once I turn it against him," Dath said sharply, stomping up to the *Red Sands* pilot.

"Captain Lhyso. On my order, you will train sonic disrupter cannon on a section of the Great Wall just before the advancing horde."

"Your will . . ."

* * *

Qasar Khan fixed his eyes on the reddish World Wall looming ahead.

Above him, death rained. Ahead, destiny lay. All was not lost. There was still survival, and if there was one thing Qasar understood, it was how to survive.

Qasar Khan never knew the source of the wide ray of blue-white light. Too many flashes of emerald illuminated the night sky. The sky pavilions overhead were releasing flight upon flight of fighting Bone Heads. They died as fast as they emerged, bringing a hard rain that was unrelenting.

The ray simply touched a section of the Great Wall before the place where it merged with the New Wall, and that section turned to hissing steam. It happened in a heartbeat: the stone gave up steam, and when the steam dissipated, there was no more stone—only a gap in the wall, smooth at both ends.

Qasar Khan's fearless heart quailed at the sight. It was too great a chasm to leap, even for Mongol horses.

And as the thunder of the Golden Horde approached it, loose rock shivered and began to break away.

On the *Red Sands*, Telian Piar watched. "Simple, but effective."

"With no other path before them, they will simply plummet to their deaths—all six thousand of them," Komo Dath said.

The Great Wall began to crumble and tumble on either side of the gap . . .

Lashing his own steed, Qasar Khan urged it to its utmost.

The horse was lathered to the point of foaming from every hair, but it responded as a Mongol horse should—without hesitation. Qasar broke free of the horde, passing his loyal companions who had been in the lead. He called back to them.

"Morning Doe! Gerel! Pilot your mounts down the sliding rock! It is your only chance. Trust them to guide you. And if you still live when you touch soil, ride for all you are worth, for the horde will come careening after you like a thousand blind dragons!"

"I hear and obey!"

Then catching up to Chino, Qasar switched mounts, transferring to the empty saddle with an effortless jump that was breathtaking.

"Now, Chino, you will show your khan that you are the horse I broke upon the steppes so long ago—or you and I will lie broken and shattered together under the Everlasting Blue Sky!"

The heat of vaporizing rock wafted into his face, turning it to sweat. It made his scorched brow pucker in pain.

Then came the gap. It was wider than it had seemed.

"Ai-Yah!" Qasar cried. And Chino seemed to drop away under him as if they both plunged into the pit of no return.

"It is the Dog Khan!" Telian Piar exploded, his outward calm dispelling.

Komo Dath whirled. "What?"

"I know that face. He rides the horse of the Dog Khan. And his brow is a black sear mark."

"He burnt off the White Card brand?" Dath roared.

Piar nodded. "Obliterating the subcutaneous homing microtransmitter."

"He is a dog unlike any!" Dath said, impressed.

Then both Martians turned to watch the tableau of death and destruction as it unfolded.

* * *

The tumbled rock had not finished shifting when Chino's hooves plunged into it. Eyes wide, the white stallion stumbled, recovered, and stumbled again, his nimble hooves instinctively picking out the most settled supporting stones. But they were insufficient in number.

In the end he slid more than picked his way down, the nearness of the horde forcing his nerves and reflexes to do more than they could normally achieve under better circumstances.

Hugging Chino's neck, Qasar simply held on.

"I will personally exterminate that abysmal Mongol if he survives," Komo Dath vowed tightly.

"His survival is likely," Piar said.

"Then his life is mine to claim," Dath retorted, going to the gunnery position and enabling the microbeam cannon.

Qasar Khan knew he would live when the clatter of rock became the soft mushy padding of hooves on loose soil.

"Ai-Yah!" he cried, spurring Chino to put distance between them and the disaster that now could not be averted.

Throwing a glance over his shoulder, he watched the other horses come down off the Great Wall, their suddenly unsupported legs kicking air.

Weak from their ordeal, they tumbled down on unsteady legs. Qasar caught a glimpse of Morning Doe as she valiantly clung to her mare. A glimpse only. Then she was lost to sight.

Rank upon rank of howling men and horses came down, jostling into one another, piling up in a screaming avalanche of men and horseflesh.

To his everlasting pride, Qasar saw that his men continued firing into the air, even as they drew their final breaths. Return fire was desultory. Even the hot-eyed Bone Heads hung back in awe of Mongol courage . . .

The reverberating sound of doom went on for a very long time. The gap between the two segments of the wall quickly filled with moaning and screaming as mortar and rock dust rose up to obscure all in billowing, smothering waves.

Many Mongols survived, and some horses, too. Most, however, did not. They piled atop one another until those at the bottom were inexorably pressed to death by those falling atop them, living or not.

But Qasar stood off from it all, knowing that if those he held dear were to survive, it would be as a whim of Fate, and nothing else.

The edge of a billowing cloud touched him and his stallion, and Qasar thought it safer to ride into it, since the sky pavilions were still hovering overhead, full of red, searching eyes.

Choking on the mortar dust, his eyes were squeezed down to slits and his brow burned hot. His voice lifted in anguish.

"Morning Doe! Morning Doe!"

No answer.

"Ariunbold!"

No reply. Then Qasar recalled that the loyal Ariunbold had been reduced to smoke so swiftly that disbelief still clung to his passing.

"Gerel. Gerel Khan. Your khan seeks you!"

"I live," a racking voice cried.

Closing his eyes, Qasar piloted his tenderfooted stallion in the direction of the voice.

"Speak up, Gerel. I come."

"Here, my khan."

Qasar found Gerel Khan lying in the rubble, dazed, his features bathed in streamers of blood.

"You are hurt?" Qasar asked, dismounting.

"No. But we are doomed."

"We live. Thus we are not doomed."

"The Bone Heads live to kill Mongols."

Qasar peered up through the rock dust. Dimly the burning jade sky pavilions loomed, unthreatening but of uncertain intent. Here and there emerald streaks rose up to touch them, without doing discernible harm.

"Your horde fights to the death," Gerel said as Qasar helped him to his feet.

Qasar smiled bitterly. "It is their duty, having sworn fealty to their khan."

As the bitter stink of spilled brains and bowels, vomit and blood, began to impregnate the dusty air, Qasar laid a hard hand on his shoulder.

"I seek Morning Doe," he said urgently. "Where is she?"

"I do not know. I was too preoccupied with my own survival to account for hers."

Qasar frowned. "I do not upbraid you for this, although—"

A searing beam touched a spot off to Qasar Khan's right.

There, a fragment of rock sublimed to steam.

"It begins," Gerel Khan said, his eyes flinching. "The slaughter of we who have cheated death only to die, unable to fight for our lives."

Another beam struck closer, almost at the spot where Qasar had stood. Except that he stood there no longer.

He spun Gerel around, bringing their faces close.

"Gerel Khan, it is here that we may or may *not* die."

"It will be as Fate decrees," Gerel agreed.

"It will be as Fate decrees, but in this hour I decree that you accept the blue and gold armor of Lord Genghis."

"I?"

"Yes," Qasar said, stripping off the cuirass with a sudden ferocity.

"I am not worthy."

"That is for your khan to say. I must seek Morning Doe in the ruins of death and cannot be encumbered. Nor will I abandon the armor I wear to a rubble heap. It is in you I have placed my trust, and so you will accept my armor."

"I hear and obey," Gerel Khan said, kneeling.

"Kneel later. Obey now. I must be off."

The last of the armor tumbled to the ground, and Qasar Khan stood nearly naked. He held the wolf's pelt that had formerly nestled within, and set it atop his shaggy head so that the wolf's half-dissolved eyes stared in the same direction Qasar did.

"See that it remains clean should I have need of it again," he said gruffly.

"Your word is my command, O Khan," Gerel Khan said, scrambling to don the hallowed lamellar accoutrements of the mightiest Mongol who ever trod the earth.

Qasar Khan strode on, feeling the heat of the Chof guns as they spat rags of green fire in two of the directions of space. The Bone Heads were pouring down emerald death. Let them.

He had gone no more than thirty paces when a searing white needle of light touched the ground behind him, and the stink of burning flesh and hardened leather told Qasar that Gerel Khan had died in his place.

As was fitting for a Mongol who believed he could walk in the boots of the *two* most powerful khans in Mongol history.

Qasar walked on.

* * *

"I did it!" Komo Dath exulted. "Direct hit."

"Congratulations," Telian Piar said thinly.

"Let the Air Death Squads mop up the survivors."

"Here it ends."

"Yes, here it ends."

They exchanged scarlet glances.

"You are certain this time?" Piar asked.

"I burned him in the blue and gold armor he looted from the tomb of the First Khan. There can be no doubt this time."

"Then there is no doubt," Telian Piar said softly.

"Morning Doe! Morning Doe!"

Qasar Khan was crawling over shivering and broken horses, many with legs bent into impossible shapes, raw white bone sticking out from the torn horsehair. He suppressed the urge to sob. Men he had seen die. He was inured to it. Mongol men lived to die. But horses should not suffer so. It was an affront to their noble spirits.

"Morning Doe!" he called again.

Oblivious and uncaring, Qasar walked on, as emerald death rained all around him.

"Morning Doe!"

A groan reached his ears. He had heard it before. Often in pleasure, not in pain.

"Morning Doe! Your khan is here!"

Another groan. He picked his way to its source.

Amid the settling dust, illuminated by intermittent flashes of electric-green fire, he found Morning Doe, her legs twisted and entangled in the stirrups of her dead and bloodied mare, herself broken on a spill of rock a ways distant from the zone of dead and dying.

"I live, my lord," she moaned, her lips overflowing with crimson.

"But not for long," Qasar said, kneeling beside her.

"I know. . ."

"Among those loyal to me, you have been most loyal."

She made a noise like a dead laugh. "I have been mostly disloyal."

"There are different kinds of loyalty. Yours I prize most, for you flung back in my face my hasty decisions, rather than obey my foolish pride blindly. A khan needs one such as you."

She nodded. "What will you do now that I am dead?"

Qasar touched her bloodied cheek. The bone gave slightly under his suddenly tender fingers.

"I do not know, but until you are dead in truth, I will not leave your side."

Morning Doe glanced up at a looming sky pavilion of jade, and pain made her catlike eyes wince.

"I do not desire to die at the hands of Bone Heads," she said softly.

"I will shield you from their angry fire."

"Nor do I wish to die bleeding and broken inside."

"I cannot fix what cruel Fate has broken, for I am only a khakhan—and one without a horde."

Morning Doe had reached up to touch his scorched brow. It was cool to the touch, even the burned skin.

"When you made love to me, a skull on your brow, I knew it was death making love to me. But I did not care. I have lived a lifetime with you in only scant weeks. There are no regrets."

Qasar took her wrist, feeling its thready pulse.

"A boon, my lord."

"Speak this boon."

"A final sweet thrust. To quench the fires that consume my brain."

"You ask much of your khan."

"If you truly and unselfishly love me, you will do this thing."

"Because I love you, I hesitate," Qasar murmured.

"If you hesitate long, your life, too, will be forfeit."

"I died for you once. I can die again."

"It is my turn to die, heart's desire." Morning Doe closed her eyes, murmuring, "I have looked upon your face for the final time. I am ready."

Qasar kissed her blood-smeared lips, tasting them, then taking his silver dagger from his boot, slit her belly open all the way across. Morning Doe contorted her face, but complained not.

Reaching in with his hand, Qasar followed the rib cage with his knuckles until he found the pulsing heart.

"I hold your heart in my right hand. And your life, too."

"Take both," she gasped.

"Good-bye, Morning Doe Khan."

"Farewell, khakhan of my heart."

Squeezing once, Qasar Khan stilled the heart that mattered most to him. The body relaxed under the gentle, merciful constriction, Morning Doe's face surrendering to a peaceful expression.

Then, withdrawing his crimson fingers, he stood up, his entire body trembling, his many-times-hammered visage a mask of metal.

He looked up.

The sky pavilions continued to rain down merciless death. Fewer and fewer bullets and arrows lifted in response.

No longer khan, Qasar walked among the unseeing dead, stopping only once to pick up a silver object from the rubble.

As the sounds of death and dying lessened, he found his stallion, Chino.

Mounting the saddle, he said, "*Ai-Yah*, loyal one! Ride!"

Through the ever-billowing rock dust they rode. A flash of green raced after them, touching the ground and leaving a smoking crater the size of a black-faced sheep.

Shifting in his saddle, Qasar reached into his empty box quiver and his hand came away seemingly empty. One-handed, he shook the sight-confounded garment taken from the Red Eye assassin and flung it over his head.

Abruptly, he vanished—all but his hands.

Shifting low, Qasar instinctively clung to the flank of his horse, hanging off the side and away from the hovering sky pavilions whose pilots, if they could see at all, would see only a riderless white stallion.

Without a backward glance Qasar lashed his steed to his greatest effort.

A tear started in one eye.

Under his breath he growled, "I forbid you to weep."

The tear tracked down to his chin, clinging briefly before falling off. No more followed.

Aboard the *Red Sands*, Komo Dath was scanning the terrain below, Telian Piar scrutinizing a monitor with his acute red orb.

"Terran life signs," Dath called.

A technician reported, "None, Commander. Only a few beasts without riders."

Dath looked to Piar. Piar nodded mutely.

"Beasts do not matter. Let them go."

"Your will," the Gnard said in a servile tone of voice.

EPILOGUE

Deep in the Hentiyn Mountain Range, behind the World Wall, a very pregnant gray steppe wolf climbed to a certain ledge on the peak known to the Mongol people as the Mountain Where the Wolves Give Birth.

Pausing at the entrance to a shadow-clotted cave, the she-wolf paused, sniffed, then carefully padded inward, her feet scratching and scuffing detritus with each cautious step.

Green eyes adjusting to the darkness, she came at last to the farthest extension of the cave where, for thousands upon thousands of years, wolves such as she had given birth and suckled their feral young.

Catching an unfamiliar scent, she vented a low growl.

From the darkness came an answering growl.

Then a voice.

"Ho, she-wolf. You have come unbidden to the cave where a wolf greater than you was born, then reborn, and now waits to be born again, as Fate decrees."

The she-wolf padded forward, baring her fangs.

And a rag of emerald flame came scooting toward her, to turn her tense, predatory form into a smoking curl of blackened bone and fur.

Before the last wisp of fire faded, a face like a bronze gong that had been hammered by adversities beyond counting showed briefly, shoulders mantled by a gray wolf pelt.

As the light at last died, a final glimmering showed twin knife slits of cold brooding menace.

Then Qasar the Khalkha Mongol curled up and slept, dreaming of his next incarnation—and of the road to empire that still called to him through the blood of ancestors without name and number . . .

Free *Mars Attacks!*® trading cards!

Just fill out the survey below and we will send you your *free* exclusive Mars Attacks® trading cards, as promised on the cover.

Age: ___   Sex: ___ M ___ F

Highest education level: ___ High School ___ College
___ Graduate Degree

Annual income: ___ $0–30,000 ___ $30,001–60,000 ___ over $60,000

Number of books you read per month: ___ 0–2 ___ 3–5 ___ 6 or more

Preference: ___ fantasy ___ science fiction ___ horror ___ other fiction
___ non-fiction

I buy books in hardcover: ___ frequently ___ sometimes ___ rarely

I buy books at: ___ Superstores ___ Mall bookstores
___ Independent bookstores ___ Mail Order

I read books by new authors: ___ frequently ___ sometimes ___ rarely

I read comic books: ___ frequently ___ sometimes ___ rarely

I watch the Sci-Fi cable TV channel: ___ frequently ___ sometimes
___ rarely

I am interested in collector editions (signed by the author or illustrated):
___ yes ___ no ___ maybe

I read Star Wars novels: ___ frequently ___ sometimes ___ rarely

I read Star Trek novels: ___ frequently ___ sometimes ___ rarely

I read the following magazines:
___ Analog   ___ Locus   ___ Popular Science
___ Asimov   ___ SF Chronicles   ___ Wired
___ Fantasy & SF   ___ Fantasy   ___ Cracked

Check here if you do not want your name and address shared with qualified vendors ___

Name_____

Address_____

City/State/Zip_____

Return completed form to:
    Del Rey Books
    Mars Attacks® Trading Card Offer
    201 E. 50th Street
    New York, NY 10022
[This offer valid through April 30, 1997.]

The worldwide invasion was quick and merciless . . .

MARTIAN DEATHTRAP
by Nathan Archer
Published by Del Rey® Books

The battleground is a huge estate, with secret passages and
trapdoors inside, giant insects outside, and death lurking
around every corner. For the Martians, the mission is to
secure the captured ground by whatever means necessary.
For the desperate band of humans defenders, the goal is to
simply survive . . .

You know how the Mongols fared. But what about the
Americans? Read on to find out . . .

DEATH ON TWO WHEELS

Bud Garcia looked up at the sky ahead and frowned. He cranked
the brake and brought the Harley to a skidding stop on the shoulder
in front of a weathered billboard reading GELMAN MANSION
4 MILES. He kept the motor running, but put down his booted foot
and stared overhead.

Lenny, Blitz, and Screwy Joe pulled up beside him. Blitz and
Lenny had their chicks with them, riding post, but no one got off;
they all stared at Bud. "What is it, man?" Lenny asked, his eyes
hidden by his mirrored shades, his head jerking nervously from
Bud to the empty highway ahead and back. "Why'd you stop?
We're in the middle of nowhere!"

Bud glanced at him. "Take a look at that," he said, pointing,
"and tell me what the hell kind of plane that is." Cruising far above
the trees ahead of them was a green and yellow aircraft in a sort of
modified flying-wing shape.

Lenny looked, then shrugged. "Crap, man, I dunno. I'm no
expert."

"*I* am," Bud said. "My old man was in the Air Force until they booted him out for drinking on duty, and I know planes. I never saw anything like that."

"It's coming this way," said Blitz's girl, Nancy. She was wedged in behind Blitz; the two of them were a lot for one bike to carry. Blitz was a hulking blond brute in black leather who always said he needed a lot of woman, and Nancy filled the bill—dark hair, tight jeans, and black leather jacket wrapped around a bountiful quantity of female flesh.

Bud looked up, squinting through his own shades. Sure enough, the strange aircraft had wheeled and was heading directly toward the bikers at an altitude not far above the treetops.

"Well, you'll get a good look at it, anyway," Lenny's chick, Marcie, said. She was thin and blond and nervous, matching Lenny point for point.

"I don't think we want to," Blitz said. "Don't that look like a strafing run to you?" He didn't wait for an answer; he kicked off and rolled, ignoring Nancy's yelps of protest at the unexpected move. She had scarcely gotten a solid hold around his waist when he veered off the road and went charging across an overgrown meadow.

The other three stared, eyes flicking from the approaching craft to Blitz and back. The thing's engine made a strange, keening wail unlike anything Bud had heard before.

"I don't—" Lenny began.

Then the aircraft opened fire, and Bud pushed off.

The greenish death-rays tore bubbling black lines of molten asphalt in the highway, and when one touched the gas tank of Screwy Joe's chopper, the tank flashed into an orange fireball, flinging Joe and pieces of cycle in all directions.

Lenny was luckier; he wasn't able to dodge completely, but threw himself and his bike sideways. The beam sliced through Lenny's foot and both tires.

Marcie fell clear when Lenny threw the bike over; Blitz and Nancy were already a hundred feet away across the weeds, and Bud had rolled away just in time, mere inches out of the line of fire.

Lenny's bike had stalled out when it fell, Bud had always liked his own chopper to run quiet, and Blitz was a field away; when the sound of the explosion of Joe's Suzuki died away, there were a few seconds of near silence. Joe himself was dead or unconscious, his face and chest burned black.

Then Lenny looked down and saw the stump of his foot and

started screaming. Marcie, who had been dazed by her fall, started shouting obscenities. And Bud looked up to see that weird thing in the sky wheeling around for another run.

"What *is* it?" Marcie shrieked.

"What'd it do to my *foot*?" Lenny bellowed. "Jesus, it shot my *foot* off! What the hell kind of cannon was that, some kind of laser?"

Bud didn't answer; he looked around, assessing the situation. Joe was out of it for good. Lenny was down—his foot had been sliced away, and while it wasn't bleeding the way it ought to be, Bud didn't think Lenny was going anywhere anytime soon. Blitz had split, rolling cross-country.

"Yo, Marcie," Bud called. "Need a lift?"

Marcie looked up at the flying death-machine as it dropped into line for another strafing run, looked at Lenny lying crippled and pinned under the wreckage of his bike, and looked at Bud's Harley. She didn't bother answering, just pushed herself up and ran flat-out toward the Harley.

"You son of a—" Lenny shouted.

Then the returning attack craft's death-ray cut him in half. Bud's Harley was already starting to move when Marcie vaulted on, and she barely made it, but the two of them skidded out of the line of fire.

Bud didn't hesitate; he cracked the throttle and headed over to see what Blitz was planning, if anything.

He didn't have to get close to see just what Blitz was up to. The big man had pushed Nancy off the bike to get maneuvering room, and pulled his shotgun from its special boot. Now he was driving one-handed while the gun waved wildly in the other.

Bud decided to just stay the hell out of Blitz's way; he roared across the field toward Nancy, though, to see if she was still in one piece.

The craft was swinging around for a third run, and Bud was suddenly absolutely certain that the pilot was just toying with them. One biker killed on each pass . . . that wasn't a serious attack, that was target practice.

And what the hell kind of pilot was that, anyway? Much as Bud hated the fighter jocks his father had once worked with, much as he despised all authority figures, he knew no U.S. pilot would have casually blown away U.S. civilians that way. Not even redneck cops would—the risks of an investigation and of catching hell for it were too high.

What foreign pilot would have been cruising along the American coast here? As of a couple of hours ago, when the six of them had eaten a late breakfast at the Motel 6 in Toppwood, the U.S. hadn't been at war, there hadn't been anything on the news on the TV over the bar . . .

And what kind of *plane* was that? It made snap turns like nothing Bud had ever seen. It bore no insignia he recognized, though there were yellow lines patterning the green belly. The airframe wasn't like anything he'd ever seen before—it was a lifting body, with the wings merging into the fuselage, but it wasn't the usual flying wing that showed up in the aircraft mags. What were those beams it fired? They weren't any sort of lasers Bud had encountered before, and besides, who had working laser weapons?

And it was making its third run while Blitz was charging across the weed-covered field with his shotgun raised and ready.

The death-rays, or whatever they were, flashed out again just as Blitz pulled the trigger—and the beams missed the biker by millimeters, as Blitz's cycle wavered wildly from the shotgun's recoil.

Blitz's shot missed, too—or at least did no damage.

Blitz recovered his balance, roared his bike up onto the highway and aimed it straight toward the flying craft. He braced the shotgun against one thigh and pumped, readying it for another shot.

"Come back here and take it, you murdering bastards!" he bellowed.

The flying craft didn't do the same graceful wheel this time; instead it flipped over in a screaming Immelmann, and Bud decided that the pilot was angry about missing Blitz and wasn't going to play around anymore.

"Nancy, get on," Bud barked, bringing his chopper to a mud-slinging halt directly in front of her.

She looked at him doubtfully. "Three on a bike?" she asked.

"It's a Harley," Bud said. "She can handle it. Hurry!"

The shotgun boomed again, but at that moment Bud was too busy getting Nancy squeezed in between himself and Marcie to look. Besides, he doubted that a direct hit would even scratch that thing's paint.

Because he didn't think it was a plane . . .

DEL REY® ONLINE!

The Del Rey Internet Newsletter...

A monthly electronic publication, posted on the Internet, GEnie, CompuServe, BIX, various BBSs, and the Panix gopher (gopher.panix.com). It features hype-free descriptions of books that are new in the stores, a list of our upcoming books, special announcements, a signing/reading/convention-attendance schedule for Del Rey authors, "In Depth" essays in which professionals in the field (authors, artists, designers, sales people, etc.) talk about their jobs in science fiction, a question-and-answer section, behind-the-scenes looks at sf publishing, and more!

Internet information source!

A lot of Del Rey material is available to the Internet on our Web site and on a gopher server: all back issues and the current issue of the Del Rey Internet Newsletter, sample chapters of upcoming or current books (readable or downloadable for free), submission requirements, mail-order information, and much more. We will be adding more items of all sorts (mostly new DRINs and sample chapters) regularly. The Web site is http://www.randomhouse.com/delrey/ and the address of the gopher is gopher.panix.com

Why?

We at Del Rey realize that the networks are the medium of the future. That's where you'll find us promoting our books, socializing with others in the sf field, and—most importantly—making contact and sharing information with sf readers.

Online editorial presence:

Many of the Del Rey editors are online, on the Internet, GEnie, CompuServe, America Online, and Delphi. There is a Del Rey topic on GEnie and a Del Rey folder on America Online.

The official e-mail address

for Del Rey Books is delrey@randomhouse.com (though it sometimes takes us a while to answer).